TEN LITTLE
BLOODHOUNDS

TEN LITTLE
BLOODHOUNDS

Virginia Lanier

HarperCollins*Publishers*

This is a work of fiction. The characters, incidents, and dialogues are products of the author's imagination and are not to be construed as real. Any resemblance to actual events or persons, living or dead, is entirely coincidental.

HarperCollins books may be purchased for educational, business, or sales promotional use. For information please write: Special Markets Department, HarperCollins Publishers, 10 East 53rd Street, New York, NY 10022.

FIRST EDITION

Designed by Liane Fuji

Library of Congress Cataloging-in-Publication Data

Lanier, Virginia, 1930-
    Ten little bloodhounds / Virginia Lanier. — 1st ed.
      p. cm.
    ISBN 0-06-017548-6
    I. Title.
    PS3562.A524T46 1999
    813' .54—dc21   98-49470

99 00 01 02 03 ❖ /RRD 10 9 8 7 6 5 4 3 2

This book is for Mary Nix, who helped me through the bad times and had a lot more faith in me than I did. I see her input on almost every page. You're truly remarkable, Mary. Thank you, with love.

Acknowledgments

I wish to thank the following people for invaluable advice, research, and encouragement:

Bruce Ludemann, Niagara County Sheriff Special Forces Unit, Lockport, New York. Officer Kathy "Kat" Albrecht, University of California at Santa Cruz Police Department Search-and-Rescue, who owns Pet Pursuit, a business that finds lost pets with a bloodhound trained to find animals, not humans.

If I thanked William (Bill) D. Tolhurst of Lockport, New York in every future book, I still couldn't convey how deeply I am in his debt for canine training tapes, scent machine advice, police procedure tapes, and all the additional lore I have learned from him. Thanks again, Bill.

I met two bloodhounds, Bogart and Columboux, at the eleventh annual Table of Content dinner on St. Simons Island, Georgia. I want to thank their owner, Brenda Brazil, for allowing them to share the spotlight with me, even though in this outing, I placed third.

I want to thank Susan Roberts, Director of Waycross-Ware County Public Library and Headquarters of the Okefenokee Library System, for all her kindness and efforts on my behalf. Waycross, Georgia, is truly blessed with excellent librarians, and Susan's star is the brightest.

I would like, to begin with, to say that though parents, husbands, children, lovers and friends are all very well, they are not dogs.

ELIZABETH VON ARNIM
1866–1941

1

"Cast Your Bread on the Waters"

October 2, Monday, 7:00 A.M.

There's nothing better than a temperate morning in southeast Georgia. The air was cool enough at this hour that I didn't need the paddle fans turning on the back porch to be comfortable. I was draped on the chaise sipping my first cup of coffee and breathing in the aromatic fumes rising as steam. My craving for nicotine had faded into infrequent nudges I could ignore. My house and business were in order.

Rudy, my large black cat, was curled by my feet at the end of the chaise. Bobby Lee, my large handsome bloodhound, was stretched out on the twelve-inch pegged board floor. They were my housemates and had returned just minutes ago from their morning run. I glanced across the tarmac at the kennel and admired the bright sunlight reflecting from the large picture windows of the common room. Occasionally a muffled adult bay and the yips of a playful puppy competed with the cheerful background of birdcalls coming from the rose garden to my left.

Wayne Frazier, my kennel manager, had tossed the morning paper on the coffee table after unlocking the two security gates, an early morning ritual. The newspaper was yet unfolded. I preferred to savor the morning.

1

The first security gate's harsh signal shattered the tranquillity.

"Just when I thought it was safe to go back in the water," I grumbled as I quickly stood, walked to the door to my office, and waited for the second gate signal that would announce the arrival of whoever had entered my compound. The reason for the alarm-wired gates and me poised and ready to make a fast dash for an equalizer was my ex-husband, Buford Sidden Jr., known to all as Bubba. He has an ever-abiding desire to break every bone in my body with his favorite baseball bat. I protect myself the way all stalking victims should, with a restraining order that isn't worth spit and eternal vigilance, and back up both with a handy loaded gun.

I recognized the battered yellow compact and its occupant, Bertie Thompson, when she turned into the courtyard. She's Balsa City's delivery person. I walked to the edge of the porch and looked up. Jasmine Jones, a dog trainer and my right hand in all matters, was framed in her kitchen window. The security alarms are also wired into her apartment. She knows Bertie, and we exchanged a casual wave before she left the window.

Bertie is short, stout, and pear shaped, with an enormous rump. We grew up together. She had spotted Jasmine.

"Nosy, ain't she?" she called loudly as she approached the steps. Her mother is hard-of-hearing and since they live together, Bertie talks louder than a drill instructor. She also cusses like a sailor, is always cheerful, rescues more SPCA dogs every year to go with her present brood of more than two dozen, and has always been my friend.

"She helps me watch out for Bubba," I explained.

"Shit!" she said in disgust. "When you gonna quit pussyfooting around that turd and blow him to kingdom come?"

"Any day now," I answered easily to divert a tirade. "How 'bout some coffee?"

"Sounds good! Here, let me give you your delivery, a telegram, no less!"

I finished filling the cup that I had brought out for Jasmine, who usually joins me about this time, and gave Bertie a surprised glance.

"A telegram? Who could be sending me a telegram?"

She shoved it in my direction and snorted.

"Only way I know to find out is to open it, dummy!"

I tore open the envelope, read the short message, and smiled uncertainly at Birdie.

"Is this a joke, or maybe one of your tricks?"

"I haven't pulled a joke on you since the sixth grade, dammit!" she yelled.

She silently eyed me, but not for long. Curiosity killed the cat.

"What does it say?"

I read aloud, "YOUR PHONE IS OFF THE HOOK. CALL ME IMMEDIATELY AT 712-5595. CELIA CANCANNON."

I didn't recognize the name.

"My phone is never off the hook! I'm subject to be called out on a search-and-rescue by three counties, twenty-four hours a day, seven days a week. I'd never—"

I suddenly remembered Rudy's anger at being startled by my cellular phone's penetrating chirp last week during one of his frequent naps. He not only knocked it off the bed; he nosed it underneath, where I had to crawl to retrieve it. I thought it was an aberration, but if he was still holding a grudge . . . I glared at his sleeping form, and spoke loudly.

"If a certain CAT that answers to RUDY has rendered my phone inoperable, he's in a lot of TROUBLE!"

He sat up quickly, artistically wrapped his tail around his paws, and stared out at the sunshine, avoiding my eyes.

I groaned. "Excuse me," I told Birdie, "I'll be right back."

Moving through my office, I stopped by my desk and replaced the receiver that was lying on its surface and not in the cradle where it belonged. I continued to my bedroom, where I saw that my cellular was missing from the nightstand. It was under the bed, near the headboard. I retrieved it and carried it to the back porch.

"So is Rudy in trouble?" Bertie was grinning.

3

"He's due for a refresher course on telephone manners." I was grinning myself. "I'm proud of him, however. He figured out the way to keep both of them from ringing. He's one smart cat."

Bertie was stroking Bobby Lee's long ears.

"It's still hard to believe that this dog is blind."

"But he isn't any longer!" I exclaimed. "Has it been that long since you were here? He's had vision for months now." I counted on my fingers. "Six months exactly, today. It was April second, and suddenly he could see."

"Just like that?" She gave me skeptical raised brows.

"Exactly. We all called it a miracle."

"What did the vet call it? You know, the one that said Bobby Lee didn't have some connecting nerves or something was missing from birth? Bet he feels stupid!"

"The vet that originally diagnosed Bobby Lee's blindness is dead now. My present vet, Harvey Gusman, accepted the former vet's findings; he didn't have any reason to disagree at the time. Harvey now thinks that a blood clot was the problem, probably caused by trauma while still in the womb. He thinks it took two years to dissolve. I personally don't care what it was, I'm just thankful that he now has perfect vision. He's a joy to behold."

"Now that he can see, does it affect that extra-special talent that you were always bragging about?"

She said it kindly, and I knew she was just joshing me.

"Not at all. In fact, I think he's better than ever!"

She drained her cup. "Got to run. I hadn't finished feeding up when I got the call to roll at six damn A.M."

She was trotting down the stairs before I could properly say goodbye. I yelled it and waved as she gunned her small car through the first gate. I would send her a half-bag of dog food I hadn't gotten around to giving her for her tip. It couldn't be a full bag, because she was proud. A true daughter of the South wouldn't accept charity. I gathered up the cups and coffee to move inside.

I was at my desk with a fresh cup of coffee reading the telegram again. I didn't know Celia Cancannon from Adam. Jasmine gave a perfunctory knock, entered, and headed for the coffeepot, giving me a silent mouthed greeting. She saw I was punching in numbers on the phone.

I studied her as I listened to the repetitive rings of the phone. Jasmine had on a pair of jeans and a simple T-shirt in coral. She looked chic. I had on the same apparel except my T-shirt was light blue, and I looked dressed to dig potatoes and hoe the corn. Either you have it or you don't. She's African-American, with soft, gracefully curled hair, which complements her long slender neck. My hair is light brown and naturally kinks into a replica of last year's bird nest when it's damp. On the twenty-eighth of this month I will turn thirty-three. Jasmine is five years younger. I grew tired of comparing. I won't even mention her body.

"Mrs. Alyce Cancannon's residence."

"May I please speak with Ms. Celia Cancannon?"

"This is she."

"My name is Jo Beth Sidden, I received a tele—"

"Oh, thank God!" she interrupted fervently. "I've been trying to reach you since late yesterday! Amelia has been missing since lunchtime yesterday and Mrs. Cancannon is beside herself with worry. The helicopter can pick you up in less than thirty minutes. Please mark an X on your lawn in an area free of trees and power lines, so the pilot will know where to land. Use anything at hand. A can of white spray paint, a roll of paper towels or toilet tissue. Use canned goods to hold the two latter suggestions in place. Can you be ready in thirty minutes? Every minute counts!"

I had sat up straight and listened carefully after her second sentence. Her voice held stress and something else, possibly impatience, I couldn't be sure. Something was very wrong with this scenario. If this was a righteous callout for a search-and-rescue for a missing person, our local sheriff, Hank Cribbs, wouldn't have ignored my unanswered phone. Hank would have roared up my drive, siren wailing, lights blazing, with loud vocal recriminations. He knew that a scent trail grew colder with each hour lost. He also knew that a decision to wait for daylight to search was only mine to make. With bright sunshine out my window and no Hank, something was haywire.

"How old is Amelia?" I asked into the building silence.

"How old?" She hesitated. "I think she's five. Can I tell the pilot to take off? Can you be ready in thirty minutes?"

The impatience came through loud and clear. *She thought she was five?* Come on. I knew that Celia Cancannon was answering the phone at Mrs. Alyce Cancannon's residence, about a five-year-old Amelia, lost since lunchtime yesterday. Maybe the same name for both didn't mean they were related, thus she could be unsure of the child's age. Stranger things have happened.

"What is your relationship to Amelia?" I asked patiently.

"What do you mean?" She sounded confused. "I'm not related to her. She belongs to Mrs. Alyce Cancannon."

Belongs?

"Then *who* is Amelia?" Shades of Abbott and Costello, with their "Who's on First?" routine. I glanced at Jasmine and lifted my eyebrows upward.

"Oh, I'm sorry. I must have misled you. We have been so upset; I didn't state the facts clearly. Did you think Amelia is a child? She's a long-haired Persian. She's Mrs. Cancannon's cat."

"A cat," I uttered flatly.

I heard Jasmine suppressing laughter, but I carefully didn't look in her direction.

"Ah . . . Celia," I said, glancing at the telegram to be sure I was saying her name right. "We don't search for animals. You see, when we train bloodhounds, we have to constantly teach them *not to follow an animal scent.* The bloodhounds only scent-trail humans. I won't be able to help you. Sorry."

"Can't you make an exception? Please?"

Now I heard only desperation. Amelia must be some cat. I looked down at Rudy, now curled by my left shoe. I wondered if Mrs. Cancannon would like to replace her lost Amelia with an independent tom who didn't like telephones.

"I wish I could help, but it's out of the question."

Her voice was faint. "Thank you anyway."

I hung up the phone and leaned across my desk and handed Jasmine the telegram.

"Where do the Cancannons live?"

"We didn't get that far to exchanging addresses. She lost me when she said cat."

"Must be rich," Jasmine mused. "Sending a helicopter when it's just after dawn? You remember how hard it is to rent a helicopter, don't you?"

I laughed. "You got me. Of course I remember my aborted attempt to secure a helicopter some months back. Trust you to remind me."

"A small attempt to teach you humility."

"Nah, you like to lecture. Admit it."

"Do not."

"Do too."

The phone rang, bringing a disgruntled Rudy to his feet, and we watched him stalk toward the bedroom twitching his tail. It also stopped our nonsensical bantering, and I caught it on its third ring.

I propped my feet on the edge of the desk, getting comfortable. It was a few minutes before eight, and Monday morning. I guessed this call was from Susan Comstock, my best friend, who had arrived early at her shop, Browse and Bargain Books, and wanted to fill me in on her weekend. I guessed wrong. The breathless voice belonged to Celia Cancannon, and she almost ran her words together in her haste.

"Mrs. Alyce Cancannon, my employer, has authorized me to hand you a check in the amount of five thousand dollars when you deplane on the island, and give you another check for five thousand if you will search for Amelia, whether you are successful or not. Now will you come?"

2

"Get Thee Behind Me, Satan"

October 2, Monday, 8:00 A.M.

My feet slipped off the desk and my jaw dropped to my breastbone. I stretched my mouth in a comic *duh!* expression for Jasmine's benefit, and strove to sound nonchalant.

"Let me see if I understand your offer, Ms. Cancannon. Five grand when I arrive, and another five grand for the search regardless of the outcome?"

Jasmine's eyes widened, her hands covered her cheeks, and her lips formed a perfect oval. Her good sense took over way before mine. She looked sad as she slowly turned her head left and right.

God, the temptation was awesome. A five-figure infusion in the constantly drained operating accounts. But it would be a pretend search, would confuse any dog I chose, and my conscience would give my gut fits. It also had the potential to swing three-sixty and smear my reputation with bloodhound people, if truth were told. I gave the offer serious consideration for several heartbeats and reluctantly declined.

"You have to do this!" Celia Cancannon insisted. "Aunt Alyce has fixated on you as her only hope!"

It took another five minutes of denials of having any involvement before she hung up in defeat. I gave a loud sigh.

"You did the right thing," Jasmine assured me.

"Yeah, broke but honest."

"You are far from broke," she chided.

Wayne knocked and entered, with Donnie Ray right on his heels.

"Hi, guys!" I spoke and signed at the same time. Wayne is deaf. Jasmine stood with her coffee cup and moved to the left, where she could watch his flashing hands. We are all proficient in signing, even the full-time trainers and most of the part-timers.

"Good morning. The first feeding and weighing is finished. The trainers are out in the field. Donnie Ray is going to be working on the evening meal. I have to go to town for supplies. Need anything?"

Wayne is young and bright and a permanent fixture here. He and his mother moved into the upstairs apartment located to the left of the kennel almost three years ago. He was fresh out of a high school for special students. Rosie, his widowed mother, moved out just over a year ago when she married our local fire chief, and Donnie Ray moved in with him. Wayne is tall, dark-haired, and weighs just over two hundred pounds.

Donnie is short, feisty, blond, and has an ego as large as Texas. He is my videographer, filming the monthly seminars and the occasional searches we use for training films. I took him under my wing and have tried to instill good Southern manners to make up for his worthless slut of a mother, who failed to teach him anything. Wayne and Donnie Ray, so unalike, have bonded and work as a smooth team. I dread the day they find girls and marry. I don't want to lose either one of them. They, along with Jasmine and Rosie, have become my family. I don't have any living relatives I recognize as family.

I consulted my "want" list. "You can stop by Office Outlet and get me a dozen small legal pads. White, if they have them. And . . . I'm almost out of candy bars."

I saw his grin and quick glance at Jasmine. She remained silent, bless her heart. She always nags me about chocolate, but she knew I had resisted a much larger temptation a few minutes ago. I was receiving chocolate for consolation.

"Donnie Ray, when do we have the pleasure of viewing your latest masterpiece? It's been a while."

He looked embarrassed. "I had to scrape it. I messed up when I tripped over Richard. It lacked continuity."

I suppressed a smile. Richard the Lionhearted was a great drug-sniffer but was clumsier than a hippo wearing ice skates. He romped with abandonment through searches indiscriminately bowling over people, objects, or anything in his path as he pursued a drug trail. He'd knocked me on my butt more than once. I could sympathize.

"F-I-D-O," I counseled.

Donnie looked perplexed. "Fido?"

"Forget It, Drive On." I sanitized the saying by using an innocuous F. After all, I was Donnie Ray's role model and mother substitute. I couldn't use the appropriate F word in his presence.

After they left I rinsed the coffee things and made a banana and peanut butter sandwich on whole wheat bread. Even if Jasmine returned and saw my breakfast selection, she couldn't fault my choice. I had fruit, protein, and a double serving of grain.

It was bill-paying time. I turned on the computer and prayed that I wouldn't mess up too badly. My computer and I despised each other. Let me make the tiniest mistake, and she would gleefully fill my screen with incomprehensible gobbledygook, and I would be forced to grovel and try to extradite myself without calling for help. Anything that had a plug-in cord or required batteries was in on the conspiracy. I was appliance-cursed and computer-haunted.

The phone called me back to the real world.

"What kind of mood are we in today?" Hank asked when I answered. "Kindly, somewhat kindly, or pissy?"

Hank was Dunston County's elected sheriff and a good friend. He wanted more than friendship, but we had been there, done that, and had the scars to prove it.

"I can't speak for you, but I'm feeling quite benevolent this morning. What favor do you seek?"

"My lucky day," he said wryly. "Do you know the sheriff of Camden County, Jeff Beaman?"

"I met him once. It was at a drug seminar . . . in Savannah, I think. It was several years ago. He seemed nice."

"He's a good guy, I've known him for years. He called just minutes ago. He needs a big favor."

"And it involves me? Fire away, although I don't know why he didn't call me direct. Does he think by any chance you have some pull with me?"

"If he does, would he be right?"

I laughed. "Absolutely."

"Don't I wish. Beaman's jurisdiction covers the small islands just off the coast. Most of them aren't inhabitable, but two of them are privately owned. Cumberland Island is the barrier that protects them. The small island called Little Cat was the topic of his discussion. It's about seven miles from shore, straight out from Crooked River Inlet. Ever heard of it?"

"Nope. I—"

I just remembered Celia Cancannon had said the word island in one of her calls.

"Hank, if the owner of the island is Cancannon, I can't help. Sorry."

"Wait," he said anxiously. "I thought you had never heard of the island. What gives?"

"I too had an earlier phone call, two in fact. We never got around to discussing her location, I had to say no. I just remembered she mentioned island. So I put the two together. It's impossible."

"Babe, please reconsider. Beaman really needs to come through on this request, he says there's a great deal at stake."

"I can sympathize with his plight," I said in a wry tone. "They waved ten grand at me and I'm still suffering mightily for having to turn it down. I wonder what she offered him."

Hank gave a surprised whistle. "Ten grand?"

"Yep."

"There's no possible way you could do it? God, ten grand! What makes it so impossible?"

"They want me to search for a cat."

"Oh. I wasn't told it was a cat. Beaman said it was a valuable family pet."

"I also don't do dogs, raccoons, monkeys, exotic birds, turtles, guinea pigs, or reptiles. Did I leave anything out?"

"Christ, Sidden, don't be snide. No one would attempt that."

"A woman in California does."

"What?"

"A woman in California searches for exotic pets. I was just reading about her business. It's called Pet Pursuit. Maybe Ms. Gotrocks could fly her in. Shouldn't cost much more than the ten grand I was offered and whatever she promised Sheriff Beaman."

"Are you serious?"

"Absolutely. If the sheriff is interested, I have her address and telephone number, which I will supply free of charge. Maybe he'll be grateful and offer you part of his 'bonus.'"

"Why don't you just fake it?"

"Can't. Wouldn't be ethical."

"Don't hand me that crap. You've broken and stretched more laws than the law allows!"

"Y'all have a nice day now, you hear?"

I gently replaced the receiver.

I went back to closing last month's figures and trying to place the correct amounts on a floppy disk for my accountant. I dropped it into the padded self-addressed envelope and placed it in the mail basket.

I picked up a long-sleeved shirt. I was going to the kennel to give three five-month-old puppies some one-on-one tutoring. They were dropping so far behind their age group that I knew without a lot of work they would never catch up. They were having trouble with the commands *sit, stand,* and *come.* I planned on giving each one patient repetition, which is the key to training puppies. Their attention span was about fifteen minutes. After that, all they wanted to do was play. The long-sleeved shirt was to keep most of their drool off my arms. I'd be covered with it by lunchtime.

At half past noon, Jasmine and I were having lunch in the kitchen. She had made a salad while I showered off puppy slobber. The salad was delicious. Small cubes of three different cheeses, ham slivers, and cherry tomatoes. A light Russian dressing. I had told her about the puppies' antics. I was concentrating on my salad when she spoke.

"Remember telling me about Ivanhoe during rounds the first week I started working here?"

I nodded because my mouth was full.

"You caught my attention when you were discussing him. You mentioned that he was your worst failure in the history of the kennel."

"You got that right. That big lummox had no desire to scent track humans. All he wanted to trail were rabbits, coons, and . . ."

"Cats," she finished.

"He never entered my mind," I said thoughtfully. "He's, let's see . . . he's about seven now. I couldn't sell him to anyone but a hunter, and I would never do that. They would run him in the heat of summer to train the puppies. They keep their dogs in small cages, feed them erratically, and never give them enough exercise. But seven? He's probably given up his love to chase cats by now. He's not young and frisky anymore."

Jasmine kept her eyes on her salad. "Wayne tells me that Rudy has a set routine every evening as he and Bobby Lee leave for their afternoon run. He stops by Ivanhoe's quarters, and they race side-by-side, two full lengths of the long run while Bobby Lee watches, then Rudy breaks off the chase and they leave."

"Wayne has never mentioned a word to me about it!"

Jasmine smiled. "He didn't want to squeal on Rudy. He says Rudy thinks he's teasing Ivanhoe, but Ivanhoe enjoys it, and so does Rudy. He said no harm, no foul."

"True," I admitted. I thought about it.

"He's had a leash on twice a day, to be moved back and forth from his quarters to the exercise yard. He hasn't been put on a trail for over four years. He's probably forgotten every command he was taught."

"You could try." She grinned and used the tag line of an old Southern joke. "And we can always use the eggs!"

I was still chuckling as I reached to pick up the chirping cellular I had moved to the table before lunch.

"Hello."

"My name is Chief Justice Constance Dalby and I wish to speak to Ms. Jo Beth Sidden."

Her imperial voice was music to my ears. In my prior relationship with the judge, I had always been the one calling her, but now the shoe was on the other foot. I had been politely blackmailing her for years. I had asked favors on only three occasions, and each time it had been like pulling teeth.

I knew of one illegal act where she had been an accomplice and if I revealed it, it would blow her out of her Tenth District judgeship seat. I would never do it because it would also snare two good friends of mine, and place my own hide in jeopardy. Thank goodness she didn't know I would never reveal her secret. Her help had been invaluable when I needed her leverage. She truly despised me.

"This is Jo Beth. How are you, Constance?"

I flinched when she hissed her answer.

"You refer to me as Judge Dalby. I will not tolerate you speaking in to me in this manner. Is that clear?"

"Certainly, Judge. So what can I do for you?"

I knew what this phone call was costing her and decided not to tweak her pride.

"I believe that you were contacted by Ms. Celia Cancannon, on behalf of Mrs. Alyce Cancannon, to perform a service for her. Is this correct?"

"That is correct, Your Honor."

"I ask you to reconsider and accommodate Mrs. Alyce Cancannon."

"Judge, I wouldn't do it for anyone else, but your wish is my command. It's a done deal."

"You will?"

Her surprise that I let her off the hook so easily was monumental. She choked out a terse thank you and disconnected.

I gave an evil smile and a wink to Jasmine, who had seemed in shock ever since she heard me use Judge Dalby's name.

"We're on," I told her.

3

"Bringing in the Sheaves"
October 2, Monday, 1:00 P.M.

My first call was to Celia Cancannon, accepting her employer's generous offer and telling her to send the bird. She sounded so relieved and grateful, it made me wonder about the aunt who employed her. She might be a tough taskmaster to serve, or maybe she was just simply a frantic owner of a lost cat.

My second call was to the grooming room. Donnie Ray answered.

"Tell Wayne to harness Ivanhoe. Pack my backpack for two days, fill a small chest with a cool-pack for Ivanhoe's food, and another iced with six Diet Cokes. Two radios, my rescue suit, gloves, and deer jerky. Ask Wayne to go through our maps and find a detailed one of the smaller islands just off the coast that are between the mainland and Cumberland Island. The one I'm interested in is called Little Cat. Did I forget anything?"

"Ivanhoe?"

"'Yours is not to reason why,'" I quoted.

"I know, I know, I just do or die. Anything else?"

"Take a jumbo roll of paper towels out to the north field and make an X so the chopper pilot will know where to land. Use cans of Coke to hold it down. Place it a reasonable distance from the kennel roof."

"Are you sure just one roll will make it big enough?"

16

"It will make two forty-four-foot strips. Ever heard the expression, 'Just do it'?"

"Yes'em."

"Good man."

Knowing the total running feet on a roll of jumbo paper towels isn't trivia that I keep stored in my brain. I had just checked on the figures in the kitchen before I called. It had only shown cms, whatever they are, and not linear feet. The wrapper happened to mention it held ninety-six sheets, eleven inches square, so I had laboriously taken a pen and notepad, multiplying eleven times ninety-six and dividing by twelve. I'm the boss and supposed to know these things.

I called Hank.

"I'm taking the assignment. Call your friend, and tell him I'm dropping by in the next hour. I'll land in his chopper space, and tell him to keep himself available. I need all the daylight I can salvage this afternoon. And tell him not to take credit for my change of mind. Someone in the food chain way over his head accomplished it."

"And you're not gonna enlighten either one of us on who it is, are you?"

"You got it. See ya."

Jasmine was packing an overnight bag for me. I went to the bedroom to check on her. She was standing in front of my closet with the double set of folding doors open, to reveal all of the interior. I glanced in the bag and saw she had the essentials.

"What are you looking for?" I asked.

"You just might be invited to dine with the hostess of this foray tonight and not have to eat in the kitchen with the servants. I can't decide between the gold lamé top and the black long tube skirt, or the violet sheath."

"The basic black dress and one-inch heels."

She acted as if I hadn't spoken.

"I think I should pack both of them. You might be there for two nights."

"Not the gold spikes!" I pleaded when I saw them in her hands.

"You've had these shoes three years, and to my knowledge you have worn them twice. Are you saving them for your retirement?"

I sighed and picked up my snub-nosed .32. I checked the load, opened the bedside drawer, fed six more rounds into the elastic loops on my shoulder holster, shrugged it on, and fastened it below my breasts.

I walked into the living room and stooped to talk to Bobby Lee. He had followed me from room to room. When I strapped on the gun he knew I was preparing for a search. He was eagerly awaiting my command for him to fetch his leash.

"Sorry, sweetheart, it's a no-no. You can't go."

He followed me to the back porch, glanced at both of his leads hanging from nails on a pillar, and back at me. He still had hope.

I said good-bye to Jasmine when she joined us. I knelt again and fondled Bobby Lee's ears. He slumped in dejection when I pointedly said good-bye to him. I knew he would wait on the porch until I returned, whether it was a week or forever. I didn't look back.

I heard the approaching helicopter as I set my case down where Wayne had piled my gear. Wayne, Donnie Ray, and I watched as it hovered, then slowly lowered and touched down. Wayne handed me Ivanhoe's lead and I eyed him critically. We were both heading for uncharted waters. Wayne and Donnie Ray humped the gear out. The pilot had the door open but remained inside. He hadn't shut off the motor. The wind from the rotating blades blew my hair in wild disarray. Ivanhoe's ears were whipsawed, and his wrinkles all but disappeared from the wash's pressure. The guys loaded the gear and backed away.

I slapped the floor, lifted the lead, and Ivanhoe landed in front of the seat. I held him tightly and climbed aboard awkwardly, spraddling my legs where I could grip Ivanhoe's bulk between my knees. I was a tight fit, but his head was above window level, and he could see the ground. I slammed the door and glanced at the pilot.

He was pointing at Ivanhoe and then gesturing toward the back. I shook my head in an emphatic *no*. He reached behind him and came up with a helmet like he was wearing. I put it on and adjusted the chin strap and pulled the small mike closer to my lips. The noise abated and I could hear him clearly.

"The dog should ride in the rear. There isn't enough room for him up here."

What he really meant was he was very uncomfortable having such a large dog with a huge head, which held big teeth, sitting twelve inches from his right knee.

"I don't think so. He's fine here." I gave him a warm smile.

"I'm afraid that I'll have to insist." He was returning my smile with equal warmth.

"Ivanhoe has never ridden in a copter before," I said casually. "He could freak out any minute and go berserk. He weighs close to one hundred and thirty pounds. I have no idea how much damage he could cause, up to and including the ability to cause a crash if we're airborne. I believe I can control him from this position. Wanna give it a try?"

His smile slipped and he thought it over.

"You *believe* you can control him?"

His voice rose slightly with each syllable.

"No promises."

"What happens if I say no way?"

"Ivanhoe and I will bail out and you'll have a lonely trip home."

"Do you have a very large personnel injury policy on your business?"

"Huge."

"Well, with that assurance and the fact that I was told not to return without you, we will begin our perilous journey. Fasten you seat belt."

I pulled the belt out to its limit, ran it under Ivanhoe's harness, and awkwardly fastened it while he watched.

"Through thick and thin," I said.

"Can he swim? We'll be traveling over water."

I knew by his tone of voice that he was giving me a chance to have the last word. I began to breathe easier.

"No, but he can dog-paddle."

He lifted us upward, then sideslipped to the right. I caught a glimpse of Jasmine and Bobby Lee quickly becoming tiny miniatures as we climbed. When he leveled off and headed east, I spoke.

"I'm Jo Beth Sidden. Glad to meet you." I held out my hand.

"Randall Finch. Everyone calls me Rand."

We shook hands briefly and his returned to the controls. With the helmet and sun shades, I couldn't see much of his face. His teeth were very white and even. He had a nice smile and a strong chin. I'd have to wait 'til later to tell if he was handsome or homely. He had on a jumpsuit of stonewashed denim. Long legs. I compared his bulk with my memory of Hank's six feet, and he appeared to be as tall, and with the same broad shoulders. I couldn't see the color of his hair.

"Do you know where Sheriff Beaman's helipad is located?" I asked.

"The one in Woodbine?"

"He has more than one?"

"He has one by his office in Woodbine, two near police departments in other towns, and one by the Georgia Highway Patrol post on State Road Seventeen."

"Woodbine. Could you please stop there? I need to check in with him."

"Sure. Be about fifteen minutes."

"Thanks."

I watch a small section of Okefenokee unfold before me. The dark inlets looked black against the foliage. The wild maple leaves were just beginning to turn. The sweet gum and vines were yellow, red, and maroon. They had reached their peak of colors; most of the vines were yellow by August. The broomgrass was golden splotches of cover against the dark green of the cypress. Next month the cypress would shed and their denuded silhouettes would mingle with the evergreens and long-leaf pines of old growth, and the planted slash pine sections. Ivanhoe was staring downward out the window at the landscape, the same as I was. I wondered what he thought about being up so high, and seeing trees and water below him. He seemed to be taking the trip well; he wasn't nervous and whining.

Bloodhounds don't have the life expectancy of other breeds. Eight to ten years is average. At seven, Ivanhoe was in his late fifties, in people years. I noticed a few gray hairs in his muzzle. My knees were locked on either side of his body. I relaxed a little, and he tried to inch closer to the glass. We were a tight fit in the small space, and he couldn't move more than an inch or two because my right thigh was resting on the door panel. I hoped my legs didn't start cramping, because there wasn't enough room to stretch them.

"Your dog looks like he's enjoying himself."

I dabbed the edge of his gums with his slobber towel. I didn't want him shaking his head and slinging drool on me, or the expanse of the glass-enclosed cabin.

"Ivanhoe is a dedicated tourist. He hasn't taken his eyes from the ground since we took off."

"Ivanhoe?" He chuckled with amusement.

"We give all the dogs a working name. Drug dogs are named after famous authors and poets, Shakespeare, Chaucer, Tolstoy, Christie, the Brontës. Scent trackers are famous or infamous characters in fiction and history, Ulysses, Gulliver, Dr. Livingstone, Melanie. Our arson dogs are paired as famous or infamous lovers, Samson and Delilah, Tarzan and Jane, Bonnie and Clyde. You get the picture. We have fun naming them."

"Have you ever thought about some of those lovers? Most all of them have the man's name first; but I've never heard anyone say, Clyde and Bonnie, it's always Bonnie and Clyde. Do you ever wonder why?"

"Not with those two. Bonnie was the stronger personality, she deserved first billing. Clyde was a wimp."

"Are you married?"

I was surprised he asked so abruptly, then I understood. I was not at a loss for words when I replied.

"I was married at eighteen, corrected my mistake at twenty-one, which was twelve years ago; and yes, Rand, I am a feminist."

"You also read minds?" He sounded piqued.

I sighed. "Only when it's obvious."

"I was going to swear to you that you were dead wrong, but it is the question that popped into my mind the second you called Clyde a wimp. I figured you were basing your description of Clyde on the fact he was an underachiever in the sex department. Was I right?"

"Christ, no wonder people think that men are from Mars and women are from Venus! His sexual prowess didn't cross my mind. He was a whiner, and she had to psych him up before each bank job. You men constantly think of nothing but sex, sex, sex!"

I suddenly shut up and stifled a laugh. I had eyed him as if he was a piece of meat not three minutes ago; and now I had the audacity to accuse him for his sexual thoughts, when my musings had been running in the same direction.

"How did we progress this quickly into talking about sex?" I giggled as I posed the question.

He gave me a wide grin. "Because we were both thinking about it, and all women do is constantly think about sex, sex, sex!"

"Maybe," I qualified. "Just maybe."

"Here we are," he said, as he turned and dropped the craft gracefully downward. "This is Woodbine."

4

"Up, Up, and Away!"

October 2, Monday, 1:45 P.M.

When we were on the tarmac, Rand smiled.

"Will this take long?"

"About ten minutes."

He shut down the engine, and I watched the blades slowly stop their rotation. Sheriff Beaman left the shade of the overhang on the building and started walking our way. I lifted my left leg clear of Ivanhoe, opened the door, and told him to unload. He dropped to the pavement like a seasoned flyer.

"I'll just stretch my legs," Rand said, joining us.

"Here," I said, holding out the lead. "Why don't you take Ivanhoe over to the edge of the lot, and let him inspect the bushes?"

"Me?" He looked startled. "I don't know anything about handling dogs. I couldn't."

"Are you a chartered pilot, or do you fly for Mrs. Alyce Cancannon? Is this her helicopter?"

"Give me a break. I work for her, but I wasn't hired to walk a monster like this!"

"It's easy, don't be such a ninny." I thrust the leash into his hands. "Just hold onto him. A bloodhound loose in traffic is a dead

23

bloodhound. I'd hate to tell Mrs. Cancannon you lost the only dog within three thousand miles that stood a chance of finding Amelia."

I turned my back on them and walked toward the sheriff.

"Miz Sidden, I'm Sheriff Beaman. We met in Savannah."

"I remember," I replied as I shook his hand.

His appearance reminded me of the Marlboro Man, only ten years older and with a slight paunch. He was dressed in Western gear, from the ten-gallon hat to his pointy-toed boots.

"Cribbs called and gave me your message. Glad you're going to try to find Amelia for Mrs. Cancannon. She's not one of my favorite people but I have two cats at home, so I can empathize. He also mentioned the amount of your fee and the fact you were wondering what she offered me."

"It's not any of my business, Sheriff."

"She didn't offer me a dime, Miz Sidden, she knows that I will not accept money from her. It's what she threatened to offer my deputy that convinced me to call Cribbs to see if he could change your mind."

"Your deputy?" He seemed to be waiting for an answer, so I obliged.

"Yes'em. This deputy has been with the department as long as I have, and he's been itching to run against me for eight years now. So far, he's known better than to try. She told me she would hire a big-time agency from New York to run his campaign and spend as much money as it would take to make him sheriff. I'm sure he would go for it, any man would."

"You think she could get him elected?"

"I spent three hundred dollars on my first campaign twelve years ago on signs and having a big public fish-fry, and not a red cent since. With enough money, she could make our local drunk the next sheriff."

"Well, Sheriff, I wish I could tell her that you were the one who changed my mind, but the one that asked me last made me an offer that I couldn't refuse, if you get my drift."

"Miz Cancannon don't hold a grudge, Miz Sidden. She got what she wanted. You're gonna help her. She'll forget all about my deputy by next week."

"That's good. I'd better go try to find her cat. If you ever need a future favor, you can call me direct. I'll help if I can."

"'Preciate it." He swept the large hat off for the second time as we shook hands.

Rand was waiting, acting uneasy, until I relieved him of Ivanhoe's leash.

"Any problems?"

"He had a nice pee, wiped saliva on my pants leg and some dripped on my shoes, but he didn't take a bite out of my thigh, so I guess you could call the adventure a success."

"Bloodhounds aren't aggressive. They're not attack dogs. If you had hauled off and kicked Ivanhoe, he wouldn't have bit you. He's a pussycat."

"I'll take your word. I wouldn't attempt to kick a dog that big."

"That's nice," I said. "Ivanhoe wouldn't retaliate, but I would."

"I don't doubt it for a minute. Shall we depart?"

"Let's."

Without the helmet, I could see his facial features and his thick dark brown hair. He was one fine-looking man. Still couldn't see his eyes, they were covered with the wraparound shades, but all else checked out just fine.

When we were seated, and I was attaching the seat belt under Ivanhoe's harness, I saw that Rand had removed his glasses, and was polishing them with a cloth.

"Rand?"

He looked up. His eyes were dark brown-colored pools that you could drown in. I took a deep breath.

"What is it?" He was waiting for me to speak.

"How big is this island?"

It was the only thing I could think of to ask and I did need to know.

"About four by six miles, maybe a little less. Roughly a rectangle with wide sandy beaches on all four sides. There's a twenty-foot bluff on the north side and a small marsh area near the south end. Everything else in between is oak, pine, cypress, and thick growth. There are some fairly large clearings. There's a herd of feral horses, deer, wild hogs, all types of small game, and large herds of wild turkeys."

"Do you have a detailed topographical map?"

"I have one on the island. I'll get it for you when we land."

"Thank you."

When we had finished climbing and heading east again, I saw the edge of the Atlantic, a bright blue expanse that seemed to cover the world. There were small green islands right off the coast and one large one that was very long. That must be Cumberland Island, where my father had painted almost all of his paintings. I had never been there, except when I looked at his oils. He was a landscape artist. He died several years ago. I still miss him.

Long before we reached Cumberland Island, Rand turned and started descending from the south, heading into the wind. We flew low, just above the treetops. Suddenly we were flying over a large clearing, and I spotted several deer racing across a dark green lawn.

"Did you see the deer?" I asked.

"Yes. Sometimes they will stand on the exact spot where I want to land and just stare at me. I have to go back up and wait till they move."

I saw the roof of a large building, just getting a glimpse through small openings in the trees as we were coming down. He set the copter on grass in front of a large shed with a shinny aluminum roof. Even with my sunshades, the aluminum reflected the sun's glare so brightly, I had to look away.

"New roof, I see."

"This one is three years old. We need a new one after each big blow."

"You should use tin. It's not as expensive as aluminum."

He laughed. "You wouldn't recommend tin if you were visiting here during a hurricane or a violent storm. A piece of tin being blown by winds in excess of a hundred miles per hour is a missile just as deadly as a Scud. It can slice through a wall, roof, or window. It can lop off mature trees till they're nothing but stumps. We had six pieces go through the main roof during the no-name storm, and destroy one of the servants' cottages. Aluminum folds and crushes easier. It can do damage, but nothing compared to tin."

We deplaned and I took Ivanhoe to smell the bushes. Rand went into the shed. When he returned he was with two Filipino men in their fifties. One was pulling a small cable, which he attached to the front of the helicopter. With Rand on one side and the two Filipinos on the other, they walked slowly along side as the cable drew the machine into the shaded depth of the building.

There wasn't anything sinister in the scene, but I felt goose bumps dance on my spine in the eighty-degree heat. I guessed it was the contrast of the brilliant light and inky darkness within the shed. Maybe it was the realization that the object that disappeared from my view was my only link to civilization.

Rand pulled out of the cavernous shed in a sparkling new Ford pickup. I could see my gear piled on the open tailgate, where one of the Filipinos sat dangling his short legs from the truck bed.

I opened the passenger door and patted the seat for Ivanhoe. He scrambled in and sat on the smooth bench seat. I had to scoot him over to have room to get in; he wanted to hang his head out the window. It was an automatic reaction that is always present in all canines, not a learned experience, because to my knowledge, he had never been in the front of a pickup before.

"Have you noticed that the man in back hasn't closed the tailgate? It's not safe for him to ride where he is now."

Rand chuckled. "He'll be fine. What are you doing?"

I was struggling with the seat belt and Ivanhoe wasn't helping. He had one huge paw in my lap, leaning over to get closer to the window.

"Stop, Jo Beth," he said, grinning from ear to ear. "The belt is not necessary."

He reached over and caught my hands in his when I continued to try to buckle up.

I went still. "Why not?"

"It's a short trip."

"That's no excuse."

"It's a very short trip."

"So?"

"You didn't notice the truck. What do you think of her?"

"It's a nice truck." I sent a fleeting glance around the cab and turned my eyes to his, and waited.

He turned on the key, and I saw the instrument panel light up.

"Look at the gas gauge."

I leaned around Ivanhoe for a closer view. The needle was resting below empty. I saw that one of the little figures that lights up when something is amiss was a glowing red. I pointed to it.

"Your gas gauge is empty," I said wryly. "Your warning light is telling you you're almost out of gas, and I bet there isn't a gas station for miles and miles. Do we walk?"

"No, I've been driving it a year. She's a gas guzzler, and by next October I'll have to put in a gallon."

I pushed on Ivanhoe to move his legs back and leaned closer to read the mileage. My eyes widened.

"You've only put twenty-one miles on this truck in a year?"

"Well, two miles of that was from the dealership to the dock, in Fernandina Beach. I only put two gallons in the tank because I plucked her off the deck of the Cumberland Island ferry two miles offshore. The ferry couldn't get any closer. I didn't want a full tank of gas in case I dropped her in the Atlantic, or on the lawn."

"You obviously didn't drop her, and you're really not going to put more gas in the tank for another year?"

"We have a pool going, and most of the people on the island have invested. I picked next October first for the day she runs dry. I've also locked the gas tank to keep everybody honest."

"How long is this very short trip?"

"Three hundred yards."

"I'll go without buckling up, I like to live dangerously."

"Atta girl!" He clamped his hand over his mouth in mock chagrin when he caught me wrinkling my nose. "OOPS! Bad choice of words. Atta person! How's that?"

"Fido!" I replied, acting haughty and pointing imperiously toward the small blacktop road.

5

"Meeting Mrs. Gotrocks"

October 2, Monday, 2:30 P.M.

Our three-hundred-yard journey was uneventful. Two short curves and we were at the door of the mansion.

"Wow," I whispered in awe.

This three-storied edifice made Tara look like a gardener's cottage. The grayish front wall loomed above us. I had to lean out the window to gaze upward to find the red tiled roof, and twist backward to see where the mixture of brick, stone, wood, and mortar of the wall ended.

"It's larger than it looks," Rand stated.

"It couldn't be, it looks bigger than the Pentagon. How many bedrooms?"

"There's twenty guest rooms, and five permanent suites for the relatives when they visit."

"La-di-da. Hold my mint julep, Colonel, while I whip my slaves."

"That won't play here. This house wasn't built until the early nineteen twenties. Miz Alyce's relatives were all foreigners or transplanted Yankees and it remains the same mixture today for the present staff, including me."

I detected a hint of coolness and felt the blush rising from my neck to suffuse my face.

"Goodness gracious!" I was suddenly a full-blown southern belle. "I've always said, one shouldn't have to apologize for the circumstances of their birth, which includes where they were born. Don't you agree?"

I had gotten carried away in my role and began to rapidly fan my face with the loop of Ivanhoe's leather leash.

Brad laughed. "I think I just dropped a couple of points in your pole."

"Only one," I replied, with saccharin sweetness, "and if you deduct one from mine it makes us even. The relatives that visit, are they her children?"

"She had no children. It's five nieces, from two of her husband's older brothers who died years ago. She partially raised them. It's four nieces that visit, all of whom are married. The fifth, Celia Cancannon, resides here permanently and has never married."

"Is there a Mr. Cancannon?"

"He died when Miz Alyce was thirty. She never remarried."

"How many servants are employed here?"

"Forty-five, which includes the gardeners, but the total fluctuates with the seasons."

"Jesus! I thought I had a heavy operating nut. Just one more question, and then we'll go face the dragon. Does she talk to you, confide, or seek your opinion on anything?"

"She prefers conversations with men. Outside of her lawyer, veterinarian, and a elderly friend from New York who visits from time to time, I'm the only man on the island she sees. We have dinner together several times a week. Why?"

If he didn't see where my questions were leading, I wasn't going to enlighten him at this point.

"Just being nosy," I answered vaguely. "Let's do it."

He hesitated when we reached the top of the steps.

"Jo Beth, I need to ask a favor. Will you take it easy on her? Her bark is worse than her bite."

"Should I bow before I tug my forelock, or after?"

"I knew I'd mess it up if I tried to explain. She's having a lot of pain from her arthritis. It makes her sound more testy than she really is."

"You like her don't you?"

"Yes, I do," he admitted. "Very much."

The question popped in my mind without thought. Did he admire her, or her money? I was irritated at thinking along those lines. I usually didn't form a negative opinion about someone that I'd just met. Why was I so skeptical of Rand's fondness for his employer? I felt an almost over-powering desire to turn on my heel and demand that he return me to the mainland immediately. Later I would curse my stupidity for ignoring my gut's strong warning. Now, I just shrugged away my reluctance and smiled up at him.

"If you like her, I'm sure I will too."

Relieved, he pushed the bell in the impressive entranceway to announce our arrival.

A short stout Filipino female opened the huge door. She was in her fifties. She recognized Rand before her eyes discovered Ivanhoe. She was swinging the door inward and her shoe slid on the entrance tile, as she hastily tried to close it in our face.

She was clattering excitedly in her native tongue to Brad. He arrested the moving door, spoke soothingly to her in the same language, as he was giving us room to enter. Ivanhoe and I entered the foyer and paused when the door closed behind us.

The woman kept shaking her head and staring at Ivanhoe. Rand spoke again. She bit her lip, gave a terse answer, whirled, and took off in a big hurry.

"None of us got much sleep last night. We all searched the grounds for Amelia. Celia is lying down, and I sent the maid to fetch her. She is alarmed over the big dog, didn't want it in the house."

"A normal reaction," I stated calmly. "I've known some men that feel daunted by his presence." He shot a swift glance my way, but my face was serene. He took too long to think of an answer and decided to keep silent. There was a large clock ticking somewhere, and I could hear faint music further away. I moved my feet and leaned against the silk-paneled wall. Although it looked elegant, it wasn't practical for this climate. I also knew I couldn't brace my foot against its delicate and pristine surface. Not practical at all.

I wondered if Amelia had ever reached up to stretch and sharpen her claws on the lush fabric.

"Where are my manners!" Rand remarked, as the clock ticked away. "Jo Beth, why don't we move to the reception room here?" He was indicating a door to the first room on the right.

"I'll stand. Thanks anyway."

I felt a tug on Ivanhoe's lead. I glanced down and he had his nose to the carpet and wanted to follow the smell that interested him. I pulled him back gently, and pushed on his broad back near his tail and forced his rear downward, into a sitting position. I was afraid to give him the "sit" command; he hadn't heard it in years. It always embarrasses me when I give a command and the dog ignores it.

The clock continued ticking. This is one of those silences that grows so heavy, you feel the need to punch holes in it, flood the silence with words; anything but simply listen to the damn clock eating up the seconds. My heart was pumping faster while I tried to keep my expression neutral. I knew Ivanhoe would smell Amelia inside the house, but I didn't know if he would react to it, and track her outside excluding all other smells, such as rabbit, coon, et cetera.

I still didn't know the answer to the latter, but this foolish effort I was attempting now seemed a little more feasible.

I don't care how much you vacuum, clean, and spray a room with deodorizer, if a cat lives inside a house he leaves a distinctive scent, as do all species of animals and Homo sapiens. A bloodhound's scent ability is over a thousand times more powerful than a person's nose. Their long dangling ears are a useful tool as they search. They stir the scent, cup it, and bring it closer to their nose.

A good ten minutes passed until a statuesque raven-haired beauty hurried toward us with the reluctant maid lagging a good distance behind her. To use the vernacular of this region, she was "built like a brick schoolhouse," which is suppose to be a compliment on one's figure, but I've never understood the connection. I'll just say she was built, period. Wide shoulders, nipped in waist, generous hips, and legs that ran on forever. I think we waited while she freshened her makeup. It was flawless. She looked like a well preserved forty, but I've always been lousy in guessing people's ages.

She tossed Rand a brilliant smile and came toward me with her hand outstretched.

"You must be Ms. Sidden. I'm Celia Cancannon, and I'm delighted to meet you, and your dog! I'm so glad Aunt Alyce's generosity finally convinced you to come to our island!"

While shaking my hand, she deftly moved to where my body was between her and Ivanhoe. I can be more gracious than a transplanted Yankee, any day.

"Call me Jo Beth," I oozed with southern charm. "Y'all have such a lovely home. Have you worked here long?"

Her smile slipped a notch. "I've lived here most of my life, and now I'm glad to be here when Aunt Alyce needs me. If you'll follow me, I'll take you to her. She's quite distraught over Amelia's disappearance. Rand can take the dog outside."

"I'm afraid not," I said with politeness, "Ivanhoe and I are in the process of bonding."

I didn't elaborate. I just let the issue hang there between us, like unavoidable flatulence.

Her lips thinned. "Surely—"

"Not a chance." I projected over whatever she was about to purpose.

I watched her haughty demeanor drop with a mental thud, and anxiety, fear of her aunt, and uncertainty return. This was the woman I had spoken to on the phone, and one I could come to like. She was showing her true self, and was being painfully honest.

"Oh God, she'll have a fit! She'll blame me for not being intelligent enough to con you into leaving the dog outside. What will I tell her?"

I grinned. "Take me up and I'll do the talking. Just shake your head and shrug, like I'm impossible."

"Bless you. I try so hard, but I never seem to please her."

"Speak up, and don't let her intimidate you. She might fire you but she would respect you more."

"I can't take the chance, I've been her doormat too long." Her plaintive answer touched me.

I turned to Rand. "Go sit in that room you mentioned, and don't wander off. I may need to make a fast getaway."

"With your attitude, you'd better be good and find Amelia quickly. It's the only way she will forgive you. If you fail, I'd hate to be in your shoes next week!"

"I'm not afraid of a millionairess."

"Try billionairess. It would be more accurate."

"You may have a point," I said, giving him a wink. "Stand by for a *really fast getaway*. She could shoot me for insolence, and get away with it."

"It gladdens my heart that you pay attention so well!"

He was irritated.

"Gotcha."

I took Celia's arm and we ascended the staircase. I had to almost pull her along. When we were on the second floor landing, she hesitated and whispered.

"We must knock and wait until she gives permission to enter."

"Is it her bedroom?"

"No, she's in her office."

We stopped in front of the door that Celia indicated. I rapped my knuckles twice—turned the knob and entered—gave Celia and Ivanhoe time to get inside the door before I closed it firmly. I turned to approach Miz Cancannon. She was at her desk and looked shocked.

It was a long walk to reach her desk. She sat in stony silence.

I settled in a large leather chair in front of her desk. Ivanhoe flopped on the Oriental carpet and prepared to take a nap. I gave Celia a pointed look, and she slowly perched her fanny on the edge of a cushion to my left.

Celia spoke. "Aunt Alyce, this—"

Celia stopped immediately, when Ms. Cancannon raised a veined hand. She was younger than I thought she'd be, she looked like she was in her late sixties. She had dark brown hair, with very little gray at the edge of her temples.

For the first time, I took my eyes from her face and saw she was sitting in a wheelchair. It was rolled close to the large desk and obviously was on a raised platform. The chair didn't make her look shorter, she dominated the desk and the room. I would guess her dress size was an eighteen. She wasn't fat; her upper body looked firm from exercise.

"My dear Celia, you don't have to identify my visitor. The bloodhound accompanying her tells me who she is. I've been sitting here contemplating her bad manners and your sudden pseudo courage to sit in my presence without my permission."

Celia jumped up, as if someone had goosed her.

"Celia, would you excuse us for a few minutes?" I asked, adding a warm smile. "Miz Cancannon and I need to talk."

She stared at her aunt with a silent plea, and hastily withdrew when she received a contemptuous wave of dismissal.

I slouched lower in my chair, rested my right foot on my left leg, and waited until I had her attention.

"Miz Cancannon, first let me apologize for my rude behavior in the way I entered your office. I was raised correctly to be polite to my elders, and I've always tried to practice good southern manners. I did it deliberately, as I wanted you to know two things quickly. You can't run roughshod over me, and also to try to put a little starch in your niece's spine. I didn't accomplish either of my goals.

36

"I wish to tell you, however, I'm sure most people who bow and scrape in your presence excuse your actions by calling them eccentric because you possess a few hundred million. Personally, I think you are a tyrannical harridan who gets her jollies by making the people around you squirm. Now it's your turn."

6

"Here, Kitty, Kitty"

October 2, Monday, 3:15 P.M.

Miz Cancannon gave me a long, calculating appraisal. *She probably knows my bank balance, to the penny. Maybe she's trying to decide if it's worth the effort of having me squashed like a bug. Or she could be mentally measuring me for a shroud.* I passed a message to my brain. *You will not squirm or blink. Look her square in the eye.*

She shocked me. She snorted in amusement.

"You have no idea how much you sound like me when I was your age. Full of piss and vinegar. Ready to tackle the world. Going to bring equality to all women, and right all wrongs. Yes, I was informed that you're a feminist. How naive you are. You have just enough backwoods smarts and gall to be dangerous, not only for yourself, but people around you. I will turn sixty-seven the twenty-ninth of this month. What does that tell you?"

"That we're both Scorpios? Is that what you're basing your comparison of the two of us on? Christ, Miz C., do you read your horoscope each morning and plan your day around it? It's a wonder you're not broke. We're nothing alike."

"We both have a ruthless streak in our makeup," she said, sounding smug. "You try to suppress yours, while I use mine to full advantage.

Case in point. Without hesitation, you shot a man three times in the chest for killing your dog, and yet you've let that psycho you married come within a heartbeat of killing you twice. You don't practice what you try to preach, Ms. Sidden. Leave Celia alone. She's my responsibility."

I stood so I would have better control of Ivanhoe. He was getting restless. He must be smelling Amelia. She might have spent a lot of time in this room. A bloodhound can nap on his feet, if he can find something or someone to lean on. They will sleep twenty hours a day if they aren't working. Ivanhoe was audibly sniffing the area of carpet around the chair and distracting me from thinking up a zinger to answer Miz C.'s amateur analysis of my character.

"I've enjoyed our little chat, Miz C., but the sun is slowly sinking in the west, and I need daylight to search for Amelia. I need to ask some questions. You do still want me to try to find your cat, don't you?"

"Of course I do!" she snapped. "That's why I offered the big bucks, which you wouldn't refuse!"

I let that one pass. This woman knew enough about me without giving her a hint about the judge. She must have checked me out when Amelia had been lost long enough to know she was going to need outside help. I could picture her on the phone about midnight, awakening sources without impunity, demanding answers and information. This made me pause. She was a formidable foe. I don't needlessly poke at rattlesnakes. I should watch my p's and q's while in her presence.

"Was the house searched from top to bottom? I don't know much about cats, but I do know they can hide in some extraordinary places if they are sick or hurt."

"I can assure you that Amelia is not inside. My entire staff combed the building. They were told if Amelia was overlooked, they all would share the blame."

That ought to do it, I silently agreed.

"What was the perimeter of the outside search?"

"Within the immediate vicinity of close buildings. I, unlike you, know a great deal about cats. I've had Amelia five years, and I haven't

39

always been in this wheelchair. She didn't like the tall grass and uncleared brush. She would never go beyond the mowed areas. When dew or frost or rain was present, she never left the house. She didn't enjoy getting her feet wet."

"There's the possibility that she was kidnapped, or catnapped, to be more accurate. Do you have any enemies, someone who might want to get even with you for anything?"

I was proud of myself in keeping a straight face while I delivered these words. I bet her enemies were legion.

"Impossible," she snapped angrily.

"Nothing is impossible," I paraphrased. "Some are just more improbable than others."

"You misunderstood my answer," she said, sounding superior and omniscient. "I have more enemies than a third world nation. That's why I have remained on this island for the past twenty years without once leaving it. I have two round-the-clock motor patrol boats three miles out, making constant surveillance of all watercraft, using both radar and sonar. The coastline was checked during the night for any boat that was rented or moored within two hundred miles in either direction. The overlook flight film didn't produce a single boat near this island for the last twenty-four hours. *That was why I stated it was impossible!*"

Good God, she must have both Army and Naval Intelligence in her pocket. Was it possible that the overlook flight she mentioned was actually our "Spy in the Sky" satellite, or our national weather satellite's orbit over this area? Hell, it might be both, or maybe she was afflicted with megalomania, with delusions of grandeur.

"Uh-huh," I muttered, keeping skepticism out of my voice. "I'll need something that Amelia touched, a sleeping pad cover or something she played with, to use as a scent article."

"Anything else?"

"No, ma'am."

She picked up the phone.

40

"Celia, come up and show Ms. Sidden out. Give her the bag you prepared of Amelia's things."

"Just remember, I have only a slim chance of finding her. This dog was not trained for cat recovery, and has been in retirement for four years."

"You must have a reason for using this particular dog. I understand you have fifty-nine adult dogs in your kennel at the present time, not counting your pet, Bobby Lee."

I gawked at her. I noted the malicious pleasure on her face. My head whirled in shock. The only way that she could know the actual head count at the kennel was from one of my employees who worked inside the compound. The number of dogs fluctuated—sometimes daily—but never remained the same for longer than a week. How many dogs we had currently wasn't posted on the sign outside my business or inside.

The only reason I'm aware of the exact count myself and knew she was correct was that Wayne had shipped Simply Simon to his new home in Hainesville this morning. The transfer of ownership papers were lying on my desk while I was totaling out September. I had entered the sale in the computer.

"Did I make any mistakes in closing out September this morning?"

I knew she had violated my computer. The only people who would have this information lived within the compound with me. Wayne, Jasmine, and Donnie Ray. I'd trust them with my life.

"How can you be certain it wasn't one of your staff?"

"Some people have loyal friends. I have many. How about you?"

She only smirked. I was at the door when she decided to speak.

"I met your father once, almost twenty years ago. I recognized he was a genius with oils and I invested in his paintings."

She's baiting you! my mind cautioned. *Don't you dare ask; and if you have to ask, for God's sake, don't beg!*

"Do you . . . still have them?" At this moment, my heart had control over my mind.

"We'll discuss them," she commented slyly, "if and when you return with Amelia."

I opened the door, pulled Ivanhoe clear, and slammed the door with all my might.

When I turned, Celia stood frozen ten feet down the hall.

"What happened?" she whispered, looking terrified.

"Why are you whispering?" I yelled angrily. "How can you stand to be around that bitch? Get me out of this maze, and give me the damn cat's scent articles, before I shoot somebody!"

She scurried in front of me, trotting to keep ahead of my long stride. I followed her blindly, choking on my anger. When we reached the stairs, I passed her at a fast clip and stopped only when I was standing in front of my gear, which had been placed against the wall in the entranceway. I popped a Diet Coke, took a long swallow to ease my dry throat, and looked around for Rand. I sat on my ice chest and started taking off my shoes. Celia approached timidly, holding a paper bag. She seemed worried.

"Are you going to search for Amelia?"

"Of course, that's what I came to do." I was calming down, somewhat.

"Rand," I yelled, "front and center!"

I had both legs in my rescue suit when he came out of a door to my right and looked at me with apprehension. I glanced at my watch before I stuck my arms in the sleeves. It was hard to believe it was only 3:30, and I had spent only fifteen minutes in the witch's presence. It had seemed a lot longer. I shrugged the suit over my shoulders, and zipped it closed. It was neon yellow with large white letters denoting SEARCH AND RESCUE on the front and DUNSTON COUNTY SHERIFF'S DEPARTMENT on the back.

"Nice suit," Rand offered.

"It's made of lightweight Kevlar. It's briar-proof, fang-proof, and almost but not quite bulletproof."

I was putting my shoes back on.

"Don't shoot anyone you run into out there. All the servants that are not on duty are scouring the brush hoping to find Amelia on their own. They think they will receive a generous reward."

"*El Grande Bastardo* will probably fire them for them not finding Amelia sooner."

Rand smiled. "They're Filipinos, not Spanish, if that was what you were trying to imitate."

"Whatever," I snapped.

"I gather the meeting didn't go well?"

"I'm proud of myself. I fought a good clean fight. I didn't kick or scream or draw my gun."

"I was hoping that you two would hit it off."

"Hit would have been a good choice. I didn't do that, either." I looked hard at him. "Are you going to be here when I return?"

"The clan is all gathering to console their aunt. If you're out more than two hours, I will be. Two have already landed at JAX. I expect the other two within the hour. I'll fly over and pick them up."

I glanced at Celia. The news that her cousins were to arrive soon didn't make her happy. She looked troubled.

"Do they give you a hard time too?" I asked her.

Rand spoke quickly. "Don't worry, Celia, I'll keep them occupied so they won't give you a hard time."

As she looked at him, her face softened. I thought, *Well, well, she really likes him. Okay,* I corrected, as she continued to gaze at him, *she really, really likes him.* I couldn't read Rand's face. His expression was a closed book.

I was loading my pockets and checking my backpack. I had attached Ivanhoe's lead to my belt. He wanted to explore the premises.

"I'll have your luggage taken up, and have the maid unpack for you. You'll be tired when you get back."

"Thanks, Celia, but don't you dare touch my things. I wouldn't spend a night under this roof for a million bucks! Rand is going to fly me home when I finish. I'm going to give this search to near first dark, then I'm coming in and Rand will take me home. Isn't that right, Rand?"

"If that's what you want."

"I just remembered. You don't have telephones out here. How did you know the clan was gathering and needed to be picked up?"

"We have a radio hookup in Fernandina Beach. They relay all long-distance calls in and out. Our radio can also reach Camden County. It's where we do our local shopping."

I pulled out my radio and arched my brows in question.

"Sorry, won't work. The closest signal tower is a good forty miles on the far side of the Camden County Sheriff's Department."

"That means I have no means to communicate. Don't worry if I don't show up tonight. If I'm not back two hours after sunrise, come looking for me in your bird. I have signal flares I will use if I can hear you. If I'm unconscious, you'll have to find me the hard way."

"If I have to look, I'll find you," Rand assured me.

"I'm counting on it."

I drained my Diet Coke, and they wished me luck.

Outside, I knelt beside Ivanhoe.

"Well, partner, we're both cherries on this adventure. You've never had a successful search for a human, and I've never searched for a cat. We're evenly matched, so maybe we'll get lucky. Let's give it a try."

7

"Cat Trailing"

October 2, Monday, 3:40 P.M.

I spent the first hour circling the house and constantly pulling Ivanhoe back on track because he wanted to return to the house, where the scent of Amelia was the strongest. I gently tugged on the leash to suggest he go left instead of right. I was walking the perimeter in a clockwise rotation.

After two circles, I moved out another three hundred yards, and tried to work counterclockwise. Not once did he go right. He kept trying to return to the house.

I stopped and presented the bedraggled hairy gray mouse that I was told was her favorite toy. The mouse no longer squeaked. It looked as if it had not been treated kindly, and had had a very bad year.

"Find the kitty, here, kitty, kitty!" I whispered with excitement into Ivanhoe's ear, for the hundredth time. Bloodhounds pick up the handler's emotion. If you act bored, they will copy you in no time, losing their enthusiasm for the search. I was trying to use the same words I shouted out the back door when Rudy had taken a powder.

"Here, kitty, kitty, here, kitty, kitty!" Ivanhoe perked up, raised his head, and pawed playfully at my leg, trying to get me to jump at him, or run away. I sighed, and again pulled out the disreputable mouse. My

45

back was already throbbing. Stooping with a thirty-pound pack on your back every three to five minutes can make you wish you hadn't, after a couple of hours.

"Let's find Amelia," I sang in a high squeaky voice. "Ivanhoe is a good dog! Find Amelia!" I took a couple of shuffling steps sideways, looking foolish, I'm sure. He sprang along with me, and poked his nose in the air with pure joy.

I put my hands on my hips and stretched. When I switched my attention back to Superdog, he began pulling on the lead, nose held high, and his loose wrinkles on his high narrow head quivering in intense concentration. He changed from dancing clown to a dedicated trailer in less than fifteen seconds.

I wasn't positive, however, about the object of his search. His head should be down near the ground. I gave him plenty of room to maneuver by feeding out slack on the long lead and letting him pull me for a change. He picked up his speed and was clearly excited. I wasn't.

Amelia would stand about a foot tall. To trail her, his nose should be active near the ground, his long ears funneling the smell from below to his nose. His huge ears were flopping with each step, but they didn't look like they were doing much scooping. If he was trailing a mother coon carrying supper back to her brood in a large nest high in a cypress tree, I was going to inform him he was now permanently in full retirement. Damn, it could also be a wildcat or bobcat. If he ran one of those guys to ground, he could get scratched eyes and a lacerated muzzle. It also could easily be a black bear on the prowl for honey. If this was what he was chasing, I hoped the bear was in good shape and could outrun him. 'Course, they usually sleep during the day and hunt at night.

We were traveling through waist-high grass, briarberry bushes, and cattails, already turning a deep brown. Plenty of titi and palmetto shrubs. Small yellow leaves were clinging to my gloves where we had brushed against vines that slowed our progress.

"Hey, big guy, halt! Halt!" Ivanhoe finally slowed, turning back to me looking impatient. "Just give me thirty seconds to catch my breath.

Jeez!" My rescue suit was breezeproof. Air couldn't circulate inside and I was sweating buckets. I could feel it trickling down my torso and running down my legs. I'd be soaking wet when I pulled off my suit. I was also wheezing like an asthmatic. The seven months I had refrained from smoking still hadn't cleared my lungs.

I looked back to see how far we had came from the house. I could see a sliver of roof and the top of a double chimney. The grade of the land was beginning to slope upward. It would make it harder for me to run and breathe at the same time. My head snapped around when I heard a large animal crashing through dry brush. It was about five, or maybe a tad later. Our scent on the air had probably spooked a couple of deer. I took another deep breath as Ivanhoe and I stared toward the east, where the cracking foliage had been trampled in a wild flight to avoid us. They were more frightened of us than we were of them.

My breath slowed and I reluctantly let Ivanhoe start the search, and labored on another fifty feet of ground that continued to present a steeper climb. I let Ivanhoe half-pull me to the top of the small cliff. The ground was turning white in spots, and I thought I saw small patches of sea oats on the next dune, which was slightly higher than ours was. We were a good two miles from the water.

Perhaps a small inlet had been formed by erosion and drifting sand. The house was less than a mile away, I had seen it just a short time ago, and I remembered it was located almost exactly in the center of the island. I should have waited for Rand to fetch his map, but my anger made me impetuous and drove me to leave prematurely. I had no fear of getting lost. Ivanhoe could lead me back to the house in minutes. I wondered what four-legged creature he was trailing. I knew for certain that he wasn't mantrailing: He had never accomplished a successful find.

As we walked closer to the open area, I noticed that the leaves and small vines had been swept neatly against the trees and shrubs, leaving an almost circular area clear of debris. The air currents must rotate up here more fiercely than in the lower areas.

Ivanhoe had his head up, testing the light breeze. Since his head was already tilted upward, I had no warning when his huge jaws opened and he let forth a loud joyous bay of success. My heart leaped into my throat. He was celebrating that he was near his target. Bloodhounds run mute. They only bay when they know they have located the origin of the scent they're seeking.

We raced over the open area, scrambling for purchase, his paws and my feet sliding in the shifting sand. He was baying continuously and I was yelling in excitement and praising him for his victory. He reached the end of his journey, and placed both paws on a man-made circular object, and continued his baying.

I fell to my knees and shrugged off my backpack.

My chest heaved from the exhausting run. Sweat was pouring from every pore. I had to cool down some before I tried to ease my constricted throat with liquid. I sat there gasping like a fish out of water. Ivanhoe finished his solo and dropped on his belly beside me. He was huffing, and puffing, as hard as I was.

"We both need to exercise more," I wheezed.

I absently patted his shoulder as we both eyed the cistern. My mind had furnished the name while I was waiting for my breathing to ease. They were made years ago, to store water, or to contain a natural spring or hand-dug shallow well. It must be old. The solid mixture of concrete and crushed seashells had a dark patina, fading from black to light gray. The outside was pitted, and had spider cracks leading to where mortar had eroded and fallen away.

It was embedded in the sand, three feet above the ground, and three feet from side to side. The top looked heavy. I was in no hurry to try to slide the cover over far enough to inspect the contents.

Ding dong bell, Pussy's in the well. Throw Amelia in the ocean, the tide might wash her back to shore. Toss her in the trash, and she might be found. I didn't know how garbage was handled on the island. Sorted and burned, buried, or Rand might airfreight it out. They couldn't use an open landfill; the animals would be at risk. With the

48

high water table here, she couldn't have been killed and hidden in the brush either. In this heat the smell would draw scavengers, and buzzards circling the area would be a dead giveaway for the search party.

So Amelia was abducted, and tossed in an abandoned cistern which, I imagine, very few knew about. No one would lift the lid to look inside. She couldn't have fallen in accidentally, then pulled the cover over her. Amelia hadn't walked here. She was carried in someone's arms. Ivanhoe had been taking the scent out of the air, not the ground.

Maybe she had been catnapped. A terrified cat can be a handful. They scratch and bite, and can seem to have supernatural powers to wiggle free if they don't want to be held. Maybe she was killed accidentally, while someone was trying to spirit her away. That would account for no ransom demand. Anyone who knew Miz Cancannon would know that she wouldn't pay ransom without positive proof that Amelia was still alive. That could prove tricky. How could someone prove that a cat was still alive without producing the cat?

Amelia was either abducted for ransom, or killed to make Miz Cancannon suffer. With her tight surveillance and security, if she wasn't blowing smoke, it had to be a servant, a resident of the island, lawyer, veterinarian, pilot, or niece. It could be a conspiracy. A stranger working with Rand. He could have flown someone in and flown him or her out. But if that was a correct scenario, why put Amelia in the well? She could have been dropped from the air anywhere on the mainland.

I was rested and was breathing normally. I had fed Ivanhoe deer jerky, given him water, and drank myself. I had stalled long enough. It was going to be an unpleasant task, but if I could recover her body, I was taking Amelia back to Miz Cancannon. I wanted her to know for sure that her cat was dead by someone's hand on the island, who possibly wanted payback. I disliked her, but it was only fair to warn her.

I pulled on my gloves and walked Ivanhoe over to a tree about twenty feet from the cistern and tied his leash securely. I didn't want him dancing around my legs while I was hanging over the well taking a look. He was strong enough at 130 pounds to push me over the edge when he was highly excited. He wasn't Lassie. If he knocked me in, he wouldn't race back to the house barking excitedly, and lead people back here to save me. He would whine a little, maybe peer over the edge trying to see me, and do something stupid like sailing over the lip and landing on top of me.

I checked the time. It was a quarter to six. I had an hour before first dark. I opened the backpack and pulled out a plastic body bag. I unzipped and spread it open.

It was large enough to hold a 250-pound human. The cat's body would look pitifully small in it, but it was all I had. I would roll it up, and seal the tiny bundle. I fished out tape, and wet wipes to cleanse my hands after, a fresh pair of gloves, and an industrial-strength pressed paper towel. I placed them all on the body bag.

I grasped the edge of the cover and pushed. I couldn't budge it. I groaned. The second time, I scooped back sand with my shoes until I had enough to brace my feet against so I wouldn't slip. I got into position and threw my 128 pounds behind my push, and grunted in frustration when I saw I had moved the sucker about an inch. At this rate, I'd still be standing here straining when Rand took to the air to search for me after sunrise. I braced and tried again, moving it another hard-fought inch. I had to stop because black dots began to float within my vision.

As I rested, I eyed Ivanhoe. When the puppies matured into adults on their first birthday, they were trained to pull the rescue sled. They were first paired with a seasoned dog, then trained solo. I had no idea if Ivanhoe had passed with flying colors or had failed miserably. I couldn't remember. It was worth a try.

From my backpack I took out a 25-foot, 150-pound test, three-ply nylon rope. I snapped it on his harness, wrapped his long lead around my waist, and brought him back to the cistern. He began to whine and scratch on the sides of the well.

Seeing him diligently trying to scratch through the solid cement to find Amelia's scent brought a fragment of a lecture I had listened to in the broiling sun of July, three years ago in Atlanta. I had Lazarus standing beside me. It was a training exercise for cadaver dogs. I could see the short, slight instructor's sweaty face as he delivered his message.

"Remember, trainers, your dog is not scenting on a human body smell here, they are searching for the smell of death. A chemical odor has been lab-produced that resembles the death odor. Once a living body dies, it doesn't produce an individual smell. All cadavers smell alike. Your scented search sample has been sprayed with this odor, as well as the dummies buried under the rubble."

His words—just remembered—gave me hope. I believed that Ivanhoe followed Amelia's scent while the abductor was carrying her. He was still trying to reach her. He had never been given any training to search for a cadaver, so he couldn't have scent memory of the cadaver death smell, so therefore—

I broke off speculating, hooked the rope tightly around the short protruding edge of the cistern's cover, and, acting animated and excited, stood shoulder to shoulder with Ivanhoe and gave the command to pull.

"Pull, pull!" I cried as I tugged on my end of the rope. It was looped around my right shoulder and padded with a bandanna. I looked at Ivanhoe and he was standing there expectantly, slowly wagging his tail, but he wasn't doing any pulling. He seemed to be waiting for me to give him a clue about this new game.

My expectations took a nosedive. He must have flunked Sled Pulling 101. Shit. I decided to move forward, so he was behind me. If he knew how to pull, me being in front of him might jog his memory. It was the trainer's normal position. In front, with him between the sled/cistern and me, I slid my feet back and forth, pretending to walk, and called, "pull, pull," and then bent to the task.

I strained and felt the line move. Without looking back, I pulled and yelled and pulled. I heard the heavy cover scraping across the edge. The grating sound was beautiful music to my ears. I kept yelling and pulling, so when the cover became lopsided, the heavy side slid over the edge, landed on the sand, and released all pressure from the rope. I hit the dirt lightheaded with success. Ivanhoe ran up and began licking my face.

I fended him off with my elbows and gave him his well-earned praise. I unwound his lead from my waist, replaced it, and unfastened the rope. When Ivanhoe was again tied to a tree, I coiled the rope and returned it to my backpack.

I pulled the flashlight out of my pocket and checked the time. Half past six. I had a few minutes of daylight left. I trudged wearily toward the well. This was the moment of truth. *Is she, or isn't she?*

8

"Delivering the Goods"

October 2, Monday, 6:30 P.M.

I leaned over the edge, making sure my body was not touching any part of the well. I wasn't sure how strong the sides were and I didn't want to put any pressure on them until I knew how stable they were. It wouldn't be any fun if I discovered Amelia was down there, then knocked half the wall in on top of her.

The inside of the well was dark, and at first, even with the flashlight, I only saw algae-coated walls and dark water several feet down. The sun was behind me, but it was still bright enough to make my light's beam look puny and ineffective. I leaned over and quartered the area. My eyes were slowly adjusting to the dim interior. I sensed movement and turned my light. Two bright green orbs were caught in its beam, and their color was reflected back to me.

"Amelia? Is that Amelia down there?"

I heard a plaintive, *"Meow?"*

"It is Amelia!" I answered, talking cat talk to assure her I wasn't the enemy and deliverance was near.

"Amelia, you couldn't prove your identity to me, you look like a drowned rat! Are you sure you're Amelia?"

I wanted to keep her looking up, so I knew where she was.

Without the reflection of her eyes, I would have trouble finding her again. She was about eight feet below, and the water seemed to be up to her neck. All I could see was a head. I hated to move the light, as she had been down there a lot of hours already, and I didn't want her to think I was leaving, but I had to get the rope and decide how I was going to get her out.

I kicked the side gingerly with my foot and tried pushing the top rim with my hand. It felt solid. I heard a small splash and looked down, and couldn't see her eyes. I finally found her with the light and sucked in a breath when I saw her struggling in the water. She was trying to get her body back on what she had been clinging to. I couldn't see what it was because it was underwater.

She seemed to be moving in slow motion, but she finally dragged herself back up on her precarious perch. She wasn't standing on the bottom, she was balancing on something to keep her head above water and not drown. I felt a lump in my throat when I wondered how many times she had slipped off and had to pull herself out of the water during yesterday afternoon, a long night, and most of today.

I still find it hard to think of man's inhumanity to animals even when I'm staring it in the face. Did he know that she would find a way to survive, or had he merely tossed her in and covered her up? I say he, although there are females just as capable of cruelty as males.

I couldn't come up with a way to lift her out. I got the rope and lowered it near her to measure the distance I would have to lower myself to the water. My estimate was close. It was seven and a half feet to Amelia's head. I lowered the rope again and tried to hold it close to her face. I was talking nonsense to let her know I was trying to save her.

"Now, Amelia, grab the rope, and stick one paw inside of the loop and pass it over your shoulder, that's right, now hold on tight and I'll pull you out of there."

All the natural oil on her skin was soaked away by now. Her long thick hair would be heavy. No wonder she was so slow in regaining her balance. I could try to place a slipknot over her head and pull her up, but I could crush her throat and or garrote her in the process. Maybe if I could get it under her chin . . . Oh shit!

She had jerked her head to avoid the rope, and was back in the water, floundering. I watched anxiously until she slowly pulled herself back on her perch, while I was practicing my excuse for Miz Cancannon. *You see, ma'am, I knocked her in the water by accident, and she drowned before I could save her.*

I ran to the backpack and dug out the ground sheet for my sleeping bag. I pulled it out and started flapping it in the air to shake loose the folds. I jerked off my gloves and fumbled with the side straps that would add four inches of space on each side of my suit. The buckles were small and haste made my fingers clumsy. I had a feeling Amelia couldn't survive more than one or two more dunkings.

I crammed the ground sheet into my suit, making a crude nest for Amelia, if I could get her into it. My belt would hold her from slipping below my waist, and the sheet, vinyl on one side and thin flannel on the other, was to protect my chest from being shredded by her claws. I zipped the suit up to hold the sheet in place.

I tied the rope to the closest tree and paced off the yards back to the well. Nine feet, I had enough. I doubled the rope and tied it around my waist and looped one side around my thigh. My body and arms were protected, but my face and head were vulnerable. I unrolled the three-inch Ace bandage and wound it around my neck, up my face, and around my head. I left slits for my mouth, nose, and eyes. I pulled on them gently to get more slack, and it just made the strips cling more tightly. It would have to do. If one of the Filipino searchers strolled by about now, I'd possibly give him pause, because I must look very strange.

I knew I could slide down easily enough, but getting back up was the problem, especially with a squirming cat. I rigged up the remaining rope, and hoped I had gotten it right, under the left thigh and over the right shoulder. I backed over the edge and started sliding down, rappelling, actually. The rescue attempt would have been child's play if the walls weren't covered with a thick coating of green growth. It was slick as owl's shit, and I couldn't get a purchase for my feet.

I had my small flashlight clenched in my teeth. The large one was in a waterproof pocket of my suit. I looked below and located Amelia. She wanted to run from me, but she wasn't stupid. She knew she had a choice, the big hunk that smelled like a dog, or the water. She tried to duck her head to avoid my glove, but had to raise it quickly because it went under the water.

I held both ropes with my left hand and my right clamped around her collar in a death grip. I pulled her clear, and with water streaming off her like she was a sodden mop, I started cramming her into the front of my suit. She fought me tooth and nail with energy born of desperation.

I'd get a leg inside and zip an inch, only to have a paw appear to swipe at my face. Sweat was stinging my eyes and the rope was cutting into my thigh. I couldn't talk to her, my teeth were clutching the flashlight. Her tail was impossible. Even soaked with water, she managed to slap it across my face numerous times.

She wanted to climb up on my head, and almost succeeded. I finally had to pop her on her nose and twist her tail to get her body parts inside the zipper. Her head was still out and she continued to strain upward. I was scared that she would notice that the Ace bandage around my throat had worked loose and my neck was a very close and inviting target. Her limbs were safely inside, but her teeth were only inches away. I could almost feel her jaws closing on my windpipe, the little vampire! I tucked in my chin and pushed on her nose the whole intense climb up the rope. I'd rather have a scar on my face than my jugular vein opened.

I clutched the top of the well casing, and pulled us up and over the edge, and then slumped on the ground. I hooked my left finger in her collar so she couldn't wiggle free, and just sat there. My arm muscles were screaming abuse, and my back was throbbing. Amelia had calmed down. She had finally gotten the message that she was out of the cold water. She was warming up within the airless suit. I pulled off the Ace bandage and wiped my face, and then used a section to gently wipe hers. She flinched once and then closed her eyes. Her battle to survive was over. Defiance disappeared and exhaustion took over.

As I moved around packing the items I had used, I was poised to drop everything and grab her if she tried to wiggle free. I worried unnecessarily. She had fallen into a deep sleep, and her head was nestled into the hollow of my throat.

All during the rescue, Ivanhoe had whined and quivered and wanted to smell his prize. Before I donned my backpack, I put a hand towel in my pocket, and sat beside Ivanhoe to feed him several pieces of deer jerky. He gave Amelia several friendly licks on her head, which made him content. Amelia wasn't aware of his display of affection; she was in the Land of Nod.

We headed back to the mansion. I was tired but the journey was all downhill, so my heart was light. I was proud of Ivanhoe. He had done exactly the opposite of what we had tried to train him to do, and had done it well. Some dogs are completely untrainable. They have the natural instinctual ability, but somehow they can't or won't conform to our training. If animals and humans had a common language and worked together, I believe we could civilize the planet.

It was half past seven when Ivanhoe and I strode across the cultivated lawn leading to the mansion. We passed several groups of three and four servants, standing or sitting under the trees near a nightlight. As I passed each group I held the hand towel to my chin, so it hung down and covered Amelia's head. My shape under the rescue suit might have looked a little more chestier than when I left, but the bulge wasn't obvious, and I didn't believe they could tell that Amelia was snoring away on my chest. My hands held only Ivanhoe's lead and the towel, and that is where they looked, before lowering their glances.

I wanted Mrs. C to know the details before everyone knew that Amelia was found. When I reached the front door, I took off my backpack and propped it against the wall before I rang the doorbell. The door was opened by another Filipino woman, only slightly younger than the one I saw earlier. I brushed past her and headed for the stairs. Celia entered the foyer from a hallway to my left. I reached the stairs before she could stop me. I sailed by her, wiping my mouth with the towel.

"I know the way," I called over my shoulder, "stay here!"

"Did you find—" I turned at the landing, and that cut off her question. I made one wrong turn on the second floor and had to retrace some of my steps, but I succeeded in finding the correct door. I rapped twice, and walked in.

As I marched to Miz Cancannon's desk, I saw two heads swivel around their chairs to stare at me, one blond and one brunette. Obviously, two of the nieces. I patted my chin with the towel, and I spoke to Miz Cancannon, ignoring the two women.

"I need to speak to you. Alone."

I heard a startled gasp from behind me, but I didn't react.

"Please wait in the library," Miz Cancannon told them.

The blond woman stood, walked around the desk, and placed her hand on Miz Cancannon's shoulder.

"It may be bad news, Aunt Alyce. I think we should stay."

"Get out!" Miz Cancannon hissed at her, brushing the hand away. "At once!"

The blond's jaw dropped, and she left without uttering another word. The brunette was right on her heels, and softly closed the door behind her.

I held a finger to my lips and tiptoed to the door. I jerked it open. They were just turning into the main hallway, and didn't see me checking on them. I closed the door and returned to the desk, unzipping my rescue suit. I saw her eyes widen when she spotted Amelia. I pulled her limp form from the warm interior of my suit, wrapped the hand towel around her, and placed her in Miz Cancannon's arms. Amelia didn't stir a whisker.

"She's wet and exhausted. She slept the entire trip back. I wanted to get her back to you and explain what I found before anyone knew she had been rescued."

I glanced at Mrs. Cancannon, and tears were coursing down her checks as she held Amelia cradled in her arms. I walked over to the fireplace and stood with my back to her, staring up at a large portrait over the mantel. I didn't recognize the name of the artist. It depicted a woman in a blue dress holding an ivory fan. I wasn't admiring the picture, I was giving her privacy.

"Ms. Sidden, I'm fine now. Tell me what happened."

I came back and sat down in front of her.

"I'm warning you, it's brutal, so brace yourself."

I described the cistern, and told her about Amelia having to climb back so often after falling off whatever she was clinging to in the cistern.

"It's a galvanized water pipe, about three inches in diameter," she said softly, remembering. "Papa had it put there with an extension coming up higher than the edge of the cistern when the well was dug. It was for a hand pump so we could have fresh cold water, when we went there for picnics. He preferred taking us there instead of the beach. We had a sandy play area, and he said he didn't have to worry about us drowning while he was taking a nap. We had a large cabana there, and beds for all of us. A hurricane destroyed it in nineteen fifty-three. We were grown then, my two brothers and I, so he didn't have it rebuilt."

She gave me an intense look.

"Was there anything around to indicate who did this?"

"Nothing. The lid is rough cement and crushed shell. It wouldn't take prints if you sent anyone out there to try. There are strong wind currents on the dune. It scoured the area clear of leaves, debris, and footprints. I don't believe a woman could have opened and replaced the lid by herself. I'm a little stronger than the average female, I've tugged on leashes pulled by strong dogs for the past six years. If Ivanhoe hadn't been available, I might have removed it eventually, or could easily have failed."

"The dog helped you move it?" She sounded doubtful.

"All the dogs are trained to pull a rescue sled. It's like a body bag with a smooth galvanized rubber bottom. I hook it to their harness when I have to move an injured person or a body out of the Okefenokee."

"And your dog led you right to Amelia?"

"Yes'em. Miz Cancannon, you have an enemy that wants to hurt you. This first attempt has been thwarted. The hate could escalate, and you could become the his next target. I wanted to warn you."

"Thank you for bringing Amelia back safely. Here are your checks." She held them out to me.

I took them from her, tore them in half, and put the pieces on her desk.

"Mail me a check for five hundred."

"Can you afford this contemptuous gesture?" She had her haughty look firmly in place. She seemed amused.

"I'm still gouging you," I said with a smile. "In Balsa City, I'd only ask for fifty."

"The money is yours, take it!" she insisted.

"No, it's not," I said firmly. "Keep an eye on Amelia. This is where we part company. I won't be back."

"Not even if I ask Judge Dalby to call you?" She sounded full of herself, and back in complete control.

"Not even then," I said with confidence.

This time I closed the door without making a sound.

9

"A Budding Acquaintance "

October 2, Monday, 8:30 P.M.

We were over the mainland, flying home. Ivanhoe was wedged between my knees and we both had our noses pressed against the window. I was watching the small points of light that signaled a house, or several houses in a clump, down below in the darkness. We passed over Highway 301, which I recognized by the yellow-hued vapor lights at the main intersections of connecting roads. Very light traffic, and long stretches of darkness with tiny red taillights going south, and white headlights heading north. A single light emitting a lonely tiny spark always drew my attention. I wondered who lived there and if they enjoyed the isolation or longed for crowded streets.

Most men in this part of the state were hunters. They made their living in a mill, a factory, or worked in timber for the large paper companies. Bored with their repetitive job routine, they would convince their spouses that pulling a trailer on a couple of acres in prime hunting territory was the best of all places to live, at least for them. They could shoot a deer on the way home from work, take long drives in their trucks on work-free stormy days, and have conversations on backwoods deserted roads with other hunters.

VIRGINIA LANIER

The trailers sprang up like mushrooms in the isolated locations. Suddenly the land was cleared, a single brave nightlight lit the ebony woods, a septic tank installed aboveground encased in tons of dirt because the water table was too high for burial, and a well was dug. A trailer would appear like magic.

Then the wife would discover that no other wives ever dropped in for a cup of coffee, and neighbors didn't visit because there were no close neighbors, and she had to drive twenty miles for a loaf of bread and gasoline for her car. The only people she saw were her husband and kids. The Georgia Power meter reader and a propane gas truck driver came by once a month. Within six months to a year the trailer would disappear and the grass would grow tall.

If they were lucky they would sell the land to another hunter with dreams of living in paradise. A different trailer would appear, the grass would be cut, and the never-ending cycle would begin again. I believed the wives' isolation wrecked more marriages in South Georgia than infidelity and money problems combined.

Rand startled me out of my reverie.

"What are you two looking at?

"I can't speak for Ivanhoe, but I was reflecting on isolation and marriage."

"The two can't be mentioned in the same sentence, they are grossly incompatible. For instance: Did you hear why Dick and Jane got a divorce? He had no income and she wasn't patable. Get it?"

"I got it," I groaned.

"Do you know what I'd like? When we get to your place I'd love to have dinner. I'm famished. I'd like to go to a bistro that stocks good wine, has soft lights and flickering candles, and dine on some good French food. Sound good?"

"Sounds impossible," I said wryly. "To make that happen you'd have to turn this bird around and fly over a hundred miles to Jacksonville, and by then everything would be closed. Thank God you didn't say you wished you had a quote, good home-cooked meal, unquote,

62

because if you had, this budding acquaintance of ours would die on the vine. I don't cook."

"You don't cook? Of course you cook! All Southern women cook!"

"Not this one. I've traded in my frilly apron, Aunt Minnie's cookbook, and having my arms up to my elbows in dishwater scrubbing greasy pots and pans three times a day. I prefer the simple life."

"What do you eat?"

"Takeout. Pizza, burgers, or maybe baby back ribs."

"You know what I'd like?" He laughed. "I'd like a well-lighted diner with indigestible cheeseburgers, greasy French fries, cold beer in a can, and a jukebox so loud the vibrations make your teeth ache. How does that sound?"

"A lot more obtainable," I said with false enthusiasm. "There are five such locations in Balsa City alone, with lots more in the county. You're in luck!"

"There's no middle ground?" He sounded wistful.

"Nope, it's goll-dern country, or there's a place you can land behind Hardee's and pick you up a burger to munch on your flight back to Little Cat Island, where a cordon bleu chef awaits to fulfill your every wish, twenty-four hours a day. Bon appetit!"

"I was just kidding!" He seemed surprised when he heard the anger in my voice that I hadn't taken the trouble to hide.

"Rand, lesson number one: When living in the South, don't make fun of the natives, they may get restless."

He lowered the helicopter slowly downward to rest near the paper towel X that was almost still in place. Only in two or three places had the paper pulled free of the Coke cans that were suppose to anchor it down.

We sat in silence while the blades slowly finished their rotations and stopped. I saw Wayne and Donnie Ray start out to help me unload. The five nightlights on the property gave us adequate light.

"I guess this means that we won't have dinner together tonight. How about Friday, about six? We'll get an early start and make

Jacksonville in plenty of time for a little restaurant I discovered recently. You'll love it."

"Not hungry."

He seemed to act as if I had a couple of loose screws for refusing to go along with his plans. I'd have to state it plainer.

"I don't think so, Rand. At least not in this lifetime. Thanks for the ride home."

I scrambled over Ivanhoe, hopped out, and Ivanhoe obliged by jumping out promptly when I tugged lightly on his leash. If I'd spent time trying to get him out of the copter, it would have weakened my exit line.

I greeted the boys. I gave Ivanhoe's leash to Wayne, and signed that he had performed really well and was now to be called Superdog by all. I strode off with confidence, knowing that Rand would follow me and try to set things right between us.

I stopped on the back porch and greeted Bobby Lee, where he had patiently waited for my return. He followed me into my office, and I began hugging him and talking sweet talk, listening for Rand's knock on the door.

When the knock came, I yelled "Come in," but it was Jasmine who stuck her head around the door.

"Are you alone?"

"So far. Come in, did you see Rand out there?"

"If you mean a man, no. However, there is still a helicopter sitting out there. Is he the pilot?"

"Yes. Come on in, I want you to meet him. He'll be along in a minute. Say hello and good-bye in less than three minutes. We've just had our first spat."

"Why am I not surprised," she said with a grin, entering and sitting in a rocker. "Is he nice?"

"He's quite a hunk. About nice—"

We both turned our faces to the ceiling when the helicopter's motor broke the silence with a *whoop-whoop* so ear-splitting that he seemed to be landing on the roof. We listened for a long ten seconds and then heard him depart, the sound diminishing and fading into the night.

"As I was saying, he's a mean-minded, antisocialist, Southern-knocking Yankee, and y'all won't be meeting him."

Jasmine winced. "Is he still a hunk?"

"Oh yes. On a scale of ten, he's a nine in anatomy, and a minus one in personality. Want a beer?"

"Have you eaten?"

"Nope, but I have to shower first. And call Donnie Ray."

"How's this? You take a hot soak. Your muscles will thank you tomorrow. I'll bring you a cold beer, and call Donnie Ray for you, and nuke you a personal pan pizza. This is offered only if you promise to relate word for word the entire afternoon."

"Deal. Ask Donnie Ray if our fearless pilot just sat like a lump, took a whiz, or said anything before he departed."

"Everything but the whiz."

"Missy Nice Nice," I taunted as I left to take my bath.

Soaking in lavender-scented bath salts, and sipping a cold one, is to wallow in sybaritic splendor. I ruminated about my white knight and decided he wouldn't be caught dead in a ratty jumpsuit astride a control stick in a whirlybird. I took a sudsy finger and drew an imaginary mark in the air in front of me. Chalk up another kill, Jo Beth. Another potential lover shot down before the heavy breathing could commence. My sharp tongue and persnickety ways were my libido's worst enemies.

I dressed in soft cotton joggers and thick lounging socks. Jasmine had the time to bake a real pizza, which I bought from Tony's by the dozen and stored in the freezer. I had beers number two and three while I ate and related to Jasmine the events of the afternoon. Jasmine had one slice to be sociable, and I consumed the rest.

I had just introduced her to Celia Cancannon when she interrupted.

"Tell me what she was wearing." She had her elbows propped on the table and had her chin resting in her hands.

"And don't you dare say it was a faded housedress. I'll strangle you!"

"It was a pale blue wool power suit, feminine, not stark. The blouse was sheer, same color of the suit, so thin you could easily see the darker blue camisole beneath it. Narrow gold choker, and small button-shaped gold earrings. The slits in the tight skirt were more pronounced than usual, showing off her really gorgeous legs. Her shoes were tiny straps of leather, dark blue, with two-inch heels. She was dressed elegantly enough to meet a queen, or to work for her billionaire aunt."

"Mine would be pale pink," she said dreamily.

"Would look really good on you," I agreed. "Just be careful of the doo-doo in the dog runs."

She wrinkled her nose. "She has a fabulous job. Where do I apply?"

"You haven't heard what a harridan Ol' Lady Cancannon is!"

"As opposed to a younger—" She smiled and didn't finish her sentence.

"Did you know that the unemployment in this county is almost eight percent?" I pointed a slice of pizza her way, to make my point.

"Finish the story," she urged.

I continued. I recounted everything and I was up to my parting shot I had taken at Rand before stalking off, expecting that he would follow me and apologize.

She threw her head back and roared.

"Okay." I drummed my fingers on the table 'til she could contain her laughter. "I bet I think it's funny too, when you let me in on the joke. I gather it's what Rand said to Donnie Ray before he so rudely buzzed the house."

"Yes," she said, struggling for control. "He . . . he asked directions to the vacant lot behind Hardee's!"

I joined her, but my sickly laughter was forced. I didn't see a damn thing funny in his remark.

10

"Judy, Judy, Judy"

October 5, Thursday, 3:10 A.M.

Heart pounding, I sat straight up in bed. Unsure of what had pulled me from a deep sleep, I didn't move but quartered the room with my eyes. Nothing. The phone rang. Now I knew that it was the first ring that alerted me.

This had better not be Bubba up to his old tricks, I thought sluggishly, still not completely awake. I stared at the clock, trying to focus on where the little hand and big hand were pointing, as I reached for the phone. The second I heard the clicking sound instead of a voice, I was elated. It was Wayne. Judy must have started labor. I listened to the taps in Morse code and translated them into letters.

O . . . n . . . e, pause, m . . . a . . . l . . . e.

I hung up, turned on the light, and started pulling on the clothes I had laid out last night. Judy had just delivered the first puppy of an expected litter of ten. You can't wait until delivery to be surprised at the number of puppies. It has to be known in advance because sometimes the last one or two can't be delivered normally through the birthway and have to be removed by cesarean section. Harvey, my vet, had confirmed the count by X ray fourteen days ago. He had first tried to palpate, but there was too many to take a chance on missing one.

As I tied my shoes, I reassessed her condition. A normal whelping can begin between fifty-eight and sixty-three days after breeding. This was day sixty-one for Judy. Wayne and I had started monitoring her temperature on day fifty-five. We keep a log and enter the reading three times a day.

The idea that prompts these readings is to recognize the drop in progesterone, which happens one or two days before whelping. Her temperature had hovered from 100.4 to 100.9 for the past six days. Yesterday morning it suddenly dropped to 99.1 and remained there all day. This was when we started 'round-the-clock surveillance; we'd keep it up until all ten are born.

I had been with her from 4:00 P.M. until midnight, then Wayne took over. We were lucky. Judy completely trusted both of us, so we could take turns staying with her. Some bitches won't allow but one person to be present when in labor. Bloodhounds have to be reassured constantly and have you near the entire time. I glanced at my watch. Judy had begun heavy panting and restlessness at 6:00 P.M. last evening. Nine hours so far. The first delivery had arrived, but she might not drop a second one for hours. Thirty minutes is average, and any delay after that we start worrying. If it went to three hours, we would panic and call Harvey and demand a cesarean, which would mean Judy was in trouble. The puppies would be at risk.

I'm a worrywart when any of the bitches are whelping. I think of all the bad things that can happen, chew my nails, and pace, as if I were a first-time expectant father.

I hurried through the hallway and Bobby Lee joined me. Rudy had been awakened by the phone and was hunkered over his dish, where he had left a few morsels from his supper. I let Bobby Lee come along. We entered the grooming room and went down the hall to the whelping room.

Bobby Lee knew he couldn't go any further. He had waited outside this door on previous occasions. He quietly settled in the hall, and I entered. I closed my eyes for a few seconds, so they could adjust to the dim lighting. Judy wanted her delivery to take place in complete darkness. This wasn't possible, but we only burned a small lamp, shaded with a towel.

"How is she doing?" I whispered, and watched Wayne's flashing hands.

"She cried and jumped into my arms on the arrival of male one. She never did that before."

"Oh no," I breathed. Bloodhounds don't usually show they are in pain. If Judy had been that demonstrative, she could be in trouble. I inched around Wayne's sleeping bag and picked up her chart from the low shelf where we keep all essentials close at hand. Wayne was on the other side of the whelping box, gently rubbing Judy's back.

Her eyes followed my movement but she hadn't stirred. She didn't seem restless or in pain. Judy's previous litters had been normal, and had gone without a hitch.

Bloodhounds can have very large litters, up to fifteen. The average is from six to eight, but ten is not unusual. In Judy's previous litters, the number of births had been seven or less. Bloodhound bitches get very big before they whelp, and Judy had been enormous this pregnancy. She had resembled a blimp. Her stomach had changed from round to pear-shaped two days ago. This meant she had "dropped normally." Harvey had examined her every morning for the past week and declared she was healthy.

I continued to read on down the chart. The time of birth for puppy one was recorded at 1:16. My eyes widened and I checked the time. It was now 3:30. Two hours and fourteen minutes ago! I looked at Wayne, who had been watching my progress down the chart.

"We still have a window of forty-five minutes. She's showing no distress, so let's give her a little longer. She has been lactating for two days. If she has a cesarean it could slow her milk. We already know we'll have to supplement the feedings. The puppies will gain weight much faster with her milk than they will on formula."

He lowered his hands again, to rub Judy's back. I reached over and wiped drool from her mouth with a towel and whispered some comforting words. I went back to her chart. Male one weighed four hundred grams. His collar color was blue, and his coat markings were black and tan with no white. He was born without a placenta. We had to keep a careful count of placentas. Leave one inside too long, and Judy could die.

It isn't easy being a midwife. I had checked on Judy first; now I was ready to see the absolute joy of all this labor. I peeked into the nursery box. It had two hot pads on low, covered with a receiving blanket. The little guy was asleep. I picked up the tiny creature and cradled him in my hands, looking for any imperfection. He was beautifully handsome and appeared flawless. We wouldn't know for sure until several months had passed, but at this moment in time, he was perfect. This litter was slated for the show ring. An impressive champion papa and an award-winning mama had gotten together to produce this small miracle.

I loved all my bloodhounds, but this litter's monetary value would be substantial if they all had the right bone configurations. The pick of the litter went to the stud owners. Nine others would be sold from a carefully culled list. The new expectant owners had already signed a purchase agreement and mailed a large deposit to guarantee ownership. This was not just the birth of some purebred bloodhounds, this was a happening!

I glanced at the preparations that awaited the future births. Nine different-colored pieces of yarn were aligned in a row. These were temporary collars so we could identify each puppy. Some litters have two or three with the exact same markings. This preserved their order of birth and helped us keep them straight when we charted their progress.

Judy stirred. Wayne and I watched while she rose to her feet and started straining. We both reached for thin disposable gloves. Within thirty seconds, Wayne caught puppy two and moved it closer to her. It was still in the sac. Judy tore it open with her teeth and chewed through the umbilical cord. Sometimes we had to help young bitches with their first delivery. Inexperienced bitches will sometimes chew too close. They can't tell where their umbilical cord ends, and start chewing open their abdomen. We watched her closely as she severed the cord quickly and neatly. Judy began cleaning her offspring. When I saw that it didn't move, I reached for a hand towel and picked up the puppy. I rubbed it briskly to start circulation. The puppy still wasn't breathing. I held its head down and swung it back and forth by its legs. When the rib cage began moving, I placed her beside Judy and she finished cleaning her up.

I stared down at the puppy as it crawled up to the nipples and started to suckle. At this point they can't see or hear, they simply move toward the heat of their mother's body, and to a certain extent the smell of her.

This little bundle of wrinkles was using her gifted nose to find the tit. I let her suckle for a few minutes, then weighed and added statistics to the chart. My little beauty, female two. I moved her littermate beside her for added warmth and watched both of them rigorously suckling.

It was now after five.

"Go have a hot bath and eat," I signed to Wayne. I climbed over the whelping box, poured cold coffee down the drain, and refilled my cup. I drew a beanbag chair closer to Judy's box and settled in comfort.

"We don't know what today will bring," I signed when I saw he was hesitant about leaving. "Get some rest."

Scratching his head, he stretched and gave me a grin.

"Want me to bring you the newspaper?"

"You're putting me on! Who can read at a time like this?"

"Promise y'all send Donnie Ray to wake me, if you need help?"

"Promise."

Things were quiet for the next hour. The puppies would suckle, fall asleep, then wake with a start and suckle again. Judy napped. She woke, wagged her tail when I rubbed her ears, and stood, stepping out of the box.

I quickly picked up the puppies and placed them in the nursery box so they would be warm. Judy was standing at the closed door. I attached her lead and took her outside.

Keeping an eye on her, I let her wander around while she looked for a spot to piddle. When she squatted, I did too, so I had a good angle to view her. Sometimes they will deliver a puppy while you think they are doing their business. She walked around for a few minutes getting some exercise. It was good for her and I enjoyed the cool morning breeze. When she headed for the door, we returned to the whelping room.

I had just placed the puppies back with her when she stood and started straining. I put the two back in the warming box. Judy strained for five or six minutes and produced male three. Male four came two hours later.

At eight, Jasmine knocked softly on the door. I stuck my head out. "Is Judy okay?"

"So far, so good," I said, knocking on the wood casing of the door for good luck. "Three males, one female. They look healthy and have good markings."

"Are you hungry?"

"Starved. I could really go for a couple of sausage biscuits."

"Coming right up," she uttered, wrinkling her nose with displeasure. "I don't think all this microwave-thawed food you eat is good for you."

"It's better than real food. Nuking it removes all the flavor and I don't eat as much."

"Sure," she drawled. "I'll be right back."

The coffee left in the pot looked like sludge, so I poured it out and brewed a fresh pot.

At nine, female five arrived at the same time as Wayne. He recorded the birth.

"You didn't even go to sleep, I bet," I accused when the five puppies were settled in the whelping box.

72

"I tried, but couldn't sleep. I'll call you if I need help, or get tired."

I didn't waste my time arguing. Wayne was more of a mother hen than I was. If he wasn't here he wouldn't be resting, but keeping up with all the other chores. Both of us were gonna lose a lot of sleep in the next ten days.

I led Bobby Lee outside and told him to go play. He ran inside the house for Rudy, and they took off on their delayed morning run. Bobby Lee had been impressive even when he was blind. Now, with his sight, he was magnificent. So far today, my tiny kingdom was intact. Five perfect puppies, and five more waiting to make their entrance.

I wondered if Rand would call me tomorrow and invite me to dinner—again—and if I would accept. I wondered about Alyce Cancannon and her unknown enemy who wanted to make her suffer. I wondered about a lot of things. I took several deep breaths of the soft breeze that carried a hint of cooler weather, and the intoxicating blend of fall odors.

I took a shower and then called Susan.

"Busy?" It took her five rings to answer.

"On a Thursday morning in October? No way, I'm putting up my Halloween decorations. I was ten feet up a ladder. Your timing is superb, as usual."

"Sorry. Want to talk later?"

"Nah, this is fine, no customers are browsing."

"So how are you?"

"Just dandy. Do you realize I'll turn thirty-four next April?"

"Since I turn thirty-three this month—"

"Mom and Dad are driving me nuts; her more than him. They want a grandchild now. I've been divorced twelve years, and haven't found someone to be the father. They are running out of friends who have friends that aren't married. What's wrong with me?"

"Nothing. You're discriminating—"

"Mother says I'm too choosy, I have to lower my expectations."

"Body by Fabio, dances like Travolta—"

"Exactly. There is no such man in this desert of suitable men. How many did you meet this week that fills the bill, just name one!"

"Actually I did meet one on Monday——"

"You did? Tell me this instant!"

My phone line double-clicked. I have call waiting.

"Susan, I have a call——"

"Don't you dare leave this line after dropping that bombshell! Speak!"

I put her on hold. It was Hank.

"Hiya, Sheriff. What's up?"

"You busy?"

"Nah, just gossiping with Susan. She'll wait."

"That doesn't sound like the Susan I know."

"This time she has an incentive," I chuckled.

"Give me time to install a wiretap. I'm curious."

"So is she, so you better tell me what you want before she puts a curse on both of us."

"I have two men cooling their heels in the squad room who wants you to do a search for them."

"Who are they?"

"Two uniforms from Moody Air Force Base. One has captain's bars, and the other is sporting eagles."

"Who have they lost?"

"It's not a who, but a what. It seems they have, ah . . . misplaced a valuable item."

"Are we playing twenty questions? What?"

"It's an F-16 Falcon fighter plane, commonly known as a Viper. They want you to find it."

11

"You Lost a What?"

October 5, Thursday, 10:30 A.M.

I scratched my head and pulled down a curl and arranged it on my forehead. I was thinking about bangs. I might give them a try when the temperature turned cooler.

"Did you hear me, Sidden? Speak up. Don't mumble, I can't hear what you said."

"O . . . kay," I drawled, waiting for the punchline. "So they've misplaced a fighter plane. Bet it happens all the time. Did a pilot forget he drove his car to work, and fly it home? Call his wife. I imagine she's cussing because she can't hang up her colored unmentionables inside the garage, 'cause it's got a plane parked in it."

"Honest, Jo Beth, it's true. This is not a joke."

"Uh-huh, then why did you word your announcement so it sounds like one?" I was being patient with him, knowing that Susan was building up a boiler of steam while she hung on to a silent phone. Hank likes to tease me, and I delight in confounding Susan. Usually they both don't happen at the same time.

Jasmine knocked and entered the office. I gave her a questioning look by lifting my brows. She shook her head and signed, smiling.

"Seven total, four males, three females, all A-okay."

"I couldn't resist, the devil made me do it," Hank spoke in my ear. "The chicken colonel is a pain in the ass. He's throwing his weight around—drumming his knuckles on a support column—doing everything but jumping up and down while he's waiting for me to call you. I'm watching him through the glass.

"Remember the crash they had last Monday week? The flameout, and then the news that the pilot ejected safely? That's the misplaced plane. They've been looking for it for ten days now. They thought they knew where it crashed but they can't find a trace."

While Hank had been talking, I had pulled over a pad and written a fast note to Jasmine, asking her to call Susan and tell her that I was stuck on a business call and I'd call her later. It doesn't pay to get Susan too upset, she's slow to forgive and forget.

"Don't they have something on the airplane, a whatchamacallit, to tell them the exact location if it crashes?"

Hank laughed. "Transponder."

"Do I laugh when you can't name a maillot, jabot, or dickey, even when I'm wearing one?"

"Yes, you do."

"Well, I shouldn't," I answered smoothly, "because it's impolite."

"All three sound sexy. Are they worn above the waist or below?"

"You're a precocious dirty old man at thirty-seven."

"Thanks for the kind words."

"Getting back to my question, was a transponder on board?"

"Some have them and some don't. This one didn't."

"Where do they *think* it came down?"

"They have some iffy coordinates. The pilot eyeballed it as it went in."

"When you said they had been searching for it for ten days, did they explain how they searched?"

"Helicopters. Three of them. They were looking for a path of destruction, but if it went in nose-down, it could be halfway to China by now."

"It's an interesting puzzle. Thanks but no thanks. They don't stand a chance in hell of recovery if they can't pinpoint the exact spot it went in. Did they ask for me, or did you sing my praises and volunteer my services?"

Silence. "Hank?"

"I said if it could be found, you're the only one that could do it."

"Tell them I can't help them, okay? Judy has delivered seven out of ten, and Wayne and I won't leave the premises for at least a week. We have ten puppies to feed."

Jasmine headed for a phone. I leaned back and relaxed in the chair.

"Are you telling me you won't be on call for a week? This is a first."

"Hank, bear with me while I explain. Judy is a good mother, but bitches can accidentally lie on a puppy. There's only two ways I know to prevent this. One is to put a rail about four to five inches wide around the perimeter of the whelping box at a height of four inches. That helps. The other is 'round-the-clock surveillance. I'm gonna use both. This is my 'Masterpiece' litter. I've put a lot of hard work and money into this dream. Can you understand?"

"Sure. You run a business. You turn out a product to sell and wanna make a profit. I can see what you're saying."

"You sentimental devil, you," I said with weariness, "you have no idea of what I'm talking about, do you?"

"Oh hell, yes," he snapped. "Don't sound so damn condescending. I know you love those hounds of yours more than you could ever love anyone else, including me. I know all about dreams. I've a dream of my own, had it for several years now, but mine sure ain't working out. I hope you have better luck with yours. See you around, Sidden." He hung up.

"Don't call them hounds," I whispered as I replaced the receiver. I always like to have the last word.

I tried to call Susan, but her line was busy. I went back to the whelping room in time to see female eight make her appearance. Wayne told me Harvey had came by while I was away and pronounced all the puppies healthy, and to be sure to call him immediately if Judy started looking exhausted.

I took Judy outside. She piddled and then seemed to enjoy the sunshine. She sat and turned her head up and closed her eyes. I didn't urge her to hurry. I wanted her to have this little respite from her birthing. After a few minutes she stood, shook her head, stretched, and looked at the door, then back at me. Her actions were so clear. It was as if she told me the sun and air were nice, but she needed to go back inside and finish her business. We walked back to the birthing room.

A short time later I heard the gate alarm. Jasmine or Donnie Ray would answer. The trainers wouldn't be back until noon. I decided to ask Windell Grantham to help Donnie Ray this afternoon. With Wayne and me out of the picture, there was too much for Donnie Ray and Jasmine to handle. We have seven puppies that are fed four times a day and forty-three adults fed twice a day. Counting the time consumed in cooking, mixing, and serving them, we have a heavy chow schedule. In our spare time we weigh, groom, exercise, and train them.

Windell is the best trainer I have. He's a retired druggist, just turned sixty-eight, who can work rings around the younger guys. His dogs are always ahead of their peers. I wish I knew his secret, I'd use it on the puppies I train.

He and Cora Simmons, another trainer, had fallen in love and were married in the common room three months ago. Cora had to relinquish her Social Security benefits from a prior marriage when she wed Windell. Everyone, including their children, had advised them to simply live together so she could keep her check. They wouldn't hear of it. They were raised in the era that frowned upon living in sin. Said it would demean their love.

I envied them. True love is hard to come by. I had always dreamed of having a home and a loving husband and two children. Susan's parents weren't the only ones who could hear the biological clock ticking. My ears were also tuned to that frequency.

I jumped when Jasmine eased open the door.

"You have visitors," she whispered.

I signed to Wayne. "I'll be right back."

"Let me guess," I said to Jasmine as we walked through the grooming room. "Two Air Force uniforms, and the older one wouldn't take no for an answer. He insisted on talking to me."

"My, your crystal ball is really accurate," she said, sounding annoyed. "He not only insisted, he demanded. Threatened to go looking for you himself, if I didn't produce you posthaste."

"Oh, he did, did he?" My voice was grim, and I could feel my dander rising and the blood in my veins felt hot enough to boil.

Jasmine stopped me with a hand on my shoulder. She gave me a wry smile.

"Sorry, I was deliberately trying to provoke your anger because the creep got under my skin. He made me wish once again that I didn't have a record. I would have loved to stomp on his spit-polished shoes. Please don't do anything rash. I'll feel like I egged you into a confrontation and that it's my fault."

"Did they stop and announce themselves at the gate?"

A month ago, my attorney had insisted that I put a two-way communication system at the first gate and a large sign explaining the procedures for gaining legal entry even if the gate was standing open. He said it would strengthen the Georgia Posted Land Statue for property owners. It would also aid in convicting Bubba if he ever again came on my property and caused damage.

"Not a peep, but you know most of our regular visitors ignore the instructions half the time. Don't toast and roast him, please."

I arranged my face into a calmer expression for her benefit. "Nonsense, I have no plans to castrate him or whatever. Hank told him I said no; but being Hank, he probably sent them here just to annoy me. He got pissed at something I said."

Jasmine shook her head, looking sad. She's been trying to get Hank and me together ever since she first met me. Jasmine was a prostitute from age twelve to nineteen. She adores the guy for helping her to get off the street and would wade hip-deep in alligators to do him a favor.

"Let's go see the colonel," I delivered in crisp tones.

Outside I saw two men standing by a dark sedan that had an Air Force emblem on the door panel. The tall younger man gave me a smile. The short older guy looked grim and stood with his arms akimbo. Jasmine and I stopped the proper distance away for polite conversation.

"I'm Jo Beth Sidden," I said pleasantly, dividing my glance between them. "You wanted to speak to me?"

The younger man answered.

"Yes, ma'am, I'm Captain Evan Danglish, United States Air Force, and this is Colonel Rupert Hayes of Moody Air Force Base command. We—"

Hayes brushed past him, invading my personal space—putting his nose two feet in front of mine—effectively cutting off both the captain's speech and line of sight.

"I was told that you refused to guide us on a search for lost high-priority national defense equipment. Is that correct?"

"Rupert, you have your nose in my face," I said calmly. "I'd also appreciate you moving your ass back to the acceptable distance for discourse, or my associate and I will forcibly eject you from these premises."

I shocked the hell out of him. His face first blanched, then started pinking up nicely, especially on his nose and checks.

"You can't talk to me this way!" he squeaked. "You don't . . . have any idea . . . the trouble I can cause you—"

I stopped him with a raised hand and pointed a finger quite close to his nose, almost touching, in fact. He had forced the words from his throat, and looked ready to kill.

I waited. He didn't move an inch and didn't seem capable of further speech.

"You've lost track with the real world, Rupert. I'm not under your command and you're the one in trouble. You're on my land illegally. After threatening me, I could shoot you where you stand. This is the last time I'll tell you, MOVE IT OR LOSE IT!"

He turned and stalked back to the car, walking stiff-necked and stiff-legged, ignoring his traveling companion, who was standing with his mouth agape.

I winked at Captain Danglish. "Y'all have a nice day, you hear?"

His gaze focused on me with a bemused expression.

"You too, Ms. Sidden."

His words were soft and polite. He hustled back to the car, slid into the driver's seat, and drove the colonel out of the courtyard and out of our sight.

"I think that went well, didn't you?"

Jasmine drew in a ragged breath.

"Quite."

12

"Pizza, Beer, and Wine"

October 6, Friday, 7:00 P.M.

I was on my knees on the office carpet astride Bobby Lee, tickling his ribs, when the first gate's alarm went off and Susan announced herself. She didn't expect an answer, so I let Bobby Lee push me away, swooped up Rudy, and flopped on the couch. I cradled him like a baby, which he rarely allows, and crooned a lullaby as I scratched his tummy. Both of them were feeling neglected, since I was spending over fifty percent of my time in the birthing room with Judy.

Rudy remembered his dignity when Susan knocked and entered. He extracted himself from my hold and began to groom his pelt back to perfection.

"Welcome to the weekly meeting of the feminist dateless losers who eat pizza and drink beer on Friday nights," I said, giving her an air-kiss on her cheek and a hug all Southern females ritually bestow on one another.

"Thanks, I love you too. A beer really sounds good."

"Make mine a glass of red," Jasmine said, entering on Susan's heels.

"Coming right up. Get comfortable."

In the kitchen I looked again at my watch for the umpteenth time in the past thirty minutes. Ten after seven. I really hadn't expected

Rand to land on my roof and whisk me away to dinner in Jacksonville as he had promised on Monday. He hadn't called all week, and even he wouldn't be brassy enough to show up unannounced after the way our first and probably only meeting ended. I shrugged and practiced an uncaring look while I watched my reflection in the framed kitchen print that I use as a mirror. Its dark surface showed me a disappointed face trying to appear indifferent. You can't win 'em all. I returned to the office carrying a tray with two beers, a glass of wine, and cocktail napkins.

I had dimmed the office lights and had six candles lit on the coffee table between facing couches. Susan and Jasmine sat opposite me, while I sprawled in comfort on the other after serving the drinks. Susan was in the middle of one of our schoolday disaster tales, and I sat quietly as she regaled Jasmine with one of our silly exploits.

Susan's hair is naturally flaming red, but she subdues it with a dark titan rinse. Our birthdays are seven months apart. She is the oldest. Her hair is shoulder-length and a mass of curls. At five-feet-nine, she's quite beautiful. She doesn't think she's attractive, and covers her insecurity with a bold and sexy voice. She's been my best friend since the first day of school. She's divorced from a creep who ran off with a high school cheerleader after seventeen months of marriage almost fourteen years ago. She claims that she can't find a man she likes. I think, "Once bitten, twice shy." We're a lot alike.

Susan had Jasmine giggling as she finished her story.

"Don't believe a word she says," I admonished Jasmine. "She greatly exaggerates."

"Don't you wish," she retorted. "I still have the scars from old Mr. Hamlick, our esteemed, and recently deceased, principal. They paddled the girls as well as the boys in those days."

"See what I mean?" I held Jasmine's eye. "It was a yardstick and it only stung. It couldn't have left a scar."

Susan gave me a dark look. "The paddle had holes bored in it. I've got two small crescent-shaped scars on my fanny."

"I rest my case," I said smugly to Jasmine. "I've seen her bare ass, and it's alabaster-white without a blemish."

I barely managed to catch the thrown pillow before it smacked me in the face.

"I never know who to believe when you two get started," Jasmine complained.

"Me, me," we both chorused, laughing.

"I almost had a date tonight," Susan announced.

"Almost?"

"A new salesman from one of my wholesalers called on me this afternoon. We hadn't talked ten minutes when he asked me to have dinner with him."

"What happened?" I asked with caution. You never know with Susan, she could be setting me up to bite on one of her jokes.

"Directly after he left my store he called on that slut that runs the religious book shop over on Fifth, you know who I mean, Jo Beth, the blond with the big boobs."

"Peggy?" I was shocked. "But she's married!"

"That's the reason I referred to her as a slut," Susan replied.

"Maybe she's separated from her husband," Jasmine offered.

"Nope," Susan said quickly, adding in triumph, "I saw her and him at Porky's last night having a gay ol' time!"

"My, my." I was smacking my lips over the juicy gossip. "Homer would strip her and stake her out over a bed of fire ants if he knew. How could she be so stupid? Are you one hundred percent, absolutely and positively sure that it was her? I gather he called you back and canceled. Did he mention her name?"

"Yes, yes, yes, and no. You decide. He called less than thirty minutes after leaving the store. He asked for directions to her place before leaving. He mentioned that he had already been to the chain out on the highway, and there are only two bookstores in town. He gave the excuse that he had to call at a store later in Waycross as the reason for canceling our dinner date. He also had the balls to ask me, and I quote, 'Knew a friendly motel in Davis that didn't ask questions if he got lucky later on,' unquote."

"What a slimeball! What did you tell him?" I was grinning with anticipation.

"I held onto my temper and suggested he try Davis Motor Inn. I told him they were very discreet."

Susan and I doubled over with mirth.

Jasmine eyed us. "What happens at the Davis Motor Inn?"

"Drums!" Susan howled.

"The Inn is owned by a elderly couple who are devout members of the Salvation Army," I explained to Jasmine.

"If they even suspect a single check-in has become a double, they will take their position outside the door. She beats the bass drum, and he preaches into a magnified hand-hailer. They're both hard of hearing and play and shout very loudly. Someone finally complains and the police are called."

Jasmine had a wide smile of amusement when I finished.

"I have the feeling that you two have experienced the drum beating and sermon firsthand. Correct me if I'm wrong."

Susan was grinning. "You're correct. In our wilder years after our divorces and before we attained our present sanity, we did on rare occasions kick up our heels. We sneaked in about ten minutes after the guys registered. We had followed them back to the Inn in my car. Our rooms were next door to each other. They were auditors down from South Carolina on a convention. We were no sooner inside when all hell broke loose outside. I heard Jo Beth knock over a large brass floor lamp in her panic to reach the door. It fell across a glass-covered dresser with a horrendous crash."

I continued the tale. "My guy had opened me a beer and after my first sip, he turned out the light. Patience was not in his dictionary. At almost the same moment Armageddon arrived at the door. The drum was booming like the crack of doom and a magnified voice was shouting incomprehensible gibberish.

"My first silly thought was a brass band was outside, that me and the auditor were winners of a contest being the millionth couple to occupy the room. I could picture reporters and cameras outside making sure that our reputations were forever branded as sluts. I freely admit to panicking, but I wasn't the only one. Ms. Susan here could be easily heard screaming over all the noise, 'Mama, is that you? How did you know I was here?'"

Susan grimaced. "I lived back at home after the divorce until I was almost twenty-one. Mama and daddy treated me like I was sixteen."

Jasmine looked wistful. "You both had families that loved you. You were very lucky."

We both knew that Jasmine's mother had tossed her out of her home at twelve and she was forced to survive by living on the streets until she was nineteen. I quickly changed the subject.

"Susan, I just remembered something you said earlier. You said you saw Peggy and Homer together at Porky's last night. Just how did you visit Porky's without me? You obviously had a date last night. Fess up! We want to hear all about him."

Dismay flashed across her features and then she shrugged with resignation. "Me and my big mouth," she muttered.

She took a deep breath. "It wasn't a date. I just met an acquaintance there. Can we drop the inquisition? Please?"

"No."

"Damn!" Susan suddenly yelled, holding a finger under her eye. "I just smeared my mascara. I'll be right back."

She took off in a fast lope for the hall and toward the bathroom . . . I hoped. Too late, I remembered what was displayed on my bed. Would she use the bathroom mirror or my makeup mirror in the bedroom? The odds were fifty-fifty, for either location. I decided not to press her about her "acquaintance."

Jasmine spoke just above a whisper. "Are you going to make her tell you?"

I gnashed my teeth in frustration. "That sleazebag named Brian Colby is back in town, I just know it!" I hissed.

"Do you remember what happened last time, when you and Hank interfered?"

"Yes," I replied, hating to admit it. "Hank ran a check on him at my request and found out that he scammed women. Then he ran Colby out of town, also at my request. It took a long time for Susan to forgive me, she was furious. She accused me of trying to run her life."

"Well?"

"I know, I know. You're right. I won't mention him to her, all right?"

"Great." Jasmine looked relieved.

I heard the toilet flush, and felt relieved myself. Susan had used the bathroom to repair her makeup, and not my bedroom. I could now tell the cat story my way.

Susan placed her bag at the foot of the sofa, sank down, folding one leg beneath her, and settled on the couch cushion. She looked at me with apparent calm.

"Where were we?" I could read the storm signals loud and clear.

"I was just about to start my cat story. Let me turn on the oven and warm the pizza."

On my way back, I replenished our drinks with more beer and wine. For the next eighteen minutes, I told my tale about the rescue of Miz Alyce Cancannon's cat, Amelia. I started with the telegram from Celia Cancannon, and finished with me stalking off from the confrontation with Rand, and my mistaken belief that he would follow me, apologize, and reissue the invitation to dinner tonight. We all chuckled about my error in judging the situation correctly.

"I know a true fact when I hear one," I said as I left the room to fetch the pizza. "Men *are* from Mars."

I placed the pizza slices on paper plates and passed around plenty of paper napkins. We dine *al picnico,* but drink out of crystal goblets. This way we can pretend we're both practical and sophisticated.

I was still on my first slice of pizza when the phone rang. I frowned.

"At this hour? Hank knows I won't take a callout, and Bubba hasn't called in over a month."

"I know a quicker way to solve the problem." Susan spoke with her mouth full. "Answer the dang phone. Hee—hee—hee!"

"Ah, so wise! Such a wit! A veritable sage!" I kissed the tips of my fingers and blew her a raspberry on the way to the phone.

"Hello."

"May I speak to Ms. Jo Beth Sidden?"

A mature male voice. No one's speech pattern that I recognized.

"I'm Jo Beth Sidden. How may I help you?"

"My name is John Jason Jackson. I'm an estate attorney from Woodbine, Georgia. I want to apologize for calling this late. For the past several hours I have been with Sheriff Jeff Beaman of Camden County, and unable to reach a telephone. I will be handling the probate of the late Ms. Alyce Cancannon's will."

"Late? She's dead?" My voice had risen with each word.

"I'm so sorry, I assumed you knew. She died unexpectedly between midnight and nine A.M. yesterday morning."

13

"Unfinished Business"

October 6, Friday, 8:30 P.M.

How did she die?" was my next question.

"This is awkward, Ms. Sidden. I'm sorry you found out this way. I assumed you knew. It was in all the papers, even New York. I do apologize."

"Rest easy, Mr. Jackson. Miz Cancannon was not a relative, not even a close friend. I've been tied up with a new litter and haven't seen a paper. I'm sorry she died, but I only met her last Monday, and didn't anticipate any future contact. If this call is about those checks that she wrote me, the amounts were ridiculous and I tore them up. She owes me five hundred dollars; but with her death I have no proof, so I won't send you a bill. I would, however, appreciate an answer to my question. How did she die?"

"I'm not at liberty to say at this time, Ms. Sidden. The investigation is not complete."

"I'm not asking for the *official* cause of death. I understand they have to wait for the autopsy, which could take days or weeks. I'm asking for the *unofficial* version. Surely you could narrow speculation a bit. Did it look like a natural death, or was she hanging from a chandelier, stabbed, suspected of being poisoned, shot, or garroted? Did I leave anything out?"

89

He chuckled. "Other than clubbed to death, snakebit, or mauled by a bear, I'd say you covered the spectrum."

"Well?"

This guy had a sense of humor. Maybe I could get a straight answer out of a lawyer . . . nah.

"Sorry, I can't explain."

"Then why the hell did you call me this late, less than forty-eight hours after she died? You didn't call to tell me of her death; you thought I'd been informed. I now know that you weren't trying to trace two checks that Celia Cancannon, her niece, has probably already supplied an adequate explanation of them to both you and the sheriff. Stop pussyfooting around, this is not a one-way street."

"I need to talk to you about an important matter."

"Ah, but the question is, who is it important to?"

"It's in your best interest, believe me."

"We're talking," I noted. "Shoot."

"This has to be a personal meeting, it can't be discussed over the phone."

"The CIA, FBI, GBI, and DEA no longer bug my phone, Mr. Jackson. It's unproductive. They've learned I don't discuss state secrets or drug shipments over the phone."

I heard a snort of suppressed laughter. I waited.

"Would you be able to come to my office tomorrow anytime after eleven? I should be out of court by then."

"Not for all the tea in China," I replied sweetly.

"May I come to your home tomorrow? I can be there anytime after eleven."

I thought about it. In court at nine, he couldn't drive here by eleven, so that meant Rand and his helicopter. Was I curious about what Jackson wanted to discuss with me? Did I want to see Rand again? Do bears sleep in the woods?

"Only on one condition, a simple yes or no. Was Alyce Cancannon in your opinion murdered?"

"I was told—"

"Good-bye, Mr. Jackson."

"Wait!" he said quickly.

"Yes or no?"

"Yes."

"I'll expect you at eleven tomorrow," I uttered as I hung up.

Jasmine and Susan had been sitting quietly, hanging on my every word.

"I need a pit stop and a beer, then I'll be back with all the news."

"Hurry," urged Susan. "I'm dying for the details."

I went first to the bedroom and grabbed the basic black dress, a black lace teddy, and the three-inch black heels that I had spread out on the bed, just in case. I'm a diehard optimist. I had listened for the whirlybird long after 6:00 P.M. I was relieved that Susan hadn't seen them, and put them away.

I got comfortable with my beer, and gave them Jackson's side of the conversation. They had already heard mine.

"I bet you're in her will!" Susan exclaimed excitedly. "Maybe she left you her fortune for finding Amelia!"

"I only met her Monday and we didn't part friends," I answered dryly. "I think not."

"You did find her cat, maybe she mentioned how good you were to her lawyer. Maybe he wants to hire you to find her killer. That sounds feasible," Jasmine reasoned.

I had to laugh. "Also a not. With her millions or billions, he could hire F. Lee Bailey, Johnnie Cochran, and a whole plenitude of experts, consultants, and investigators. Tracking down a cat with a bloodhound is not on par with solving a murder.

"Y'all wanna know what I think? I think he's been told that I spent about thirty minutes with her alone after I brought the cat back. She really wasn't a happy camper when I warned her that she had an enemy who might wish her harm. I think that she was spitting tacks over someone almost drowning her cat, and the agony that poor Amelia had to endure for hours.

"I think she must have taken her anger and frustration out on all

91

of them after I left the scene. I imagine that anyone as rich and powerful as she was, and remember she's had both money and power all
her life, finally gets to the point where they believe they are godlike.
Think about it. I bet she jumped down their throats, all of them. She
may have sealed her own doom by talking about harsh penalties when
she found out who had catnapped Amelia. She might have threatened
to cut them all out of the will until she could find the guilty party. I
think Mr. John Jason Jackson, Esquire, simply wants to pick my brain.
He wants to know what I said and what she said during that thirty
minutes. Wanna form a pool? We put in five apiece, and the one who
comes closest to the answer wins it all."

"You always win," Susan grumbled, but she was digging in her
large suede carryall for her wallet. I walked over to the desk and lifted
a five from the petty cash fund. I turned to tell Jasmine I would trust
her until tomorrow because she never brings a purse with her. I stood
there speechless, staring at her with my mouth agape.

Jasmine had one of her polished loafers in her lap and had peeled
back the insole. She slipped out folded currency and peeled off a bill.

"Anyone got change for a hundred?"

"You bank out of your shoe?" I blurted without thought.

Stupid. Stupid. Stupid. As soon as I uttered the words my brain
told me why.

Susan was cawing with laughter and pointing a red-tipped talon.
"I'm not believing this!"

"Susan," I warned, to silence her.

"Oh, Jasmine," I said, feeling sad for her. "After all this time?"

Jasmine smiled bravely. "I never have left home without it since I
was nineteen."

"I'm in the dark here, ladies." Susan looked from me to Jasmine,
waiting for an explanation.

"It's bail money," I said softly. "In case she's arrested."

"They wouldn't dare!" Susan sputtered. "Hank would skin them
alive!"

"Hank's not always available, and doesn't control the neighboring counties' deputies," I explained. "Both Jasmine and I have enemies who wear a badge. They could possibly try getting even with me by harassing her. God, Jasmine, I didn't know that it still troubles you."

"Hey, cut it out," Jasmine demanded. "Sometimes I go for days and don't even think about it. I honestly thought you both knew I carried cash for an emergency, or I wouldn't have exposed my stash."

Liar, I thought sadly. Seven years of dread, and she had exposed her worst fear in one careless moment of forgetfulness. All because of a silly bet.

I had dreaded Bubba's attacks much longer than she had dreaded being picked up and thrown into a cell. I could empathize. She had told me once, this new Jasmine born after leaving the streets, that she could not survive one night of penal confinement. I believed her.

I mentally promised once again that I would protect her from all harm. I would also keep my guard up twenty-four out of twenty-four and not turn complacent about Bubba. He hadn't forgotten his burning desire to destroy me. He was out there—waiting.

We rehashed everything we knew of Alyce Cancannon's suspected murder, and then started discussing the new litter.

"Did all ten arrive healthy?" Susan asked as she tilted her empty beer bottle in my direction.

Jasmine grabbed it before I could and went to get refills. I noticed that she took her goblet with her. She limits herself to two glasses at meals and on these pizza nights. This would be her third. If she brought me back one, it would be my fourth. I was beginning to feel mellow.

"Five beautiful females and five handsome males, all perfect and healthy—at least—so far." I reached over and rapped the wood coffee table for good luck. "The last one arrived at one A.M. this morning, almost twenty-four hours after Judy delivered the first one."

"That sounds like a long time, is it normal?"

"Yep, Wayne and I had our usual bet. He said before twenty-four hours, and I took after. I lost by sixteen minutes."

"Good!" declared Susan. I stuck out my tongue. She gave me an evil grin. I knew right then I was in hot water.

"You always act so righteous! You never admit you're vulnerable and can be conned just like the rest of us. You were so quick to figure out I went to meet Brian last night, and so tactful about not pursuing the matter."

"Susan—"

"Hush!" she sang, delighted and determined. "I want Jasmine to hear this. You were so careful when you explained earlier to Jasmine and me how you didn't give a good goddamn whether you ever saw your flyer hunk again. Total indifference is what you pictured so eloquently. You know what was laid out on her bed for a quick change, Jasmine?"

Jasmine shook her head, remaining mute.

"Her 'Come hither' black dress, teddy, and spikes!" she cackled. "Now tell us dear, if flyboy had descended tonight, would you have gone and left us to consume the pizza?"

"You're sneaky, you know? You flushed the toilet to make me think you hadn't seen them."

I tried to sound indignant. Susan was enjoying herself, and she had every right. She had nailed me fair and square. I wouldn't give in too easy.

I squirmed. "I changed my mind *after* I put them there."

"Answer the question, *would you have gone?*"

I sighed. "In a New York minute. Now are you satisfied?"

"Gotcha," she laughed with satisfaction. Jasmine joined her.

All things considered, it was a nice evening.

14

"The Battle Is Joined"

October 7, Saturday, 10:00 A.M.

I spent Friday night with Judy and the puppies. Other than two quick early morning phone calls, I had remained at her side until a few minutes ago, when Jasmine had called me to breakfast. We had finished eating and I was sitting in my office admiring my father's paintings.

Jasmine entered quietly.

"Would you like me to come back later?"

"Sit," I told her as I reached behind the window drape and pushed the button to conceal them. The panels slowly lowered over the four oil paintings with only a small hum of the motors. They should be in a museum, but I couldn't bear to part with them. After my death they would belong to the masses, but right now, for my too few allotted years, I would use them to sustain me against loneliness and all the dark nights when demons came calling.

"I'm going to confide one of my secrets that I haven't told another living soul, aren't you lucky?"

"Hmmm," she answered.

"That sounds noncommittal to me."

"That's what I was aiming for."

"Well, I'm gonna tell you anyway. Have you ever heard of Little Bemis?"

"No," she answered with conviction, "that name I would remember."

"He's not called Little Bemis because he weighs over three hundred pounds, it's because his older brother is Big Bemis." I looked at her.

"Haven't heard of him, either."

"I'll give you the short version. Big Bemis played fullback in high school. All-State three years, and the alumni's great white hope to put Balsa City on the map when he went to U of G. South Carolina offered him a black Trans Am for signing, so he jumped ship. Four glorious years of college and three years in the pros before he ruined his knees and was forced to retire."

"This left the alumni with Little Bemis," Jasmine stated.

"Are you sure you haven't heard this story?"

Jasmine smiled. "Proceed."

"In his freshman year Little Bemis was just as good or better than his brother. The alumni were drooling, hope springs eternal. At Christmas Little Bemis was given a computer by his brother. When school started, Little Bemis quit the football team and took a computer class and refused to play football. The whole school went berserk. They made a pariah out of him. They didn't acknowledge that he was still on the planet. It warped him and changed his personality. He has to this day attended every home game wearing his brother's football jacket, to which he added special panels so he could zip it—driving a new black Trans Am—which he trades in each year for the latest model."

"Good for him," Jasmine clapped. "Is he really warped?"

"The rumor is he presented himself to the personnel department out at Apex-Semex when he was eighteen and demonstrated his skill with a computer by entering all their secret chemical files without them giving him passwords—also opened their competitors'—so they could compare. They hired him on the spot. He's been a productive citizen ever since, with one small exception."

"Ah, we're down to the nitty-gritty."

"He thinks he's the last great spy left in the universe. Since I discovered his quirky operation purely by accident, and worked out the correct approach, he's been securing every bit of information I want for several years now. It's accurate and complete and best of all, free. I just feel so silly abiding by his rules."

"This is the quirky part?"

"My code name is Lila. I have to work out the code name from a codebook and use it in a sentence when I call him. I have to couch the reason for the information in figures from nursery rhythms or mythology. I need 'Jewels rescued from the dragon,' or 'The princess must be returned to the castle.' You get the picture."

"You have got to be putting me on," she giggled.

"Scouts honor. Then I have to follow his instructions to the 'drop,' where he leaves the information for only so long. If I don't pick it up on time, he'll consider me compromised—deactivate my code name—and I'm shit out of luck for any future information. But he's accurate and fast."

"How do you know he's accurate? You can't double-check his information."

"You tell me. I asked him for a quickie when I called. I asked him for your current bank balances. He says you have eight hundred in checking and thirteen thousand in savings, which you should put most of in CDs. You're losing interest daily."

Her eyes widened. "That's illegal!"

"True. Unfortunately, all computers leak information like sieves. Little Bemis is just one of the determined hackers out there with a bucket and sponge. I know of three different ways to secure your bank balance without using Little Bemis."

"Tell me."

"One, pretend I'm you, call up the bank, and ask for it. I know your mother's maiden name, your account numbers, and the amount of your last deposit, because I write your check. Two, I call and say I'm

Sears from Waycross and want to verify a check. We're all a close-knit community here. Sometimes they'll do it. If not, I tell them I'm running a credit check and give them the name of my business. They won't give the actual balance, but with the figures they release, you can come close. They say high three figures, medium four figures, or low five figures. Three, I can hire a private detective and receive the information in thirty minutes. I have no idea how they do it."

Jasmine appeared pensive. "I've wondered where you got those thick computer sheets that you studied from time to time. No offense meant, but I knew you hadn't generated them."

"I can't help it that this miserable computer has gremlins that hate me. No offense taken, you're just grounded for a week right *after* you retrieve the information packet from the 'drop.'"

"Don't ground me," she whined. "You're a computer genius!"

"You're forgiven. Did you bring your map?"

She swept it off the sofa and advanced to the desk.

"You mark your map while I read the directions. Go south on the Woodpecker Route until you reach the third dirt road on your right and turn right, which will put you on One Hundred Fifty-third Street NW."

I heard her snickering. I stopped reading and looked at her.

"I can't help it," she said, giggling. "I laugh every time I see those new street signs on every small three-path road in this county! They look so strange. Some of them are twenty-five miles into deep woods yet peter out in less than fifty yards!"

"Jasmine," I lectured with a stern face, "Dunston, and all the surrounding counties, even in North Florida, have been brought into the twentieth century. It's not nice to make fun of progress. The federal government in its infinite wisdom has given grants to each county so their streets can have signs. By God, *all* our streets now have signs. You should be grateful that now when we get lost, we'll know the name of the street that we are lost on!"

"I won't think they're strange anymore," she said with a straight face and immediately started giggling again. I ignored her.

"After you complete the turn, go exactly five-eighths of a mile and look for a cross on the first pine tree in a row to your right. It's made out of white adhesive tape and both pieces are only two inches long, so they are hard to see. Better change into old jeans. There is thick growth between the trees down most of that road. Walk to the fourth tree and the package will be wrapped in plastic and leaning against the back of the tree. Got it?"

"Got it. For Pete's sake, why doesn't he just put it in a post office box? It would be a lot easier."

"Silly you, what decent spy would use the U.S. mail? It would cut out all the fun."

"Silly me. Anything else?"

"Raise your right hand," I ordered, "and repeat after me. I solemnly swear that I will eat my driver's license and credit cards if I see I'm about to be captured."

"And swallow my poison capsule?"

"That goes without saying. Now, get out of here!"

I had Donnie Ray on watch for the helicopter, with specific instructions. When I heard it approaching from the west, I walked to the front window and peeked from a tiny part in the drapes and watched it land. Donnie Ray had removed the battered paper towel cross, but Rand sat the bird down where it had been. I watched the blades stop and both men alight. Donnie Ray walked toward them and gestured to Rand. He should be telling him where the door to the common room was located and that he could wait for Jackson in there.

Rand ignored him. Donnie Ray said something to Jackson, and hauled buggy toward the office.

"He said he wanted to say hello to you," he repeated breathlessly when he skidded to a stop in front of me.

"Go back, say hi from me, and tell him to wait in the common room! Be firm! Hurry!"

He tore off to do my bidding. I checked the action from my peephole in the drapes. Donnie Ray ran until he was six feet in front of

Rand, stopped, and lifted up an officious hand to stop him. I smiled. Donnie Ray is seven inches short of Rand's six feet. It made me think of David and Goliath.

Rand looked toward the office and gave a casual wave. I jumped back, even knowing it was impossible for him to see me. By the time I could peek through the slit again, he was leaning indolently against the wall of the grooming room. He was staring across the tarmac toward the window he thought I was using. Jackson and Donnie Ray were almost at the office door.

Good. Things were looking up. At least he hadn't stalked back to wait in the copter. This meant he was going to give it a second try to see me.

I ran light-footed back to my desk and sat up straight staring at my screen saver, which was my favorite picture of Bobby Lee chasing butterflies. I jiggled my mouse so that text would appear.

When Jackson's discreet knock sounded, I was typing THE QUICK RED FOX JUMPED OVER THE LAZY BROWN DOG over and over on my December's projected tax totals. I'd have to remember to clean up the page before Jasmine saw it.

"Come in," I called, and kept typing.

"Am I intruding?"

I looked up, startled. "Forgive me, you must be Mr. Jackson," I said, rising from my chair as I typed a final line. "I had to get this into e-mail," as if I were on the Internet and knew what I was doing.

"Sit in this chair," I offered. He was across the desk from me, so he couldn't see my silly typing. I slid my chair a foot to the left because the computer blocked his face.

"What did you want to talk to me about?"

I wanted to seem like a businesswoman whose time was just as valuable as his own. He was in his sixties, looking prosperous and proper from his manicured nails to his expensive tasseled loafers. Brown sport coat and tan pants, white shirt with the collar open sans tie. Casual Georgia elegance on a Saturday morning.

I was in a hunter green wool sheath, lime green scarf, pantyhose, and black sensible pumps. My stomach muscles were sucked in so tightly I feared cramps. I had tamed my frizzy tresses with styling mousse and hairspray and applied serious war paint. We were even on appearance, but I had home turf advantage. He dispensed the fluff first.

"I realize you run a business and I appreciate you seeing me on such short notice." He glanced around the room. "I'm familiar with your father's work, and greatly admire his paintings. Mrs. Cancannon owned four. Do you have any here? I'd feel deeply honored if you would allow me to see them."

"Mr. Jackson, I'm afraid that you have wasted your time and mine," I chided. "I wish you had told me over the phone the purpose of your visit. I have none of my father's paintings that you can view, and I was aware that Mrs. Cancannon owned some. She mentioned the fact during our only meeting on Monday."

I stood. "If there's nothing else?"

We bared our teeth politely at each other, but he ignored my broad hint that the meeting was over by remaining seated.

"I was informed by the Jacksonville Museum curator that you personally possess four oils, titled 'The Four Seasons.' He said you wouldn't sell them. Don't tell me you keep them in a bank vault?"

I laughed. "Mr. Jackson, in trying to spare your feelings and not be rude, I qualified my statement to you about my paintings and obviously it sailed right over your head. I will repeat my sentence about my paintings for clarity. I said, 'I have none of my father's paintings that you can view.'" I repeated, "That you can view. Get it?"

"Got it!" He was angry. His face flamed to the roots of his perfectly styled gray hair.

He sat up straighter in the chair.

"Ms. Sidden, I don't give a good goddamn about your father or his paintings. I noticed that you looked uptight. I mentioned your father's paintings because Mrs. Cancannon told me that they were important to you. I was trying to put you at ease and got insulted for my efforts!"

"That's more like it," I said in an approving manner. "Cut out the bull and tell me why you are here."

"Fine." His voice had turned crisp. He had dropped the snake-oil ooze. "I was staying at the house with Mrs. Cancannon when you were there to search for Amelia. She approached me just before dinner and told me to come to her room after everyone was asleep. This didn't happen until after one A.M.

"When I sneaked into her room, she was very upset. She took your warning that she had an enemy who might harm her to heart, and acted fast. She demanded that I write a new will on the spot, so she could then tell her heirs that she was disinheriting the whole bunch until she found out who tortured Amelia. I begged her not to act hastily, at least not when she was so upset.

"To calm her down, I instructed her in writing a holographic will. This had to be entirely written by her, as testator, by her hand alone, and is legal in this state, without witnesses attesting to her signature. She also added a codicil. She had me make a videotape about the codicil. I explained that this video would not legally be accepted in a court of law. She said that its legality wasn't necessary, that she had to 'bait the hook.'"

He stopped and shook his head dramatically.

"Anyway, we finished just before dawn and we were both exhausted. I pleaded with her not to alienate her relatives and accuse them without any proof. I said her enemy might be a business rival, and she could drive her nieces away. Alyce loved those girls. She had raised them since the oldest was fourteen. She has always trusted my judgment. I had to return to the island Thursday on another matter. She agreed not to say anything or accuse anyone until Thursday, when I could be with her for the confrontation.

"I wanted her to have a cooling-off period. Everyone arrived by Wednesday who believes they are an heir. Something happened from Tuesday morning when I left to Wednesday noon which upset her and made her break her promise to me. At lunch, everyone agrees that she taunted them with the fact that she was *going* to change her will Thursday when I arrived. She didn't mention once that *she had already done it!* If I had not made her promise not to tell them, I believe she would still be alive. I feel responsible for her death. They all knew at noon on Wednesday that she was going to write them out of the will on Thursday. She died between midnight and nine A.M. Thursday morning. I arrived at nine, and they had just found her. I was told she had coffee every morning at seven, but she didn't answer the maid at seven or eight. Just before nine they became alarmed, went in, and she was dead."

He didn't look as elegant as he had when he arrived. It was like he had lost stature in telling me the story. I felt a twinge of sympathy.

"You're not responsible for someone killing her."

"Thank you for saying that. It's what Sheriff Beaman said also, but I still feel guilty."

"We all get the guilts from time to time. I have a doozy of my own." I was thinking about Leroy. "I appreciate you coming over here to tell me these facts. I could claim some of the blame myself, for warning her, but I won't," I said with a smile.

"Mr. Jackson, I'm sorry, I still don't see why you felt you had to tell me this. I'm not involved."

"I'm afraid you are, Ms. Sidden, whether you care to be or not."

He reached into a pocket of his sportcoat and produced a videotape.

"Do you have a VCR handy? I'll let Mrs. Cancannon tell you."

15

"A Voice from the Grave"

October 7, Saturday, Noon

I pointed silently toward the TV and closed the drapes. I could understand now why Jackson had insisted on meeting with me and telling me what had happened in the wee hours of Tuesday morning. It all led up to this tape I was about to see.

I bet Miz Cancannon would be shocked if she could have known that it would be viewed so soon. With her money, I would have packed a bag and chartered a jet to some safe haven far from harm's way. I have a few bucks and also have a determined enemy. I mentally laughed when I pictured me on a plane winging to safety with fifty-seven dogs, seventeen puppies, and a cat. I have too much baggage to travel and would have to remain earthbound. Maybe that was the way Miz Cancannon felt.

But we people in peril don't really believe deep down in our hearts that the grim reaper is going to come calling on *us*. It always happens to someone else.

Jackson and I sat opposite each other on the oyster-white couches and he started the tape.

Miz Cancannon appeared on the screen looking a lot different than she had the last time that I saw her early in the evening on

Monday night. I had left her clutching Amelia with a haughty expression. I would have preferred to remember her that way.

Two days of anger and fear had shrunken her cheeks and hollowed her eyes. Only her voice remained unchanged.

"A good reporter will always put the five W's of journalism in the first paragraph of his story, who, what, when, where, and why. Unfortunately, I only know the victim . . . me. I have no knowledge of the other four. I also want you to find the how.

"It is obvious to you at this point I have died under suspicious circumstances. Everyone may know by now most of the answers, but some are still unanswered, or you wouldn't be viewing this tape.

"I charge you to find my killer. I am willing to pay handsomely for your services. I have instructed my lawyer to release ample funds for your investigation. Find out who prematurely stole my right to die a natural death, whether it's a month from now, or years in the future.

"I only met with you briefly, but I know enough about your character to make an informed decision. You're brash, prideful, and stubborn. You would not take money you felt you hadn't earned. You were not afraid to judge me and tell me what you thought. I know you didn't like or approve of me, yet you took the time to return Amelia secretly, so I would hear your assessment of what occurred and offer me some advice before the others knew.

"If you think I'm seeking revenge and retribution, you are absolutely correct. You may not be able to supply either one. It may be impossible to find my murderer and prove it in a court of law. This is not a condition that has to be met before you are compensated. I want an honest effort. My lawyer has been authorized to offer you twenty-five thousand dollars to investigate, and another twenty-five thousand if you succeed.

"Sitting here, I can almost predict your argument *against* even trying to find a solution. I know that you aren't a qualified detective or have vast resources of information available. Mr. Jackson will handle your inquiries and personally pass them on to a large reputable agency that can find out anything you wish to know.

"There is no time limit. I know you cannot work full-time on finding a solution. You have your business and your bloodhounds. I know they will come first with you. If you are wondering why I should care about justice for the guilty party, as I will not know if you succeed or fail, I'll explain. At this moment I feel better in knowing that I have hired a person who will try diligently on my behalf to find the answers surrounding my death. As they say, you can't take your wealth with you, so there is no reason for me to haggle over costs.

"I also know what you are now thinking at this moment. You have independent means and cannot be bought for a possible fee of fifty thousand. I understand this, Ms. Sidden, and I have baited my hook with the means to secure your services. I saw your face when you discovered that I owned four of your father's paintings. You adored your father, and love his paintings. You know that you can't be bought. I hate to disillusion you, but anyone can be bought if you know his or her price. I know yours.

"Mr. Jackson has been instructed to hold the four oils your father painted in a trust for one year. If you try and succeed or fail after one year from this date, you may choose your favorite from the four, and it is yours, tax-free.

"Good-bye, and good luck."

I saw her make an angry gesture toward the camera and watched the picture fade, leaving only the static sound of a continuing reel. Jackson ejected the cartridge and cut off the machine without rewinding the tape. He walked to the windows and opened the drapes. He was tactfully giving me time to recover from hearing her demands.

I felt as if I was walking out of a movie theater after viewing a double feature in the daytime. The sunshine was too bright. I was disoriented and reality was slightly askew. The bitch really knew how to turn the screws. I went back and slouched in my chair behind my desk. Jackson sat silently across from me.

I gave him a smile. "You have to give the ol' gal credit. She knew how to push the right buttons."

"I'll never forget the first time I drew the line and said no to her," he reminisced, giving me a rueful grin. "She didn't argue, and seemed to accept my decision gracefully. I went home and found my wife, Carolyn, ecstatically sporting a tennis bracelet with a total of two carets of exquisite cut diamonds that had been delivered that very afternoon.

"Enclosed was a charming note from Alyce telling her how happy she was that she and I always agreed on business matters. Carolyn has a great weakness for expensive jewelry and I have a great weakness for Carolyn, so I never said no again."

I shook my head in understanding and grinned.

"I'm afraid, however, that there is a quirk in my personality that Miz Cancannon didn't know about when she made her horseback estimate of my character traits."

I leaned back in my chair and braced my feet on the desk. I was enjoying this.

"You're going to turn down the offer?"

He seemed taken aback.

"Not hardly," I drawled. "I'm not stupid, just nosy. I would have paid money to be able to dabble in this case, even on the edges of it unofficially. Here I'm given unlimited funds, plenty of time, and the right to pry officially. Who could ask for anything more?"

"I don't think Alyce would be overjoyed with your answer. She loved to manipulate and control her employees. She would be very unhappy if she knew your feelings right this minute." He looked amused.

"Good. Let's get to work. How did she die?"

"She was shot above her right ear at close range with a small-caliber round, probably a twenty-two. Her doctor thinks she was asleep and died instantly."

I stared at him. "Shot? This is the cause of death that you think they can keep a secret? I bet everyone in Camden County knows it by now. I thought there was a chance of natural death, or some hard-to-diagnose poison. Shot? I'm not believing this!"

"Only the sheriff, the doctor, and I were told the method of death, and now you. The sheriff seems to think that one of the suspects might slip up if everyone is kept in the dark."

"Tell me another one," I said with disgust. "This is a small town in South Georgia. Where do y'all live, on the moon? The EMTs told their co-workers, the doctor told the coroner and hospital morgue staff, and they all told their families. How often does a billionaire recluse get murdered close by? Also, the sheriff's deputies, reporters, the media, you told your wife, and she told the beauty parlor regulars. Ten-year-old boys are reenacting the crime by shooting their buddies in the head with imaginary guns, and sprawling across desks in the classrooms. You're probably the only man in the county who thinks the cause of death is still a secret."

"I didn't tell my wife the cause of death," he answered stiffly.

"Then I'm sorry I misspoke," I said, laughing. "Alyce died Thursday morning, and it's now shortly after lunch on Saturday." I picked up the telephone receiver and held it out to him. "Call your wife and ask her how many different opinions about Alyce's shooting has she heard." He didn't reach for the phone, and after a couple of heartbeats, I replaced the receiver. I changed the subject.

"It's a shame, really, how few mantrailing bloodhound teams are now working in Georgia for local city, county, and state law enforcement. There have been tremendous advances in forensic evidence gathering in just the past five to ten years, including crime scene scent evidence. Would it surprise you if I said that if the crime scene had been handled correctly and with the latest techniques in use, there would have been an excellent chance to point out the killer with the use of a bloodhound and a machine that costs less than five hundred dollars?"

Jackson just looked at me with a quizzical expression. He had no idea what I was talking about. It never hurts to let the person who was gonna pay the freight know that you were knowledgeable in what you do. I made him ask.

"What kind of machine, and how could a bloodhound find anything after the killer had gone?"

"That would probably be the exact question that Sheriff Beaman would ask, and it's ironic. Scent at the crime scene is the forgotten evidence. We now have the ability to gather scent, store it, and use it in the future to convict a suspected killer."

"How?" He seemed surprised. "And why doesn't Sheriff Beaman know about it?"

"It's been available for several years and has actually convicted suspects, but they can't see it, feel it, or hold it in their hands. Law enforcement officers can't envision what a great tool it is and they spend their money on what they understand."

"Explain what you are describing."

"Scent. Scent left in the air hovering over the murder scene. Let me give you a hypothetical scenario. Suppose the sheriff employed a good handler with a trained mantrailing bloodhound, and the handler had a scent machine and knew how to use it. This scenario would also suppose that the sheriff's men would be trained to protect the scene from contamination.

"A call comes into the station that Mrs. Cancannon had been found dead. The sheriff immediately orders the room to be sealed, with no one to traipse in and out of the room. She's dead, right? What's the big hurry and bustle about? If the room is immediately sealed off and if platoons of people aren't in and out, looking, touching, standing around and contaminating the room, the killer's scent is all over the victim, the bed linens, the floor, and permeating the *air itself.* The dog handler arrives with the scent machine.

"Picture the machine in your mind. It's slightly larger than a twelve-volt car battery. It can be operated with electricity or on a battery. It is carried into the room, set near the victim, and turned on. It runs from five to ten minutes, depending on the size of the room. It is sucking the air into the machine like a vacuum cleaner. The air has to pass through a sterile pad. This places the scent in the air in a concentrated form onto the material. This piece of evidence is stored in an airtight bag and can be frozen *indefinitely!*

"In some random killings they have no idea who did it, but years later they may have a suspect, say a serial killer with not enough evidence to place him at the scene. If the scent material is thawed out and presented to a trained bloodhound, he can pick him out of a lineup of several people. That's corroborating evidence that will nail him.

"In this supposed case, the sheriff has ten suspects. Ten people who are heirs apparent and under suspicion. A bloodhound could clear nine people in a lineup and give you the correct suspect. This person couldn't be convicted on the dog's testimony alone, but when you're positive who did it, you can narrow the search for corroborating evidence and usually turn it up. This same method can be used on lesser crimes, armed robberies, residential break-ins, you name it."

"Then why isn't it used by every law enforcement agency?"

"It's fairly new. There's no twenty years of precedents in court cases. Each case has to be won individually on its own merit. Judges, lawyers, law enforcement people, and possible jurors have to be educated in the bloodhound's abilities.

"To all the people who judge, it sounds unbelievable. And, as I said before, so many officials want to purchase the flashier tools: the German shepherd who works to catch fleeing suspects and guard his human partner's life, and who also can be used for crowd control and other duties."

I laughed. "A bloodhound would hunker down and hide his eyes with his paws if someone tried to knife his handler. They are gentle and aren't aggressive."

"How about all those old movies with a pack of howling bloodhounds chasing a prison escapee?"

"Hollywood has a lot to answer for in relation to the public's perception of bloodhounds. Using their noses to find a person exhilarates them. When they find them, they don't attack or bite or hold them with their teeth. Detection is their only function. They just find them and when they do, the bloodhound's job is done."

"You lost me back there in your scenario when you said the bloodhound handler could have captured the killer's scent in Alyce's bedroom. Wouldn't the machine have pulled Alice's scent from her body, and given him two scents to look for?"

"When a person dies, the body doesn't give off an individual scent anymore. It instantly begins to decay and only gives off the scent of a decomposing cadaver. Cadaver search dogs are trained with actual human bones and the smell of decomposing flesh. The laboratories have invented new chemicals now that replicate the smell of decomposing bodies and bones. If a child is believed to have drowned in a pond, you don't scent the bloodhound with a child's sweater. That's the way they find live people. To find a dead one, they are given the scent of a decomposing body. Mrs. Cancannon's dead scent wouldn't have been confusing, even mixed with the suspect's scent."

"Couldn't you still try it, even though two days have passed?"

"I could try it successfully a month from now, if the room had been properly sealed, with only the body removed, but that's not what happened. I'm sure the room has had heavy traffic, people taking photographs, dusting for prints, family members coming in to see where it happened. The maid has cleaned the room and changed the linens. The scene is too contaminated with different and more recent scents. Also, the murderer was probably in the room with the rest of the family, at least briefly, gawking as the others did. An identification now would be suspect. The forgotten evidence of scent has been lost forever from Alyce's bedroom."

Jackson sighed and shook his head.

"It sounds to me like most unsolved crime statistics could be cut in half if all officers used the machine to collect the scent first, and investigated afterward."

"That's right on the money."

"You know what? If this came to pass, it would also cut out half the judges, half of overcrowded court dockets, half the lawyers' fees, and half of the law enforcement personnel. It will never happen, trust me."

"You have a point," I agreed.

16

"Will He or Won't He?"

October 7, Saturday, 1:00 P.M.

I walked Jackson out, and when we reached the back porch he stuck out his hand.

"The minute any information that you requested comes into the office, I'll forward it to you immediately."

"Whoa," I said, acting confused. "You must have misunderstood me, Mr. Jackson. I'm relaying my first request through you just to get the system working and for them to be informed the bills go to you, but all the information comes to me."

"I thought we'd both read them and discuss . . ."

His voice trailed off as he watched my head moving slowly back and forth and the solemn expression on my face.

"It ain't gonna happen, Mr. J. I don't work well with someone watching over my shoulder. You set up the account where whoever is in charge knows that I'm the boss and the only one they take instructions from. Have the person call me and I'll relay what I wish them to investigate. That will prevent any confusion further down the road, okay?"

"I really think we should work together on this. I know all ten suspects. I have knowledge that would be valuable for you to know."

"Sorry."

"Will you please tell me why?" His voice was petulant and annoyed. He wasn't taking me cutting him out of the loop with good grace.

"Certainly. I'm going to invade these people's past and present life like it's never been done before. If they think that Alyce spied on them, they'll decide she was a kind ol' aunt before I'm done. I can't do the legwork personally, so operatives will and report to me. I don't think a second party, you, and possibly a third, your secretary, should also know their secrets. You've admitted you have personal knowledge of most of them already.

"The important fact to remember is that *nine* of these people are innocent, and we assume one is guilty. They are all strangers to me and if they are innocent, I don't want their personal lives aired to anyone, including you, if it is unnecessary. Do you get my drift?"

He did, but he sure didn't like it. I could see him reluctantly swallow his objections. In his lawyering mode, he was probably already marshaling his thoughts for a future confrontation in which he could change my mind.

I thought I knew why he wanted to know every scrap of information I obtained. He knew that whoever ended up inheriting the fortune, the other nine would surely contest the will. Knowledge is power. I personally didn't give a fig which one inherited. I just didn't want to give him information that could effect the outcome of a protracted court battle. Fair's fair. As a stranger their secrets were safe with me if they weren't the one who eliminated Miz C.

"I was going to say, keep me posted, but I understand that is not going to happen. So I'll say, we'll be talking in the future." He gave me a frosty smile.

"You can count on it."

I watched him walk across the tarmac toward the helicopter that was partially blocked from view by the corner of the grooming room.

Now I would get the answer to a pressing question: Will Rand still attempt to speak to me? My pride had dictated that I would rebuff his first attempt, but I was rooting for him to try again. I stood a long thirty seconds before I ducked back inside my office. I didn't want to be caught waiting for him on the porch.

"Damn!" I had no sooner sat down at my desk when I heard the whine of the helicopter's rotor increasing, 'til it was shattering the peace and quiet over my head. He was leaving, the schmuck! I gnashed my teeth in anger and disappointment. His ego was obviously in direct proportion with mine, big. Very big, maybe even bigger. At this rate, I'd never get to see that quaint little restaurant and the St. John's River in the moonlight. A person could starve to death waiting for another invitation. I could dry up and blow away while we played silly games.

"What did he say?" Jasmine was breathing hard. She must have trotted across from the grooming room. She eyed me expectantly as she advanced into the room.

"Not a dang syllable!" I muttered. "He leaned against the grooming room and waved at me while I hid behind the curtain. I had Donnie Ray stop him from entering before Jackson. Afterward, I expected him to try again, but he flew away obviously sulking."

"That sure reminds me of someone. Who could that be?"

Her head was cocked to the side and her eyes were sparkling with good humor.

"Don't nag me, I feel rotten."

"I'll change the subject. I retrieved the info from the master spy. It's in the car. Donnie Ray wants to name the last female puppy Caboose. You said this was going to be Judy's last litter."

"Over my dead body. We can't call her the runt, either, she weighs the most."

"Let's discuss naming her over lunch. Hungry?"

"Getting thwarted always makes me hungry," I declared.

Just after three, the detective agency based in Washington, D.C. called. The male caller identified himself when he was assured he was talking to me.

"Ms. Sidden, I'm Chester Adams. I'll be your personal representative here at the agency. I will be handling your inquiries and instructing the operatives who will be securing the answers to your questions. If you'll tell me the names of the people you would like to have a dossier on, I'll get started."

"Certainly," I replied. He held while I found my list. I read the names of Miz Cancannon's five nieces, their four husbands, and Rand.

"I want this as detailed as possible, by next Friday morning. Call first and speak to me, then you can fax what you have on them. Never fax any information without checking first, so I will be the one receiving the information. Do not give out any information to anyone who calls for it if it isn't me. The lawyer who is paying the freight is not privileged to receive any duplicates. Is this understood?"

"Absolutely. The best method is to use a code word, one of your choice, and it's to be mentioned in your first sentence to me, or the call will be terminated."

"Bobby Lee."

"Very well. I would like to mention that six days is not enough time to completely cover every facet of their lives. An in-depth study will take longer."

"How much longer?" I asked.

"It will depend on whether there are blanks in their histories, and if they lived or worked in Europe or Asia."

"Fine. I'll expect your call next Friday before ten A.M. If you don't mind my asking, I seem to hear a Southern accent in your speech."

"You do," he answered. "I thought it had disappeared, but hearing your voice must have made me revert back to it. I spent half my of my life right outside Atlanta, in a small town named Tucker. When I graduated from high school, I moved to D.C."

"You don't know what you're missing," I replied.

"Oh yes, I go back to visit several times a year, Mom, and old high school buddies."

"No old sweethearts?"

"They have all vanished by either moving away or into marriage and motherhood."

"Time marches on," I commented. "You'll get back to me next Friday?"

"I'll call you by ten. Nice doing business with you, Ms. Sidden."

"Jo Beth."

"My name is Chester, but everyone calls me Chet."

"Good-bye, Chet."

I looked at the clock. I had been up since midnight but wasn't sleepy. If I took a nap, it would mess up a good night's sleep later on. I decided to go help Jasmine and Donnie Ray prepare the feed for the evening kennel rounds.

Windell was working, but he would leave at five. My masterpiece litter was throwing all our schedules out the window, but they were worth their weight in gold. I giggled aloud. Maybe the day they were born, but not now. Puppies doubled their weight in the first week. These sweethearts were filling out very nicely.

The phone rang as I was crossing the back porch. I hurried back. "Hello."

"May I speak to Ms. Jo Beth Sidden?"

"I'm Jo Beth Sidden."

"We met briefly Thursday mid-morning, Ms. Sidden. My name is Captain Evan Danglish, USAF. Please don't hang up until I tell you, I'm the good guy. I was with Colonel Rupert Hayes, USAF. He was the bad guy."

"I'm still listening, Captain. How's the colonel doing?"

"He's muttering and scowling, as usual. I wanted to apologize for his behavior. Almost all Air Force personnel here at Moody are professionals, but we have a couple of rotten apples in our barrel. The colonel is one of them."

"I accept your apology on behalf of the Air Force, Captain. This call wasn't necessary, but I appreciate the effort. I bump into species like the colonel on a weekly basis. All is forgiven."

"Thanks for understanding. I know you're very busy, but I wondered if you could spare me a few minutes. I was the pilot of the missing plane. If it's not found, I figured out that it will take me around two hundred and thirty-two years to pay for it out of my salary."

I laughed. "Surely you jest?"

"Yes, ma'am, but until that plane is found and they determine the reason for the crash, my future as a pilot in the Air Force is on hold."

"I'm sorry to hear that, Captain, but there is nothing I can do to help you. Without a pinpoint location within a few hundred yards' diameter, my bloodhounds couldn't find it. With you seeing the plane going straight in, it could be buried completely, maybe as much as twenty-five feet deep. That's just an estimate, however. I don't know how to figure the speed and the terrain it encountered.

"It could be underwater, or entangled with huge cypress trees several hundred years old, *and* below ground several feet. For every yard the search area is widened in a circle, you could begin to multiply the hours of search needed by one thousand.

"I was about three hundred feet up and looking right at her when she went in. You could call it a bird's-eye view. Maybe I could describe the area? It's crystal clear in my head and printed indelibly in my mind."

I sighed. People can't grasp the enormity of the swamp. I'd humor him a little longer. His career was in jeopardy, and he was hurting.

"Let's say you can describe it. I can too, and I didn't see the plane go in. It had lots of tall cypress, some water in small sloughs, a stagnant skim on a fairly large pond, acres and acres of planted slash pine, and lots of vines concentrated here and there almost covered in yellow leaves. From the air, it seemed the patches of vines were large areas of bright yellow flowers. The cypress and old growth trees had long strands of Spanish moss, all hanging from the south side, and the same amount drooping from the old growth section of long-leaf yellow pine. Sound familiar?"

"I couldn't have described it better. It's exactly what I saw. How did you know?"

"Because there are five hundred and fifty thousand *square acres* of the Okefenokee that look almost identical to the uninitiated and ones who are not flora experts. Does this put the impossible task more in perspective?"

"But . . . there was a tree I remember. I kept my eyes on it all the way down. I thought it could be used as a marker to find the spot. The plane crashed about thirty yards to the right of it."

His voice quivered with desperation. He was now grasping at straws.

"And what was so special about this tree? Is it extra-tall? Full of limbs? It didn't have any moss? Come on, Captain, you haven't been listening."

"I focused my eyes on it when I was following the plane's straight in approach. It . . . it was dead. Bone white, all the bark had fallen off. Tall, maybe forty feet."

I blinked. There were hundreds of dead bone-white trees still standing as if they were sentinels; guarding flora and fauna from encroaching chemical plants and careless hunters who built fires on dead grass in small clearings. I knew of one special one that had helped me once.

It was a fanciful thought, but I had felt safer sitting as close to it as I could—leaning against its dead trunk last October—when I was mantrailing Silvers, who had flipped out, shooting his mother and his first cousin and seriously wounding one of Hank's deputies—but it couldn't be *my* tree.

My tree had listed about five degrees, like it could give up the ghost any second and come slowly downward. A fallen guardian, the sound muffled by thick trees and a foot of humus. It had protected me from prowling scavengers, and at early dawn, the eager bow-hunters who crept in and sat in a tree stand and fired at any movement.

In the early predawn, I had patted its massive truck and found Silvers less than two hours later sound asleep. It was an uneventful capture. My tree had a V in the top that looked like a two-pointed crown for the dead giant. It was possible it was still standing. Some stayed upright against all laws of gravity for several years.

"Ms. Sidden?" The captain was wondering if we had been disconnected.

"Sorry," I replied, "I was daydreaming. Did your large dead tree have anything more unusual, maybe a few small white limbs near the top?"

"Yeah. No dead limbs, but the top had broken off in a distinctive V pattern, just like someone had carved a notch in it. I saw it from the east. Facing it, the whole tree leaned to the left a bit. Not much, but it was noticeable."

"Are you Irish by any chance, Captain?"

"No ma'am. I was born and raised in Chattanooga, Tennessee."

"Well, you certainly have the luck of the Irish. I know exactly where the tree stands that you described. In fact, I spent a miserable wet night at its base one night almost exactly one year ago."

"Does that mean you can find the plane?" His voice was hoarse with excitement. "You think we have a chance?"

"If your extraordinary luck holds, it's almost a dead cert. What are you doing next Tuesday morning? Care to come with me? We'll go find that Viper of yours."

"What should I tell the colonel?"

"Not a whisper to the colonel! In case you were giddy and got your coordinates wrong and got turned around, or the distance is greater from the tree to the plane than you estimated, it could take us a month of searching. I don't enjoy looking the fool. We'll have the exact location and a trail blazed to the nearest road before we tell the colonel anything."

I explained to him how to dress, and how to handle the scent article. I told him to arrive at dawn, and to come alone. He promised he'd be here if he had to be AWOL. I didn't doubt him. In fact, I pitied anyone who tried to stop him.

17

"Two County Sheriffs"

October 9, Monday, 8:00 A.M.

I had relieved Wayne at ten the previous night and he in turn woke up at five, and ran me out of the birthing room at six. I had a long soak in the tub and then cooked myself a huge breakfast of canned hot biscuits, scrambled eggs, and bacon. I was feeling almost human. I yawned and fought the urge to crawl into bed and take a short nap.

I settled in my desk chair and got comfortable. The coming conversation with Hank would take a while. It seemed lately that I had to constantly soothe Hank's ruffled feathers. He took offense more easily and took longer to forgive me. Hank wanted a wife and a family, preferably two sons and a daughter, and I was the one he wanted to marry.

We had a rocky affair, riddled with fights and accusations, for a brief period of six weeks over a year ago. Our friendship had suffered. He wanted to resume the affair and tie the knot. I had pointed out our rocky romantic interlude and rejoiced that we hadn't inflicted fatal damage on one another. He closed his eyes to our vocal mauling and disparaging remarks that could have sunk us forever, and pooh-poohed the idea that we couldn't live in peace and harmony.

Hank and I were too much alike to join in matrimony. We were

120

fiercely competitive, had sharp tongues, and used them often. I admitted only to myself that I sometimes longed for him. His shy grin and dark piercing eyes could squeeze my heart, and other times I could cheerfully provide him a slow and lingering death. I shook my head in sadness. Desire was not enough. Did I truly love him? I didn't have a clue. Sometimes I thought I did, but that wasn't enough either.

He grew furious at me during our last conversation. He hadn't called me in several days. Was I trying to hang onto him by constantly reconciling our differences? You bet. I didn't want to lose him. I could feel him slipping away more each day now. He wasn't going to wait forever and I couldn't make up my mind.

I rubbed my temples and frowned at the phone. I decided I would take a dose of the fizzy stuff before I attempted to call him. I had foolishly eaten four strips of bacon and four of the small biscuits, loaded with whipped butter. My stomach was now warning me that it was a major mistake.

Jasmine knocked and entered. She sniffed the air as she approached.

"Bacon? You ate bacon? How many strips?"

"You can't possibly smell bacon in the air," I stated, feeling smug. "I aired out the kitchen ten minutes with the exhaust fan over the stove and the overhead paddle fan, and opened both windows!"

She squealed with delight. "I was only guessing, but you've just admitted it. Your conscience should be hurting!"

"I'm hurting," I said, bending a little in the middle and rubbing my stomach as I headed for the kitchen, "but it's my gut. I have no conscience when it comes to food."

"Have you called Hank this morning?"

"I haven't got that far. I've only been *thinking* about calling him." I eased down in a kitchen chair.

Jasmine fetched a glass of water and added two Alka-Seltzers and handed me the glass.

"This has ceased being funny," she said, softening her voice. "You should go lie down."

"I'll be fine, if the fizz does its job. Let's move to the office. I have to call Hank. What are your plans this morning?"

I managed to walk straight and didn't clutch my stomach. Mind over matter, I cautioned my gut sternly. Behave yourself.

"I skipped two routine searches last week. Wayne says with Donnie Ray, Windell, and Harvey helping out when he doesn't have a patient, they can hold down the fort, so I'm going to try to catch junior high, Phillips Industries, and the sewing plant."

"Why don't you leave the sewing plant until this afternoon? Are they still running three shifts?"

"Yes, but I did the swing shift last week. The morning shift has hasn't been searched in almost three weeks, they should be first."

"Yeah, but your right arm is going to be several inches longer than your left when you finish that agenda. Ulysses really drags you around at a breakneck speed."

"I thought I would take Violet this morning. She hasn't had an outing in a month and she's twenty pounds lighter."

"Smart. You're always one step ahead of me when you plan your day. How would I ever do without you?"

"I don't plan to give you a chance to find out. I'll be back around two. Take care of the tummy."

"It's been told to behave," I said to her retreating back.

I dialed Hank's number.

"Cribbs."

"Hi, it's me. How you doing?"

"Peachy."

"Still mad at me?"

"Yep."

"Come on, Hank. You know I say things sometimes without thinking. I didn't mean to offend you. I'm sorry. Does that help?"

"Not much."

"Have you heard from your buddy, Sheriff Beaman?"

"He called about thirty minutes ago. Says he wants me with him when he comes to call on you, and that he'd be here to pick me up in time to get there by eleven. He also told me you have been hired by the estate to investigate the shooting, and was told to cooperate and not get in your way."

"How is he taking it?"

"Well . . ." Hank drawled, sounding amused, "he had to spit first before he could finish telling me, so I don't think he's taking the news too kindly."

"Does he dip snuff?"

"He spit to show disgust, Jo Beth," he explained.

"I knew that, I just wondered if I was gonna have to lug around a spittoon so he wouldn't kill the grass."

Hank snorted. "I forgot. You know everything, don't you?"

"Not hardly," I said, trying to pacify him.

"I bet you don't even know that I had a date with that little blond that works at Pete's Deli. We did the town last night."

"The one with foot-long eyelashes, a ten-inch waist, and a forty-four-double-D cup? Billie? You went out with Billie Jean Crews?"

I knew my voice had risen with equal parts of disbelief and annoyance. I decided I'd better tone it down. The things I have to do to keep this teetering relationship functioning sometimes appall me.

"Jealous?"

"Of course not," I said quickly. "You know she just broke up with that bruiser who lives over in Collins. I'm just worried that he might return and break his guitar over your head."

Hank chuckled with satisfaction. He had received conformation that I was still interested.

"Jeff and I will be there around eleven."

"Hank, will you do me a big favor?"

"It depends."

"Ask Sheriff Beaman to leave the helicopter there and let you drive him out here. It's only three miles."

"Why?"

"There are ten suspects, and the pilot is one of them. I don't want to meet him in a social situation where I would be forced to shake his hand. He may be the perp."

Hank accepted my explanation and agreed.

That should thwart Mr. Randall Finch if he was planing on meeting a simpering grateful woman who would fall all over him for an invitation to dine. I smiled with relish.

Sometimes I'm much too devious for my own good.

When Hank and Beaman arrived, it was obvious I would have my work cut out for me. The sheriff was on his high horse and not being subtle.

"Glad you could come, Sheriff. I appreciate you bringing me a copy of your files," I said, beaming, as I offered my hand.

He ignored both my hand and my gracious smile.

He spit.

"I didn't have a choice in the matter," he uttered, looking over at the kennel.

"Howdy, Jo Beth!" Hank was acting friendly and pumped my hand several times. "You sure have a nice place here."

I gave him a severe glare. You ought to know, you ninny, you lived here once for six weeks!

He was tall, slim, and trim. He wore a uniform of tailored gabardine. He didn't have to wear a uniform, but he knew that the long creased lines showed off his lanky figure to perfection. His dark hawk-like eyes and ebony hair, his gift from an Indian ancestor, made him tall, dark, and handsome. There was only one problem: He knew it.

I had to bite back a retort. He was enjoying his friend's sour manners.

"Would you like me to give you a tour of the kennels, Sheriff?"

"Never could abide bloodhounds," he commented, not facing me. "Hard to raise and a mangy breed. Never used them and never will. They are lousy with coons, and can't fetch a squirrel if you drop one at their feet."

He punctuated his comments with another spit, looking at Hank for his approval. Hank gave him a wan, noncommittal smile. He was careful to stay neutral. He knows how far he can push and my low boiling point when someone shows contempt for my animals.

Now I can abide an angry attack on me personally, but my bloodhounds? Never!

"Sheriff, you have every right to be angry with me. You don't want any woman poking her nose into one of your cases. I can live with your disapproval of me, but don't disparage my bloodhounds. Every word you utter about them points out your ignorance of both law enforcement advances and the breed."

"You calling me ignorant?"

"If the shoe fits," I said, giving him a Cheshire grin, "then wear it!"

"Well, that sure is something, you getting hot and bothered about those hounds of yours. Jackson came back from seeing you, and gave me a cock-and-bull story about how those bloodhounds could have found Miz Cancannon's killer if they could smell the air in her bedroom. You ought to be shamed of yourself, telling such big whoppers, and the damn fool believed you. I can't get over it, thought he had more sense."

"Every word I told him was the gospel truth. Several cases have been written up and published in most of the periodic police journals, which you obviously don't read.

"The man I bought the scent machine from lives in New York. He has personally presented bloodhound evidence to the courts in over three thousand cases, in which he achieved *convictions in every case!* Quite an enviable record, don't you think? I'll give you his name and address, if you wish. You just might learn something to help you get a conviction now and then. And one other thing. Bloodhounds' testimony were convicting felons in court a hundred years before you were born!"

Beaman turned to Hank. "I'll be in your car, when you're ready to leave."

He turned and trudged back to Hank's car.

I threw up my hands in disgust. "Leave!" I yelled. "You just might learn something if you stay!"

"Hush," Hank hissed softly, "you've done enough damage for one day. Don't make matters worse."

I glared at him and stalked back inside. I slumped at my desk. No reports, and no statements of alibis. Sidden's big mouth strikes again. I was a total screwup. I tried to laugh and ended up with my head on my desk, bawling with frustration.

I heard the door open, and Hank enter without knocking. I jerked my head up and surreptitiously tried to wipe my tears while I pretended I was straightening my hair.

Hank advanced with a bulging file folder.

"Beaman asked me to give you these," he said, placing the file on my desk. He looked up and noticed my tear-stained face and probably red eyes.

"Hey," he uttered softly and came around the desk with his arms open. I slid into them like it was a common occurrence. He held me, murmuring my name. It felt so good, I put my arms around his neck, pulling his face toward me. He kissed me, and it felt better than good.

Hank groaned. "He's waiting on me."

"So go." I pushed him away with a smile.

"I shall return," he promised.

"Not tonight, big guy. I was up all last night with the puppies."

"I'll call you."

I watched him hurry out. Another complication in my busy schedule, but I'll tell you true, it was a great kiss.

18

"Searching for a Viper"

October 10, Tuesday, 6:05 A.M.

Jasmine and I stood on the back porch while I gave her instructions on the search. It was a cool forty-seven degrees, with hardly any wind. I had on my bright rescue suit in neon yellow. It felt good now, but later in the morning I would be sweating heavily. The temperature could get up in the eighties. All the gear was packed; I'd checked the puppies, and I was trying to point out our departure spot to Jasmine.

"It's no use, I'll have to call you when I reach where we'll be going in. Since they have put up all those new street signs on every turn-in in the county, I have no idea what the sign says."

"When did the county say they would have the new maps?"

"When I called last week, they said it was at the printer's and promised they'd be ready in six weeks. I know it's the third dirt road to the right off the Woodpecker Route, after you pass Tom's Creek Road."

"If it becomes necessary, I'll find you," Jasmine assured me.

"I know. I hate to leave the van exposed during hunting season, or I'd leave it in open sight. It's only legal for bow hunters now, but they shoot and then look to see if it looks like a deer."

I looked down at Bobby Lee. He was wiggling his whole body in

127

anticipation, clutching both leads in his jaws. I had on my rescue suit and he knew I was going to work, and unfortunately, he thought he was going also.

"Oh God," I murmured to Jasmine. "Look who thinks he's going mantrailing."

"I'm glad I'm not the one who has to tell him," she whispered, and quickly moved a discreet distance away.

"Bobby Lee," I said softly as I knelt beside him, "you can't go. It's a no-no. You can't go."

I removed his leashes from his mouth and hung them back on their respective nails. I didn't look down at him when Jasmine returned, I knew what I would see. He would sit there looking forlorn in a constant vigil until I returned.

"You're nervous about this search, aren't you?"

"Nah, just getting more careful as I mature," I said, smiling.

I was antsy, and didn't know why.

"Don't get alarmed if we don't come out tonight; there's a possibility that we'll camp out. If I think we're getting close, I want to use all the daylight I can, instead of hiking out and then hiking back in."

"*If* the radio doesn't work, and *if* you don't show up tonight, when should I start looking?"

"If I haven't contacted you by six P.M. tomorrow, send in the Boy Scouts. Where is the captain? It's six-fifteen already. I thought he would be here with bells on, as gung-ho as he seemed yesterday."

The first gate alarm sounded.

"About time," I grumbled.

I walked to the back of the van and peered through the aluminum cage.

"You ready to go, big guy?"

Stanley's nose was pushed against the wire. I slipped a finger inside and rubbed his face. I watched Captain Evan Danglish, USAF, drive across the tarmac.

He left the car and walked over.

"Am I late?"

"Not enough to matter. Ready to find your plane?"

"I sure am," he replied.

I looked him over. He had on fatigues and boots, with the pants tucked in tight. I reached into the van and pulled out a rescue suit, holding it out to him.

"No thanks, it looks hot. I'll be fine."

"I wasn't offering you a choice," I said. "Put it on. It deflects blackthorn barbs and snake fangs. It's supposed to be bulletproof, but only for small-caliber rounds. I don't think it will deflect a forty-ought-six rifle cartridge or a steel arrow, but at least it lets them know you're not a deer, if they bother to scope your movement before they fire. Personally, I wouldn't stand in the middle of the Woodpecker Route road, which is forty feet wide, with camouflage markings like you're wearing for a million bucks. We *want* them to see us, we don't want to hide."

"Hunters wear camouflage," he protested mildly.

"And get shot with increasing frequency. I'll make you a deal. You don't tell me how to conduct a search in the Okefenokee, and I won't tell you how to fly a plane safely back to your base."

"Low blow."

"I thought you were in the Air Force. Don't they teach you how to follow orders without question?"

"Yes, ma'am."

"Well, adopt the same procedure here. I want to pull a Frank Buck, and 'Bring 'em back alive!'"

"Yes, ma'am!" He executed a snappy salute.

"That's better," I said with satisfaction.

After I pulled out, I started telling him the rules.

"You walk behind me and don't wander off of the trail. Watch for snakes. They feed at night, and continue until full daylight. They sometimes hang from low limbs and thick brush. Don't brush against anything if you can avoid it.

"After the dew dries from the foliage they are less of a threat. When you walk in water, drag your feet slowly, and don't make splashing noises. It attracts alligators."

"You're kidding, aren't you?" He looked uncertain.

"About the snakes?" I was being deliberately obtuse.

"Alligators," he replied with a grimace. "They wouldn't attack us, would they?"

"Only if they're hungry and puppies and piglets aren't available, and they're always hungry," I answered wryly. "Don't you view scary swamp movies?"

"Not if I can help it," he replied.

I laughed.

"Did you bring a scent article?"

"Sure. Have it right in my pocket." He patted his chest.

"Let's go over the procedure on how you collected it," I suggested.

"I put on thin rubber gloves, reached way down into the rag bin, and grabbed a handful of waste that hadn't been handled. I dabbed it on a small oil spill, and then poured jet fuel on it. I quickly closed it up in a Ziploc storage bag, and sealed it."

"You did good. This is what I'll let Stanley sniff, so he will know what smell he is seeking. If you had touched it with your bare hands, he would have smelled your scent and pointed you out, thinking he had done his job. Stanley has a lazy bone or two in his body. He likes to knock off early."

"I thought bloodhounds were trained to find people by smelling their body odor."

"That's true, and I wouldn't have even attempted to have one of my other mantrailers smell oil or jet fuel to find a plane, but Stanley is different. He was first started as an arson dog. Rosie, a former employee of mine, handled him, and became impatient because he acted lazy, and didn't pay much attention.

"I switched him to drug work, and he picked it up fast. A while back, I had him on a drug sweep when he alerted on a lunch box, which contained no drugs, but was a homemade bomb. He has a 'scent memory' for several types of fuel. It's a rare gift. Only one other dog I've ever trained has this talent, but his is with human scent."

"Does Stanley bite?" I saw him glance back and eye Stanley briefly.

"No. Bloodhounds are gentle and are not trained as guard or attack dogs. He would lick a burglar in the face if he were breaking in."

"Ugh!"

"A little slobber won't hurt you. Just say to yourself, this is the dog that's gonna try to find my plane. That should make him look a lot better to you.

"Another thing I forgot to mention. Be careful to watch where you are stepping. Avoid fire ant beds and a leafy path. The ant beds could collapse, and leaves can hide vines and armadillo holes. If you turn an ankle, I'll have to drag you out on the rescue sled. It wouldn't be any fun for either of us."

"I've heard that some people who live here eat those animals."

"Armadillos are big in Texas. They have hunts, and barbecues. Some people like them around here. I had two brothers that cleaned ten for me once. The meat is supposed to taste like rabbit. I cooked the meat for safety. Had it ground, and mixed five pounds of pork shoulder with it, then mixed it with dog food.

"I had this plan that would cut my meat bill in half. Not a single bloodhound ate it, even ground with pork. I've been told that no breed of dog will eat it. I decided that any meat that a dog won't eat would never appear on my menu."

"Nor on mine," he agreed.

I was driving down the Woodpecker Route, checking out the street signs without slowing my speed from thirty miles per hour. It was the best speed to navigate this road. It was forty feet in width and alternated from soft, deep white sand to hard-packed red clay. This is our dry season and the rains would start soon. When dry like it is now, the deep ruts from logging trucks become hills and deep valleys of slippery shifting sand. Meet a deep rut head on and the sand would jerk the wheel and try to slide you sideways into a deep ditch.

I had to slow often to keep the van on the road. This road compared to a wide boulevard in the city. Small three-path roads radiated like spokes from a wheel in every direction. Some were so narrow that you had less than a foot tolerance on each side of the tires, and this slim margin of safety could have deep washed-out gullies. Hit one of those babies wrong, and you usually deposit two wheels in a ditch.

North Florida county roads, now all sporting signs, had been labeled sensibly with numbers. So when you're far out in the boonies and you chance upon 145th Street NE, you can reasonably assume that the next parallel road would be 144th or 146th, depending on which direction you are driving. Not so with South Georgia. They kept the old names that people called the roads, whatever that might be.

I was passing signs with Big Gator Road, Cow House Lane, Pineland Bluff, and Pokey Spillway. I couldn't wait to see the road map they would produce. They may get it correct in the next millennium.

Bumping along on a small three-path road named Bees and Bears, I spoke to the captain.

"I could ask you if anything looks familiar, but it would be laughable to think you could recognize where we are. We have almost arrived at our jumping-off place."

"I haven't a clue. I couldn't even find my way back to civilization driving this van. You lost me after nine or so turns. If it weren't for the sun, I wouldn't even know which direction we are currently traveling. It sure looks different from down here than it does from up there."

"Captain, you have said a mouthful quite succinctly."

"Please call me Evan."

"Fine, I'm Jo Beth. And Evan, we have arrived."

19

"The First Leg"

October 10, Tuesday, 7:30 A.M.

I had pulled just past a turnaround and stopped.

"Evan, are you in shape; do you have a regular routine of exercise?" I asked as we both exited the van.

"I do some isometrics, run a few laps on a cinder track at the base from time to time, nothing elaborate."

I was glad he wasn't trying to pass himself off as an athlete. You'd be surprised how many males standing at the start of a search would lie through their teeth about their physical condition.

"I'm afraid you're gonna think I'm a direct descendant of the Marquis de Sade before we return to the van."

"I've been dreading this since yesterday. At least I'm in better shape to hike than I was two weeks ago, I still have some fading bruises to prove it. I landed in a pine tree and snapped off several limbs on my way to the ground."

He helped me unload two backpacks, the rifle, two machetes, and four water bottles. I pulled the zipper of my jumpsuit to my waist, pulled up my T-shirt, and untied the large red bandanna I had fastened around my middle. I carefully placed it in a closed Baggie and tucked it under the driver's seat of the van.

Evan watched my actions with fascination. He had seen the .32 snub-nose in its holster, and was curious about the bandanna. "Why did you do that?"

"It's a precaution I hope is never needed. If we don't return in the allotted time, Jasmine, my assistant, rides to the rescue."

"The bandanna?"

"I've worn it since I dressed this morning to place my scent on it. Jasmine lets the bloodhound smell it, and he mantrails right to us."

"I'd think he knows your scent already."

"All of them do, but we don't speak bloodhound and bloodhounds don't speak English. How else can she tell him she wants him to find me?"

"Makes sense."

"Bloodhounds are smarter than we think. Sometimes when we ask them to find us, they think we're pulling a prank and pay us back by racing to find the first available coon."

Evan laughed.

"When we're getting the dogs certified in field trials, it's a bad thing for a bloodhound to anticipate and reason. Some judges lay out a ridiculously easy trail over open ground for beginners. The smart bloodhounds can tell the person they are tracking is moving in a circle, and sometimes they leave the trail, take a short cut, and find their target's scent by cutting straight across the field and picking up the scent again. They are immediately disqualified. They don't get their certificate for being bright, they have to correctly follow the scent to qualify."

He acted reluctant about mentioning the gun. He took a breath and decided to ask.

"Do you normally carry a handgun with you when you search?"

"Yes. The twenty-two rifle is for snakes, the thirty-two is for snakes-in-the-grass."

He didn't look satisfied with my answer. I walked to Stanley's cage, where he was restlessly whining, wanting to get started. I attached his long lead and wrapped the short lead around my waist.

"Unload." I patted the floor of his enclosure. He didn't need any urging. He bailed out, ready to go to work. He cheerfully danced in circles, anticipating action.

"You really enjoy working with them, don't you?"

"It's all I've wanted to do since I was ten years old."

I dug the radio out of my backpack to call Jasmine.

"We have fun with our radio call handles. Promise not to laugh."

"Viper to Mirage. Over."

Upon hearing the names, Evan's eyes widened and he started grinning.

"Viper to Mirage. Over," I repeated.

"Don't get worried if I can't make her hear me, these woods out here are spooky on radio transmissions. Sometimes it won't work here, and will connect a quarter of a mile down the road."

"Mirage to Viper, you're breaking up, over."

Jasmine had heard me, but the words weren't clear.

"Viper to Mirage, B&B, two-tenths, left hide. I repeat. B&B, two-tenths, left hide. Convey back. Over."

"Mirage to Viper. B&B, two-tenths, left hide. Over and out."

"Viper to Mirage. Out."

She had received and understood our location. It was a load off my mind.

Evan was amused. "Are you French?"

"No, I just know they think their Mirage outclasses your Viper."

Evan chuckled derisively. "They're wrong. Why do you use code?"

"We try to keep our transmissions both cryptic and brief. We've been hassled enough by hunters who patrol their leases all during the year, but during hunting season they go ballistic when they catch us in their territory. We try to keep our location secret. We don't wish to have rabid hunters finding the van or us. It isn't healthy."

"But why should they care if you're searching for something out here? They only lease the hunting rights, and you're not shooting their deer or turkeys, are you?"

"Not hardly. They are very territorial. The lease rent makes them act as if the land has been in their family for five generations. It's a very large county and we're virtually isolated from everyone. It would be easy to have a 'tragic hunting accident' out here. I told Jasmine we are on Bees and Bears Road, two-tenths of a mile in, and the van is hidden on the left."

Evan was shocked. "Are you telling me that they might physically harm you, for just being out here?"

"There have been several incidents in the past." I was choosing my words carefully. "Why take chances?"

I didn't tell him about the suspicious shooting last year of a local man, found dead near an unclaimed deer stand. The rumor, couched in Southern lingo, "He was in the wrong place at the wrong time," seemed to be true. I didn't doubt it, and also didn't expect the shooting to be solved.

"You have to hide the van?"

"It's either that or a ruined paint job, broken windows and windshield, burned-out shell, or possibly riddled with bullet holes."

"They can be arrested, and could go to jail! You would prosecute if they did something like that, wouldn't you?"

"Evan, within a twenty-five mile radius of where we stand, over one hundred shotguns and three hundred powerful rifles are in sweaty palms or a truck's gun rack. Who would you have me file charges against? Anyone I could ID would have twelve hunting buddies to testify he was fifty miles away, or that he didn't leave Jacksonville all week."

Shaking his head, Evan disagreed.

"I can't believe this area can be so lawless, it allows these things to happen."

"The DEA, FBI, GBI, and Bureau of Alcohol, Tobacco, and Firearms would disagree with you, and they have the statistics to prove it. Don't fret, we should be perfectly safe. I've been doing this for almost four years now, and I haven't permanently lost anyone I've brought in here with me."

"That's good," he murmured. He didn't seem reassured by my statement.

I stood over his pack and explained how to sheath the machete, and held the pack while he slipped it on his shoulders and buckled it around his waist.

"How much does this thing weigh?"

"Properly packed, thirty-two pounds. It now holds a little less, and mine a little more."

"Taking it easy on a beginner?"

"Not at all. I haven't explained about the machete. It's your job to hack us an opening if necessary, and to mark the trail going in. They will have to move in heavy machinery to dig out the plane and haul it out of here.

"Since I know where I'm going, I'll try to lead us in the way of least resistance. Coming back we can change the markings, if we slipped up and marked a more difficult route entering. I don't want to have to come back and lead them in, possibly meeting the colonel. I have no desire to cross his path again."

"I don't blame you there."

"I'm going to ask you to back the van into this road, because backing a van isn't something I excel in. I back like a snake, I'm afraid, all over the road. I jumped ahead of myself, you'll have to remove your backpack to be able to sit behind the wheel, sorry."

I was, at first, not about to admit I had a weakness to this pilot, but I had second thoughts when I viewed the road up close. If I backed into a ditch, I would look even sillier, and cost us lost time in getting it out.

I stood by the packs holding an impatient Stanley and watched him roar smoothly backward, showing off his manly skill of expert control. I wrinkled my nose with envy. He made it look so damned easy.

When he returned, I swung my pack up and fastened it. I let him put his on unaided. I'd teach him to show off. I demonstrated reaching over my shoulder and pulling out the machete from its sheath on the pack with a smooth motion, then skillfully returned it. I made him practice, with four miserable tries, before he halfway completed the maneuver with any success. I was satisfied. We were even.

I slid the rifle from its sheath and ejected eighteen magnum-jacketed hollow point rounds onto the hardpan. I inspected the barrel and it was clean. I squatted and fed them back into the magazine as I counted. Donnie Ray had a habit of taking the rifle out behind the lumber sheds and shooting woods rats. Sometimes he forgot to clean and replace a full load.

"That's only for snakes, huh?"

"I use the heaviest load available for this rifle. Aimed correctly, it will stop a snake, deer, bear, wild boar, alligator, and man."

"And how many of the species have you shot?"

He was only asking an idle question, and I should have given him an inaccurate answer. I have but one excuse. The devil made me do it.

"All of the above," I said softly, and walked away.

20

"The Journey"

October 10, Tuesday, 8:30 A.M.

Evan caught up with me. "I'm sorry, did I say something to offend you?"

"Of course not, *my* answer offended me. I sounded as if I was bragging about shooting a man. I wasn't. I shot him because he killed a wonderful dog. This caused a distraction that possibly saved four lives, and one of them was mine. I'm the one who should be apologizing. Forgive me for answering flippantly."

"Hey, no sweat. Are we okay?"

"We're okay, but we have to go back and get our water bottles."

We hooked them to our belts, and he followed me when I went to lock the van and pocket the keys. I glanced around.

"Is the van hidden well enough?" He was now on the side of caution. Good.

"It can't be seen from the road. It should be fine. Are you ready?" I'd noticed he was doing some tugging on his backpack shoulder straps.

"Ready. Just trying to distribute the weight more evenly."

"Let's do it."

At the first tree in the row I halted and pointed toward it.

"Remove the bark on this side only. Head-high, and down for about a foot. Don't cut too deep, just enough to expose the wood."

He began to cautiously chip away the rough bark. I watched for a while, and decided he needed to be shown how to do it quicker.

"Let me," I said, walking forward and grasping the sharp machete. I took four swings and had cut a sufficient amount of rough bark that it would be noticeable.

We were walking westward, with the sun on our backs. The temperature was rising and the dew would soon dry the foliage. These were planted trees we were passing, and the undergrowth had been burnt within the past year. Our forward movement was not hampered by thick brush.

We made fairly good time for the next twenty minutes.

Sweat was running freely down our faces, and I could feel it trickling down my thighs in the airless atmosphere inside the rescue suit. The temperature had risen. It was about seventy-five degrees already, I guessed.

Evan was audibly panting and taking constant swipes at the mosquitoes and gnats. They weren't too worrisome for me, but he seemed to have a cloud of the critters hovering around his head like a cloud.

"You forgot what I told you yesterday, I bet. Did you wash your hair this morning, and omit any grooming product that has a scent? What was it you used, a creme rinse? Styling gel? Hair oil?"

"Yeah." He was too busy to elaborate.

I giggled. "You have a swarm of devotees who just love the way you smell."

He didn't answer. I looked around, but there were no eucalyptus bushes handy, so his relief from flying insects would have to wait. Stanley was thoroughly enjoying himself. He pranced around bushes and through the tall grass like a champion. Head held high, tail aloft, he moved briskly and hated to slow his pace for us. His nose was testing the almost nonexistent breeze. He was in doggie heaven.

When he strayed from due west, I would tug him back into the general line I was taking into the swamp to reach my special tree. It was odd that, even dead for years, the tree was serving a function for humans. It had given me comfort on a long lonely night and could be the beacon that led us to Evan's plane, if it was the same tree. The tree he described was like my tree, but it would be quite a coincidence if our two trees were one and the same. We would have to wait and see.

I didn't call a halt for another thirty minutes. I was pushing while we were on level ground with fairly easy going. The terrain would become dense on uneven ground as we penetrated deeper into the mire. Its earlier inhabitants, the Seminole Indians, called it "the Land of the Trembling Earth." We butchered the spelling in the translation into English, and it can still be found in the history books spelled seven different ways. The government in its infinite wisdom decreed it should be spelled Okefenokee, and uses this version on all maps, but a lot of historians still disagree.

I called a halt at 10:00 A.M. Evan slumped to the ground and leaned against a tree without removing his backpack. I helped him remove it without him having to get up.

"Did you have any breakfast?" I inquired as I reached into my pack.

He shook his head, as if it took too much effort to voice a no. He still had his winged escorts. His face was blotched with red spots where the tiny sand flies had zinged him. These lumps were hard to see, since his whole face and neck were an alarming red.

"Drink more water," I urged. "Are you all right?"

"Are you sure," he panted, trying to suck in oxygen, "that *this* is all you ever wanted to do since you were a kid?"

"Absolutely," I said, amused.

Evan gave me a weak grimace.

"You're out of your mind."

I laughed, and held out a foil-wrapped package. "I have here a frozen biscuit and sausage that has thawed to the perfect temperature for an epicurean's palate."

"Which means?"

"You won't break a tooth. Eat it, it'll give you strength, put some food in your stomach so you won't get nauseous from the heat and exertion."

"Twenty-four hours' bed rest would do the same." He was regaining a normal breathing pattern, but hadn't touched his food.

I felt the gentle pressure of a large paw on my thigh.

Stanley was sitting less than a foot away, eyeing my biscuit.

"This is people food," I informed him. I leaned on my elbow and unzipped a slash pocket on my hip. I fed him two pieces of dried deer jerky. He inhaled both of them without a token chomp. "That was dog food." I took a bite of biscuit and looked away, chewing. The pressure of his paw increased.

"Remove the paw," I ordered, sounding stern. He picked it up, but only so he'd have leverage to nudge me more insistently.

"Bad dog," I scolded. He gave a body quiver and a pitiful whine.

"If I give you one bite, will you behave?" His answer was to scoot his rear end six inches closer in anticipation.

I broke off a bite of biscuit and he opened his mouth.

"Hold!" He sat still as a statue with the biscuit on his tongue.

After an eternity of four seconds, I said, "Eat." He swallowed the morsel politely.

"See how well he minds me?"

"Which one of you did you say was trained?" Evan inquired with a straight face.

"Eat," I replied with mock indignation.

"I can't," he admitted. "I'd choke on food right now. I'm feeling that nausea you mentioned."

I leaned over and inspected his face. He was still too hot for me to see if his red face was a rising temperature and if the bumps were swelling. "You're not allergic to sand fly bites, are you?"

"Not that I know about," he answered, stifling a huge yawn. "Any chance of a short nap?"

"Slim and none," I answered absentmindedly. I was reviewing the skimpy files in my brain regarding medical abnormalities I had gleaned from the annual Red Cross first aid course I took every year in the high school cafeteria. I knew CPR, how to splint a broken leg, and the proper way to hold an infant, but my knowledge of anaphylactic shock was nonexistent. I was surprised that I could recall the name. I thought it meant a violent reaction to bee or insect bites, but I wasn't even sure about that, much less how to treat it.

I vaguely remembered some of the symptoms: swelling, fever, and inability to swallow. With studied casualness, I leaned close, searching his face intently.

"Swallow for me, and tell me what you feel."

He stared at me, alarmed. "What's wrong with you?"

I gave him a hollow laugh. "Please try swallowing," I insisted. "Does your throat feel scratchy and constricted? Do your bites itch or your tongue feel thick and bloated?"

"Jo Beth, do you feel all right? You're beginning to scare me." His eyes widened and he sat up straighter and assumed an attentive expression.

"Answer me, you turkey!" I yelled, losing it. "I'm worried witless that I have hauled you out here miles from medical help and you're having a violent reaction to your sand fly bites. Answer my damn questions!"

"You think that I . . . I thought you might start foaming at the mouth any minute!" He collapsed on his side, shaking with laughter. "If you could have seen your face! You were looking at me like a lovesick cow!" He howled.

"I was a worried-sick basket-case sick cow, you ninny. It's not funny, Evan. Knock it off."

I was too relieved to be angry. The adrenaline rush from my fear was already dissipating from my system. I was thankful that he had only been pooped from the unaccustomed exercise and not ill. I wouldn't be vindictive and march him till he dropped. I would let him rest again when we stopped to eat lunch.

I watched him with amusement as he tried to feed Stanley his sausage and biscuit. Stanley stared at the tempting food and didn't move a muscle.

I leaned over and whispered in his ear. He eagerly scoffed up the whole biscuit and gulped it down.

"Why wouldn't he eat for me?" Evan asked.

"One of the dogs was fed a hot dog laced with LSD during a search of a bar for drugs a while back. We immediately began training all the others not to accept food from anyone but the trainers."

"What did you whisper in his ear?"

"I told him in my opinion it wasn't poisoned, but he would have to decide for himself."

"Really?"

"Nah, I just said eat. You notice I didn't have to repeat the command."

We resumed our trek. The trees and high growth closed in on us, and slowed our progress to a snail's space. We had to blaze more trees more often. Evan seemed to get his second wind, and kept up with Stanley and me without grumbling. Maybe it was testosterone or he felt bad about thinking I was bonkers. Whatever the reason, I was thankful.

I decided we'd better stop and eat before we both fell over in a dead faint from lack of food. I'd had half a biscuit and Evan hadn't eaten anything. We worked our way around a small slough and approached a fairly large shallow creek covered with green scum. It was about thirty yards wide. I scanned the bank on both sides quickly and studied the small canals of criss-crossed clear waterways, and decided we'd eat on a small rise in the clearing under some trees about twenty yards to our right.

"Let's eat over there," I said, pointing, and started walking toward the trees. I heard a small splash, and I whirled in alarm. Evan was not behind me. He had waded out several feet in the stagnant water, and was clearing an area free of the scum.

"Be there in a second, I'm gonna wash the gunk out of my hair," he called out to me.

I began running as I reached back and jerked out the rifle. It felt like I was running silently in slow motion. I clicked off the safety and positioned it chest high and held it with both hands. Finally I was standing on the bank.

"Evan," I hissed as quietly as I could. "Listen to me. Walk toward me. Don't splash. Drag your feet. Do it now!"

I saw him straighten in my peripheral vision. My eyes were frantically searching the banks for any sign of movement.

"What's wrong?"

I saw a log slide into the water from the far shallow bank.

"Get out of the water! Run!"

I couldn't take my eyes off the log, to see if he knew what was happening, but I didn't hear any noise. I risked a quick glance. He was staring across the creek looking in the direction I had been, and was frozen with fear.

I switched my vision back to the log that was now definitely not a log but a gator. He was moving slowly, parting the green scum cleanly to produce the same channel that I had recognized earlier as a sign of his passing. Now all I had to do was locate his eyes, which would be slightly above the dark sludgy water. It's not as easy as it sounds. I threw up the rifle to my eye. Now I had to find the reptile eyes in my sights. When you're looking at an object, then switch to the scope's view, you sometimes waste precious seconds locating the target.

The sun wasn't helping. The rays were reflected from the clear path. I focused on the path and tracked the opening until I found the two protuberances. When the gator's knobs popped into place I was shocked at the magnification. It was a prehistoric nightmare moving slowly toward us. I decided to risk a shot. I had eighteen. Maybe the noise would unglue Evan's feet and get him in motion.

I wanted him out of the damn water and up on dry land far

enough to be safe. I had another problem. So far, Stanley had behaved admirably and followed my every move with just a short tug on the leash. I couldn't drop the leash, he would bolt if the gator charged, and he would be dragging a trailing lead. He could be lost forever.

I didn't have all day. I fired.

21

"Mr. Gator's Revenge"

October 10, Tuesday, Noon

I missed. Stanley didn't budge an inch, but the explosion achieved one goal. It galvanized Evan into action. He came out of the water as if he'd been shot out of a cannon. He ran past me for a few feet before he could stop.

"Run!" he yelled. "It's still coming!"

I didn't have time to answer him. I wanted to tell him that I couldn't outrun a gator if I didn't have Stanley tethered to my waist, and didn't have the backpack weighing me down, and had on track shoes. A gator can sprint from water to land and can achieve speeds up to thirty-five miles per hour for a short distance. I also wanted to inform him that gators preferred dogs over human flesh any day of the week. It would go for Stanley first. The gator would lock his jaws on Stanley's leg, drag him back in the water, and drown him.

"Evan?"

"Hurry, Jo Beth! Run!" he screamed.

"Shut up! Can you unhook Stanley from my belt and then run?"

"Not without you." His voice was closer.

"I have to kill the gator; just do it!"

I was thankful the gator hadn't made up his mind to charge. He

147

was still drifting toward us slowly. Evan grasped my arm, intending to take me with him. I sank my right elbow into his gut and frantically brought the rifle back in position.

"It's Stanley he wants, you idiot! Move!"

I felt him fumbling at my belt to release the catch.

"Don't turn him loose, don't drop the lead," I prayed as I repeated the litany, twice.

"Okay, okay, I've got him. I've got him!" Evan sounded just as scared as I did.

I had to place at least one, preferably two, of my seventeen remaining rounds into the killing spot to stop him. His brain was located just behind the knobs. I aimed between his eyes, drew in a breath, and let half of it out. I began pulling the trigger. It rose out of the water on the fifth shot, seemingly unhurt. I fired as fast as I could, as he loomed larger and larger in my scope. I brought down the rifle when I realized I was still trying to pull a useless trigger on an empty gun. I stared down at the alligator flipping and flopping in its death throes practically at my feet. Even while dying, Mr. Gator managed to avenge his death. His contorted body flipped over facing away from me. A savage swipe of the rigid tail caught me with a flat hard blow across my calf and knocked me off my feet. I went out like a light.

Fine drizzle just slightly more than a mist fell from dark low clouds, which threatened to dump heavy rainfall any second. Lightning lit up the drab scene momentarily and was followed immediately by a long jarring roll of thunder. I viewed the sad gathering with puzzlement and felt dismay creeping into my soul.

I recognized everyone, though most were bundled in rain gear and several were holding brightly colored umbrellas close to their bodies to keep the rising wind from whipping them away. This was wrong. They had no right to be standing here at this time and place without my knowledge and consent.

I moved a little closer so I could view the expression on their faces. Why would they even attempt to keep this event from me? I scanned the first-row faces, searching for a clue. Jasmine had her head lowered with her eyes closed, but I still caught the glint of tears slowly sliding down her cheek. Wayne and Donnie Ray were dry-eyed and looked glum. Could they be the culprits?

My befuddled mind cleared and I gasped in pain. *Please God, not Bobby Lee, not Bobby Lee!* I lowered my eyes and spotted him immediately. He was harnessed and on his short lead, sitting quietly, and seemed wrapped in unnatural stillness. I drew in a ragged breath of relief.

I knew now that this crowd had gathered to attend the burial of one of my dogs. We were a hundred yards behind and slightly to the left of the kennel. This plot near the timberline was edged with Bradford pear trees. It was my pet cemetery. It was for the puppies that died during or shortly after birth, and the dogs that died of old age. My sweet Bo was the only exception. He rested a few feet away, killed by a prison escapee during a search mission.

Just as I decided to call out to announce my presence, and the fact that it would be wise to get indoors when Mother Nature was displaying such a pyrotechnic warning of an approaching thunderstorm, the small group turned and began to leave the area. I watched them pass me without a flicker of eye contact. First came Jasmine holding Bobby Lee's leash. He turned his head in my direction, stared beyond me, and with a soft whine padded after Jasmine. Next were Wayne and Donnie Ray. They were dressed in their best under their London Fog raingear that I gave them last Christmas.

Susan walked alone, the wind whipping her fashionable rain attire open to reveal a drop-dead red dress of soft wool. She was wearing her funeral face, impassive and aloof. She hated to show her emotions in public. Next came the six full-time trainers, several part-time employees, and two local deputy sheriffs. This left Hank standing alone over the mounded earth.

Wait. This didn't add up. All these people would not have appeared to honor a dog. The only human who could be legally interred here was the property deed holder, and even with this distinction, it took some serious wrangling with the state to get permission.

I am the owner of record. I had expressed my desire to rest eternally with my dogs to my co-workers and heirs, Jasmine, Wayne, and Rosie. I suddenly realized whose burial they had attended and who they were mourning. It was me.

I licked my lips and gingerly cracked open my eyes to blinding brightness. Someone somewhere above me was voicing an indecipherable message. I mumbled a response in a raspy whisper.

"I didn't hear you, Jo Beth. What did you say?"

I didn't recognize the voice. His features were obscured by the bright halo of light behind him. I squinted and tried to bring him into focus.

"Why did you wake me up?" I grumbled. My mouth was dry and speech was difficult. I had no idea who he was, or what I was doing flat on my back. I fought to clear the cobwebs from my brain. I realized I had a horrendous headache. The implications of a stranger looming overhead and me in a prone position started my heart thudding in rhythm with my head. I struggled to sit up, but strong hands forced me to lie back.

"How are you feeling?" the voice inquired.

I wasn't about to tell this joker I didn't know him from Adam. I had to find out what was going on. A delayed thought reminded me that he had called me something, but I couldn't recall the words.

"What did you call me?"

Christ! That was brilliant! You didn't want him to know that you didn't know who he was, but you've now informed him that you don't know who you are!

I didn't know who I was. Who am I? The question brought tears to my eyes. Everybody knows their own name. I'm . . . I whimpered and crouched inside my brain and decided to keep my mouth shut.

"I called you Jo Beth. How are you feeling?"

His voice attempted to soothe me, but I was hung up on semantics. I silently rolled the two words around on my tongue and tried them out. Jo Beth. Jo Beth. Nope, neither of them rang a bell. I decided to ask the obvious question.

"Am I hurt?"

I knew I was hurting, but I didn't know why. Maybe he could jog my memory.

"Your leg has a nasty bruise and is swollen, but I don't think it's broken. The tail struck you a glancing blow," he said, sounding concerned. He released a nervous giggle. "Frankly, I expected to find your leg lopped off at the knee when I pulled off your suit. That monster really gave you a whack with his tail! You fell on your side and hit your head behind your right ear. There's a lump, but the skin wasn't broken. I unrolled a sleeping bag and carried you over here, underneath this tree. I washed your face with a cloth from your backpack." He glanced at his watch. "You've been out twenty minutes. I've tried to raise your assistant on the radio at least three times, and didn't hear a thing." He let out his breath with a grateful sigh. "I'm really glad you're awake. I've had a survival course in case I ditched, but it didn't tell me what to do with an unconscious female."

I lay there quietly and digested his news. He seemed worried about me, and didn't look threatening. I had peeked at him through a narrow opening of my eyes, his face partially obstructed by my eyelashes. I decided he meant me no harm. I breathed easier knowing that I wasn't in immediate danger. The rest of the message could have been spoken in Swahili for all it told me. I remembered the key words and tried to string them together for a rational explanation. Monster's tail, sleeping bag, radio, assistant, and backpack.

As soon as he mentioned my bruised, swollen leg, I became aware of the pain pulsing in my lower left limb. I hadn't really focused on it until this moment. I had a more pressing pain in my head, which had taken my knowledge of past events and hidden all of it out of my reach. I still didn't want to admit how helpless I felt knowing nothing about a trip, which accounted for the sleeping bag and backpack. Had the two of us gone camping? Were he and I friends, lovers, or, oh God, married? What kind of monster was he talking about? I fought down my panic and decided if I could ease the pain, I might be able to remember.

"Is there anything in the backpack for pain?" I asked, trying not to sound too desperate.

"Good question! I'll check. I've been busy with getting you over here and checking your injuries. I'm glad you reminded me. I should have thought about it myself."

I heard rustling noises and waited impatiently.

"Let's see. We have a small bottle of aspirin and three tablets labeled Percodan, sterile syringes, and two vials of liquid. One vial is marked SERUM."

"That's for the dogs," I said. How did I know that? "What dogs?"

"Ah," he said with relief, "does that mean you remember Stanley?"

"Stanley who?" I blurted, giving an audible gasp from the pain. It was intensifying with every breath.

"Jo Beth, I have been aware since you woke up that you don't know who I am, and who you are, and what we are doing out here. I've been trying to give you time to remember on your own, but we've run out of time and we are now approaching a crisis. This vial is labeled MORPHINE. I'm no medical expert, but I do remember something from my survival course that you shouldn't be sedated if you have a head injury, and not to let you go to sleep. Am I correct?"

I gritted my teeth. "Give me the damn shot. Left hip. Roll me over on my side, and I'll point out the spot for you to inject. Do it now before I shoot you!" I yelled.

"When I removed your suit, I took the gun and holster off because I wanted you to be comfortable. Now I'm glad I did. I'm sorry, Jo Beth; I'm not going to give you morphine, or anything else. I believe it would be dangerous."

I cursed him as I writhed with pain. After what seemed like hours,

I felt a soothing warmth spread over my skin, and most of the pain disappeared. In my growing stupor, I felt languid and lightheaded. I smiled with morbid satisfaction when I sensed the darkness enveloping me. I had beaten Mr. Smarty-Pants Medic. I was sliding down a slippery slope into blessed unconsciousness, and there wasn't one damn thing he could do to stop me.

22

"Sleeping Beauty Awakes"

October 12, Thursday, 4:30 P.M.

When I opened my eyes, I was between white sheets and still had the lousy headache. The light was subdued somewhat by the blinds, but I could tell from the sun leaking around the edges that it was afternoon. I was one of the lucky ones who had a built-in sense of direction. Even in an unknown location I knew north from south, and could recognize that the brightness was coming from the west.

Jasmine was sitting in a straight-backed chair reading a magazine. I felt a surge of elation when I knew who she was. I was Jo Beth Sidden, and the future was looking brighter with each tick of the clock on the metal bedside table on my right.

"Hi," I said. I was testing my voice. It sounded okay to my ears.

Jasmine looked momentarily startled, then she gave me a wonderful smile and moved to my side. My mouth was dry.

"Could I have some water?"

I needed to lubricate my throat before I could ask questions and answer the many I knew she would ask. I was also stalling for time. I might not want to know the answer to some of them.

"You're in Dunston County Hospital and it's four-thirty P.M. on

154

Thursday, October the twelfth, and I'm really relieved to see those dark brown eyes staring up at me."

I frowned. Her eyes were bright with unshed tears. I drew in a shaky breath. The last I could remember was standing on the back porch with her early Tuesday morning waiting for someone to arrive. But first things first.

"Water?"

"Oh," she breathed and turned from me.

I strained to remember more, and only succeeded in increasing the crashing symbols thumping in my ears. I made myself relax. I'd hear the answers soon enough.

Jasmine was holding a glass of water with a bent paper straw. I sucked down the liquid too fast. I fought nausea by closing my eyes and taking shallow breaths.

When I lifted my lids, I stared into her eyes.

"I'm afraid to stretch. Are all my moving parts still working? Fingers? Toes? Arms and legs? You know, just the essentials, I'll worry about breaks and fractures later."

Jasmine gave a nervous giggle. "You'll be cracking jokes at your funeral. You are completely intact, but be careful when you try everything out. Your left leg is going to be very painful, I imagine. It's not broken, but it's bruised and swollen."

"Let me see," I demanded.

When she mentioned *funeral*, I had seen a misty, rainy scene flash into my mind. I had been attending a funeral recently, and somehow I knew it was mine. I groaned.

Jasmine had pushed a button and the head of the bed was raising me into a sitting position. She had carefully lifted the sheet and uncovered my left leg.

"It looks much worse than it is," she said quickly, squeezing my shoulder. "It will work and shouldn't take long for the swelling to go down, honest."

She thought my groan on catching a glimpse of my funeral had been for my leg. I stared at it, and sucked in a sharp breath. From above my knee to the sole of my foot was three feet of swollen, colored eggplant and as large as a bushy foxtail in winter. I groaned again, and this time it *was* for the leg.

"I'm not about to move that sucker," I stated grimly.

I rubbed my temples with both hands. The pain was reclaiming my attention.

"Why does my head hurt so?" I asked querulously.

Jasmine had a guilty look. I bet she had saved the bad news for last.

"Let me get Dr. Sellers for you. He can explain it much better than I."

I grabbed her hand quickly, before she could leave.

"I'd rather hear you tell me now than waiting for them to locate Dr. Sam. You know that could take hours. Spill it."

"When you fell, you landed on your right side. You hit your head on a small cypress tree, right here."

She pointed behind my right ear, and I raised a hand and gingerly traced the outline of the swollen lump. It was tender and sore, but the skin wasn't broken.

"This caused a concussion. Not serious," she hastened to add, "but it did cause your brain to swell a little. That's why you can't remember some things, but Dr. Sellers will assure you the memory loss is only temporary. All your memory should return in a few days."

I grimaced. "Been there, done that," I uttered. "Remember when Bubba forced my van off the Tom's Creek Bridge?"

"Those memories never came back," Jasmine added softly. "Don't let it worry you, it's only two days this time, and Evan can tell you every detail."

I felt uneasy, and I might as well bite the bullet and tell her while I was hurting. Maybe she would forgive me faster, knowing that I was ill.

"I have a confession to make, Jasmine. I did remember it was Bubba in just a few days, but I had a good reason for not telling anyone. I had rather he dreaded my memory returning than admitting I remembered, and lose the case in court. You know how lawyers can twist things around. Forgive me?"

"You let me silently worry and stew for months on end about your lost memory, and didn't tell me you remembered it all? How could you!"

"Don't yell," I said, making my voice quiver. "Oh, my head!" I moaned.

She wasn't buying it. "More than your *head* will be hurting before I'm through with you!"

"Jasmine, I didn't know you were worrying about me, you should have told me and I would have enlightened you."

"Now it's my fault that I suffered?"

"You're beginning to sound just like Susan," I murmured waspishly. "Did you know that she wore a *red* dress to my funeral?" I'd had another flash on my interment.

Jasmine voice softened and she gave me a false smile of forgiveness.

"Forget what I said, I was just kidding." She thought I was babbling nonsense.

"Thanks," I weakly agreed. Peace had been restored.

"Who is Evan? Oh, you mean the pilot from Moody? He's the one I was waiting for on Tuesday, wasn't he?"

"Yes." She breathed with relief that my mind was now functioning correctly. "You're remembering!"

"I'm still on the porch last Tuesday morning. I just recognized the name from him apologizing for his colonel's rudeness over the phone to me on Monday. All the rest of Tuesday is a blank. Care to fill me in?"

"Evan's sitting in the waiting room right now. He could give you more detail than I can. He also came yesterday. He's been very worried about you."

"I'd rather hear it from you."

"He could do it better."

"Jasmine, you know I have a rather large ego. What if I screwed up sometime Tuesday? I want to know the facts so I can have a rebuttal in place, if I did."

"According to Evan you behaved admirably, *he* was the one who screwed up."

"You tell it, please?"

"I will, after I call a nurse to see if you can have something for your headache. You're almost cross-eyed with pain. I can tell by the way you're scrunching your eyes."

"Won't happen, but you might get the ball rolling. He hasn't penciled in pain medication orders on my chart because I've been unconscious. Now that I'm conscious, he'll have to have more tests before he'll prescribe anything, either an X ray of my cranium or a blood test, or a personal inspection of my eyeballs."

"How do you know?"

"Trust me. I'm an expert on hospital procedures. Ask me anything. I've been down this road many times."

"It won't hurt to ask."

"Fire away."

She picked up the phone and asked for the nurses' station for the second floor.

I inspected the IV stand, and the length of tubing running from bottom of the saline solution bag and into my arm, in relation to the distance to the bathroom. I had to pee, but I would just tighten the puckering strings. It was either unplug the IV machine and listen to a constant irritating beep until a nurse strolled in and adjusted it, or a bedpan. I didn't fancy either choice.

"Jo Beth Sidden is awake and needs something for her pain. She's in Room Two-ten. . . . Thank you."

"She's checking my chart," I said.

"Do you have any idea when he'll come?" Jasmine asked, sounding subdued. Then she said, "Thank you."

"I have to wait for Dr. Sam when he makes his evening rounds. He usually makes them between five and six-thirty. He has to eyeball me personally, right?" I shot her a triumphant glance.

"I shouldn't have bothered," she said, nodding. "How about food, are you hungry? I might be able to order you a tray. I see they eat supper here real early, they are delivering trays now and it's only five!"

"They're running late, usually you're fed at four-thirty. To get a hot meal for supper, the order has to be in the kitchen before three-thirty. After the order is written that I can have food, and it trickles down the chain of command, I'll be lucky if I get a cold sandwich or maybe some crackers and milk by eight P.M."

"I'll take your word for it this time," she said.

"Drag up a chair, and tell me a story."

It took Jasmine twenty minutes to relate what had transpired up until I shot the gator. I interrupted her.

"Did you see him? How long was he? I sure would have liked to save the hide. I could have had it stretched on a big board. Have you seen one made like that? They take these slender new nails, and place them real close together, and leave them in the board. Looks real neat. I bet y'all didn't give it a thought, did you, about saving it?"

"Sure we did," Jasmine muttered sarcastically. "All the time that the medics were working on you so you could be medevacked out by helicopter, all of us discussed the pros and cons of field-skinning your gator. We finally decided we'd save you!"

I assumed a hangdog look. "Forget I mentioned it."

"Certainly," she breathed, with fire in her eyes.

She resumed the tale.

"Evan couldn't raise me after you were in the land of nod, so he systematically began putting out a mayday on every channel whether he received an answer or not. After about six tries, he lucked out and tuned into the Georgia Highway Patrol's emergency channel. They told him to keep the channel open, and called Hank. Hank called Moody and requested a chopper with medics. They couldn't refuse, especially after they discovered that one of the victims was theirs and you both were searching for their downed aircraft. Hank called me and Circe and I stepped into the helicopter when it landed by the kennel, just like we had been doing it all of our lives. It was the first airlift for both of us. It was really scary for me. Circe took to flying like a duck to water. It wasn't too hard to find the van because Hank was there and had the area lit up, but finding you two was a doozie. They insisted on flying a twenty-mile grid, not five miles, like Hank and I suggested. They didn't believe that you couldn't walk twenty miles on land using a trailing dog, much less through the Okefenokee. You only carry three night flares. After Tuesday night, I think you ought to carry ten. Evan had fired the third one before we spotted the glow.

"Anyway, by the time you were loaded and on board and we were out of there, it was midnight."

"Thanks, Jasmine. I owe you."

"Just promise me one thing, and we're even."

I had a suspicion about what she wanted me to promise. I quickly slipped both hands out of sight under the sheet.

"Just ask," I vowed.

"Don't ever lie to me again."

"You've got it," I promised, crossing my fingers.

"I want to see both hands in clear sight when you repeat that," she demanded.

"God, Jasmine, you wound me!"

I looked her straight in the eye, and said the words again. I had hooked one toe over the other on my right foot but the left was too sore to cooperate. One toe cross should be enough for little white lies that were for her own good, shouldn't it?

23

"Making Friends Far and Wide"

October 16, Monday, 9:30 A.M.

I sat with my gimpy leg propped on an upside-down trash basket with a pillow on top. The small side chair was rigid and uncomfortable. *Hospitals suck!* I gave a disgusted look at the lump that was supposed to be a cushion to support my injured leg.

In the five days I'd been an unwilling visitor, I had experienced a new marvel of hygienic efficiency, the disposable pillow. It was disposable waste they couldn't find any other way to dispose of, encased in a paper and plastic cover. After two hours of trying to sleep on it and plump it up, it lumps and clumps and is unrecognizable as a bed pillow. Obviously they had an inexhaustible supply. I had one under my leg, and three on the bed. I had been told they had to leave with me, whether I wanted them or not.

Then there was the large five-inch-thick slab of blue foam. It was rolled up and awaiting disposal, and I was the designated disposee. It was as bulky as a bale of hay, and just as ungainly. Sitting on the floor near the door was a book bag, a shopping bag, my overnight case, three potted plants, and two half-dead bouquets. I tried to picture Jasmine and I rolling down the hallways with the wheelchair and a teetering mountain of baggage.

I picked up the phone. It still held the residual warmth from my hand in making prior calls. I hesitated. I had called her twice already . . . I dialed the number.

"Hello."

"You haven't left yet? It's almost ten!"

I heard Jasmine's patient sigh.

"Has Dr. Sellers been in?"

"Not yet, but he's due here any second!"

"Then when he's examined you, and deduced that you're able to leave, he'll then continue his rounds and when he finishes them, he'll sit down within the nurses' station area and write up all the orders, for medication and possible discharges, right?"

"Yes . . . but . . ." I could see where this conversation was headed.

"Then the nurse comes in and says you're free to go home, and sends for an attendant and a wheelchair to escort you to the curb, which usually takes thirty minutes from request to fruition. I'm ten minutes away from your room. Fifteen minutes after the request is when to *call me, right?*"

"Right."

I listened to the dial tone. Jasmine was getting testier every day. She had been just as anxious to get home when she was in here with a broken leg. How quickly they forget! I reached for my address book and looked up Sheriff Beaman's number, again. He sure worked bankers' hours. I'd been trying to reach him since seven damn A.M. After holding a long while, I finally heard his voice.

"Sheriff Beaman, this is Jo Beth Sidden calling. You're hard to reach!"

"Sometimes," he answered cryptically. "I was informed of your four prior calls, Miz Sidden, but I've had a busy morning. Now that we are connected, what can I do for you?"

"We are still speaking to each other, aren't we? You're not dodging my calls, by any chance?"

"Since we're talking to each other now, I think that takes care of your first question. Surprising as it may seem, I'm not dodging your calls, Miz Sidden. We had an armed robbery at a convenience store just after six A.M. I've been working the case."

"Did he drive away or was he on foot?"

"I beg your pardon?"

"You heard me," I said calmly. "Humor me, I have a reason for asking."

"On foot."

"Did the description of the perp sound something like this: lone male, black, five-foot-seven to five-foot-ten, weighs around one hundred fifty pounds, loose T-shirt, jeans, and very expensive athletic shoes?"

"Right on the money."

My heart began to pound against my ribs. This sucker had struck twice here, in Balsa City. We hadn't caught him, but I had two frozen pads in the freezer in the grooming room of the kennel that would nail him for two local robberies. Now to make sure it was the same one. I was already relishing the amazement that would be in Beaman's voice when I sprang my surprise.

"Did he also wear a bright yellow bandanna tied over his nose like the old Western bandits, and come into the store clutching his own bank bag to carry away his loot?"

"Yep."

"You don't sound surprised at all!" I accused, suddenly smelling a very dead rat.

Sheriff Beaman roared a booming laugh. "Don't stop now, Miz Sidden, I sure was having a good time. You know, Hank and I were sharing all-points bulletins on our various crimes long before you started training bloodhounds. We have helped each other from time to time. By seven this morning I recognized that Hank had some visits by the same perp. We had a lucky break. I had an officer cruising two blocks west of the robbery, as it was going down. He turned the corner, and there were three teenagers scattering in all directions like crows. He collared all three. We also found the money bag and bandanna less than a block away, stuffed down in a trash dumpster.

"I gather that Hank hasn't told you about it. He said you're in the

163

hospital with an injured leg. He won't be able to bring the dog and the handler over here until two, so we're just waiting to find out which one of the three boys is the culprit."

I was boiling, but held on to my temper.

"I've been out of the loop for the last few days. Thanks very much for answering my questions, Sheriff."

"Did you want to ask me anything else?"

"No . . . just checking. Talk to you later, Sheriff. Thanks again."

"It was my pleasure," he answered wryly.

Hank. That absolute worm! He was going to keep this from me, and Jasmine was aiding and abetting him! They were planning on sneaking Jasmine out this afternoon with a dog and identifying my perp. They had another think coming. I had spent long hours trying to trap that sucker, and they thought they were going to be in on the kill without me? No way. I punched in Chet's extension at the agency in New York.

"This is Jo Beth," I told him when he answered. I didn't forget the code. "Bobby Lee is doing fine. I'm still at the hospital, but I'll be home before noon. Have you heard anything new?"

"Good morning, Jo Beth, how is the new litter doing?"

"Great, I'm told." It's hard to be civil when you're fuming. "I've read the reports that Jasmine brought up here Friday, and frankly, they're skimpy at best."

"I know, but it's like I explained to you, we're gathering information daily. My desk is piled high this morning. I'm going through the reports that came in over the weekend. I should have the information compiled by this afternoon. I'll call you when I'm ready to fax."

"Anything interesting in what you're reading?"

"Nothing that raises any alarms. The Kingsleys, Catherine née Cancannon and Lawrence, her husband, filed for bankruptcy last year, but withdrew it from court records less than two weeks later, and promptly paid all the debts listed, something like ninety thousand."

"Auntie Alyce bailed them out."

"Most likely, but we're checking it out. Guess what they did the following week? They flew to Port Royal for ten days, while they both were unemployed, and ran all their credit cards up to the limit."

"South Carolina, or Jamaica?"

"What?"

"It was a joke, Chet. You said Port Royal, like everyone in the world should automatically know its location, and I bet only less than ten percent of the populace knows it's the former capital of Jamaica. I said South Carolina to show off my knowledge that there were two Port Royals . . . I was . . . It's hard to explain a joke," I snapped testily.

"I get it, I get it," he chuckled amicably. A representative of a large estate with bottomless pockets is treated like a VIP, whether he understood my sarcasm or not.

"Just call when you're ready to fax."

"I sure will," he returned and I hung up.

I sat and drummed my fingers on the phone held in my lap. Should I or shouldn't I? I should. I called Hank.

"Hank?"

"It's me. How are you feeling this morning?"

He automatically lowers his voice to almost a confidential whisper when he recognizes my voice. I had always thought that he didn't want any of the others who might possibly overhear his conversation to hear anything they could rag him about, like calling me sweet stuff or babe, some endearment. A new thought flashed in my mind. What if it was because he didn't want them to hear because he was ashamed of me? It dried up my usual banter in a heartbeat.

"Honey, are you all right?" I hadn't answered fast enough.

"A nurse just walked in, I'll talk to you later."

Suddenly I couldn't bear to hear his voice.

Time dragged as though I were in solitary confinement. There was a great deal of traffic in the hall, and plenty in and out of my room. I sat like a sphinx, ignoring their chirpy greetings and disgruntled servitude. I asked for no riddles to be answered. Dr. Sellers arrived and departed, accepting my silence as punishment for being late. Jasmine loaded up what she could handle, and made a second trip for the rest of the baggage after I was installed in the front seat.

She shot quick glances at me from time to time, but didn't ask me what was wrong until we were alone.

"Will you please unload the pillows, that roll of foam, and the dead flowers here at the curb?" I asked.

"Here?" She looked startled. "I can take them to the dump—"

"Here." My voice was polite but firm.

"But it's littering!"

"We are on hospital property. I feel no compunction to haul off unwanted items. They can cut costs some other way than trying to get their patients to do their chores. They are being well compensated for my stay."

"They'll know it was you." She was trying to change my mind, and sounded amused.

"Do you think they'll arrest me for littering? I would welcome the challenge, I'd bury them at trial."

"What's gotten into you? You're not acting like yourself. Anything I can do?"

"Unload the trash at the curb, please."

She still hesitated.

I reached for my door, and cracked it open.

"All right, all right!" she said, throwing up her hands. She emptied the offending pieces and piled them neatly on the sidewalk. She slammed the van door on her return.

"Thank you."

"You're welcome." Her voice was harsh as she concentrated on backing out of the space. We rode home in stony silence. She circled the courtyard, and parked with my door in front of the stone path leading to the porch steps. She placed her hand on my shoulder.

"I know hospital rules really bug you, but you should have handled it differently."

I ignored her remark and gave her a brief smile with no warmth.

"When Hank arrives, and you have the dog of your choice loaded to travel to Woodbine, please come and tell me. I'm going with you."

"Oh boy," she groaned. Jasmine realized that the shit had just hit the fan.

24

"An Uneasy Trip"

October 16, Monday, 11:00 A.M.

Jasmine was silent as she held open the screen door for me as I hobbled in on the crutches. Just letting my leg hang down hurt like hell. I pasted a serene look on my face and fought back a scream of anguish when I bumped it on the edge of the desk. I eased into my chair, knowing that Jasmine was only waiting until I was settled before she explained her duplicity in consorting with Hank.

She perched on the edge of the armchair in front of the desk and gazed earnestly into my eyes.

"Hank wanted me to help him do a lineup with the scent machine evidence. We both knew that you shouldn't move around on that leg. Even Dr. Sellers told you that you needed another week of bed rest and to keep off of it.

"We knew that you would insist on going if you were told, so, yes, we agreed to sneak around and not tell you, but it was for your own good! You know, Hank has the right to try and protect your health; he's going to be in your future, and he loves you very much."

I let my eyes widen, and a quizzical expression suddenly appeared on my features.

"Where in the world did you get that information? Have I given you any indication that Hank was part of my future?"

She closed her eyes briefly, and sadly shook her head.

"Don't do this, Jo Beth, you can't give him a reason to hope and keep yanking it back when he does something to displease you. All during your stay in the hospital he was worried about you, but floating inches above the ground with happiness that you were receptive and kissed him last Monday. Don't toy with him and mess up this latest chance to reconcile. Hank's the best thing that ever happened to you. I know you're angry, but please don't take this attitude with him. He deserves better, and I think you know this."

The reason that her explanation made me so angry is that I knew she was perfectly correct. My stupid ego was bruised and their devious plotting had hurt me. My pride blinded me.

"Hank had no reason to assume he was in charge of my fate, or the kennel's. It would be wise for you to reconsider if this problem ever presents itself again. I am the one that gives orders around here, and only me."

My voice was soft and sad. I was full of self-pity.

Jasmine sat a few seconds, and suddenly jumped to her feet, yelling.

"Will you cut out this self-righteous crap! Curse me! Curse Hank! Vent your anger! Anything but sitting there with that damn martyred expression!"

Her anger fueled mine.

"But I feel so alone!" I wailed. I bit my lip. I didn't mean to show my true feelings. I quickly held up my hand, trying to stem the compassionate feeling that was emanating from her in waves. The last thing I wanted from her was pity. I chose my words carefully.

"I don't appreciate Hank telling you every detail of our love life, such as it is, but I will inform him of this when I next speak to him. All I want from you is that you continue doing the excellent work that you have in the past and follow only my orders."

"My Lord," she voiced with sarcasm, "it sounds like you're willing to throw away our friendship of two and a half years for a silly and inconsequential misunderstanding!"

"We were good friends, weren't we?" I said quietly, ignoring my yammering heart that was screaming at me to shut the hell up.

She sank back in her seat looking defeated.

"Do you want me to leave, is that what you're telling me? Over this?"

"Of course not," I said reasonably, "you do good work. As long as we understand one other and follow the rules, we can continue like this incident never happened."

I lowered my eyes to my telephone messages lying in front of me on the desk. I pretended to be engrossed and ignored her continued presence.

"Incident?" Her laughter was hollow, chilling my soul.

She stood and drew herself up to her full height.

"I'll stay until you're back on your feet, and the puppies are out of danger."

I didn't look up or answer, and presently I heard her leave, closing the door softly behind her.

I heard the outer gate alarm at 12:30. I didn't scramble to see who had come calling. If it happened to be Bubba and no one stopped him, then so be it. I felt lower than a snake in a ditch. My mood swung from morose to blinding anger at Hank. He had started throwing orders around before he even knew he was moving back in. I heard a few snatches of raised voices before Hank threw open the door and charged toward me.

"What in the hell do you think you're doing?" he thundered when he placed his hands on the desk and towered over me, scowling. "Jasmine tells me that you've found out about the search; you're mad at both of us, and want to tag along for the lineup. No way! You're not up to it, and that's final. I know damn well that you owe Jasmine an apology from her demeanor. If your leg is hurting you that badly, I need to take you back to the hospital. Now tell me where you have the frozen scent pads, which dog you're sending, and I'll go get them while you tell Jasmine you're sorry."

"I'm in charge during a search or rescue. If you can't follow this rule, then the dog and the scent articles do not leave this kennel. Is that clearly understood?"

I had delivered this ultimatum calmly in a normal voice, and sat quietly waiting for his answer with a raised brow of inquiry.

"Are you out of your mind? You don't treat your friends this way just because you're pissed at us!"

I waited.

He slapped the desk in anger. "The scent pads were gathered during two searches that are still open cases. You're hindering ongoing investigations!"

"Arrest me."

"You're violating your contract with the county!"

"Sue me."

Hank took a deep breath, and tried a different approach.

"Look, Jo Beth, I'm sorry I came in here yelling at you; I know you must feel lousy. Is your leg hurting? Can I get you some water? I'm also sorry that I talked Jasmine into going along with not telling you about the search; will you forgive me?"

Bluster and threats hadn't worked, so now he was trying the soft soap.

"No."

"No what?" He now sounded bewildered.

"No, my leg isn't hurting. No, I don't want water, and no, I won't forgive you."

He threw up his hands, exasperated. "When you're ready to go, I'll be in the car." He headed toward the door.

I punched in the grooming room's number.

"Donnie Ray, please bring the two frozen scent pads from the freezer and load Marjorie in the sheriff's car. Don't forget both leashes and deer jerky."

"Jasmine picked up the scent pads about five minutes ago. She told me to load Caesar and I just got back. Did she change her mind?"

"No, forget Marjorie, Caesar is fine. I didn't know she had already taken care of it. Tell Wayne I'll be back around six or seven. If he needs me I can be reached at the Camden County sheriff's office."

"You're going too? Jasmine told me to check on you often while she was gone. What gives?"

"Mixed signals. Hold down the fort, I'll be back around seven."

"Yes'em."

Little Miss Hurt Feelings had been very sure that Hank would prevail, and I'd curl up in bed indisposed. She should have known better.

I reached for the crutches and made my way to Hank's car and stood by his left rear door. Jasmine crawled out of the back seat to see what I wanted.

"Jasmine, I'd appreciate you staying here. I can handle a lineup. Chet will be calling this afternoon with material to fax, and one of us has to be here to give him the code word. Do you mind?"

"Not at all," she murmured smoothly. "Good luck."

"Thanks." I clambered aboard and slammed the door before she could reach for it. We were being so polite and considerate, it made my teeth ache.

Caesar had been leaning over the seat sniffing the deer jerky when I slid in the back. I bent over to pick up the Ziploc from the floorboard and Hank's sudden acceleration would have broken my neck if I hadn't been prepared for his childish display of bad temper. I had a death grip on back of the headrest of his contoured seat.

Caesar wasn't as lucky. The thrust took him off his feet, and the economy Chevy that the county provided didn't have a great deal of space in back. He had rebounded off the back of the seat, rolled forward, and was jammed in the narrow slot for knees and shoes, frantically fighting to regain his feet.

"Slow down!" I yelled angrily as I gripped Caesar's harness to pull him back up on the plastic beside me. Hank's quick use of his brakes gave me the momentum to pull him free and back up onto the seat. Caesar weighs right at one hundred thirty pounds. My right arm felt stretched out of shape.

"What's going on back there?" he asked as he sought to find my eyes in his rearview mirror. He had slowed to a crawl.

"Your asinine driving threw Caesar off his feet. This isn't a pissing contest. Try and use some judgment!"

"Sorry, Caesar," he said, raising his voice and turning to see if he was okay. "It's your mistress's fault, she's driving me crazy!"

I didn't bother to answer. Hank raised the speed to sixty and kept it there for almost two hours. I had lowered the glass over halfway on Caesar's side, and he had his head out and his long ears were blown backward from the rushing wind.

As Hank approached small towns and sped up upon leaving them, he had no jerky stops and starts, just one continuing smooth movement. He was an excellent driver. I must have stung his pride on deriding his driving skills.

We didn't speak again until he glided to the curb in the visitors' row of parking spaces at the Camden County Court House in Woodbine.

"How are we gonna handle the next step?" Hank questioned, politely. "You have the crutches to contend with. Who handles the pooch?"

"Don't call him a pooch," I uttered with dignity while I scrambled for an acceptable answer. Where was my brain when I informed Jasmine I wouldn't need her services? Stupid move, but I had to live with it.

"Would you please take Caesar's lead until we're in front of the lineup?" I asked politely and hadn't scrunched my face in disgust at my forgetfulness.

"I'd be delighted." He walked around behind the car and opened the door.

"Come on, pooch, let's take a walk."

25

"Fruits of the Scent Machine"

October 16, Monday, 1:15 P.M.

I kept silent and made an awkward figure struggling out of the cramped back seat. Some of the swelling had gone down, but the color of the leg was still eggplant, black and blue. Jasmine had slit my jeans up to my knee so I could dress myself and then had wrapped adhesive tape around it to keep it together. If I made any kind of a fashion statement, it would be disheveled and wind-blown. My hair had suffered so Caesar could enjoy the wind. I decided to avoid looking in mirrors or reflecting glass. I wasn't up to pulling myself together; all my energy was focused on pulling myself across the pavement.

Hank was letting Caesar smell the small plot of grass sloping up to the steps. I stood and counted the white marble risers. I wanted to whimper; there were twelve of the damn things.

"Why don't we take the elevator?" Hank said, appearing at my elbow.

"Thank God," I said with a grateful breath.

He led me around some shrubbery and into a tiny cage.

"You're white as a sheet, Sidden," he said, sounding gruff. "Didn't Doc Sellers give you something to take?"

"I'm saving it for hard times," I commented as the elevator rumbled open. Hank slowed his steps to match my snail's pace down the hall and into the sheriff's office.

Sheriff Beaman was sitting behind his desk and rose to greet us. He was dressed as I saw him last, like a sheriff of the ol' frontier, and his slight paunch was evident in the tight-fitted Western-cut shirt. I wasn't one who should be noticing such things, since I didn't look too snazzy myself. They shook hands and Beaman nodded at me as I sank gracelessly into a metal side chair.

"Hear you had a tussle with a gator," Beaman said, beaming at both of us.

"He won," I commented, trying to prop up the crutches on the wall beside me. Both of them laughed and I kept an insipid smile in place. I know how to play the game, I just don't do it often; it galls me.

"How do you conduct this experiment, Hank?" Beaman asked, while relaxing backward in his large executive chair.

I glanced humbly at Hank, like asking for his permission to speak. I was perched on the edge of my seat because my left leg was throbbing from the knee downward, not because I was anxious.

"Why don't we let Jo Beth explain?" Hank said, being generous. He was pleased as punch with me. I wasn't embarrassing him in front of a friend.

"Let's hear it," Beaman acknowledged with an expansive gesture.

"Well . . . we really need an outside source as a witness, someone like a newspaper reporter or a sitting judge, so we won't look biased, and I think the accused should have a lawyer present, you know, to advise him. A lawyer could tell him how much the evidence could or couldn't weigh in court. What do you think, Sheriff Beaman?"

I channeled all my attention on him, waiting nervously for his valued opinion.

"I can handle that," Beaman said, including Hank and me with a satisfied smile. He picked up the phone. "After all, we want to *appear* unbiased, don't we?"

I swallowed bile as I bathed both of them in my warm glow of approval and gratitude.

Thirty minutes later we were gathered in an unused courtroom. Sheriff Beaman, Hank, and I, with Caesar lying near my feet, sat at the prosecutor's table, and two young men looking no older than the eight black teenagers presently ensconced in the jury box sat at the defense table.

One of the young men at the table was a cub reporter from the *Camden County Crier*; the other was a hastily recruited defense lawyer from the Georgia Defense League, who had been given five minutes to confer with his possible future client. We were waiting for an ADA from the District Attorney's office.

I glanced around the room. There were several policemen and deputies sitting in small cliques around the room. I decided it must be near a shift change, or they had an unusual amount of the hangers-on that populate small Southern courthouses.

A man, equally immature as the others, ran into the room, skidded to a stop, and proceeded decorously to Sheriff Beaman's side and pulled up a chair. In the hushed silence of the room, we all heard his stage whisper.

"Has the suspect been read his rights?"

A very good question. I saw Beaman's angry countenance, and knew this was something he hadn't taken care of. I glanced quickly to my right, and one of the young men at the defense table had dismay prominently displayed on his face. I now knew which was which, even if we hadn't been introduced. The lawyer had been secretly hoping that this obvious duty had been overlooked, so that anything the suspect blurted out here could be excluded from the teenager's future trial. I don't believe he had any doubt that the kid was guilty, so he had been counting on them screwing up before they tried him.

We all waited until the teenagers filed out, with the lawyer, then Sheriff Beaman bringing up the rear, so he could ream some asses, and after several minutes all reappeared.

Sheriff Beaman arose and addressed us.

"We have a lineup here that we want to conduct without bias, so no one can say it was handled incorrectly. I'm gonna let the dog handler explain the scent machine and the scent evidence she will be using." He nodded my way.

I stood and turned, leaning my butt against the table to support me. I didn't touch the crutches.

"My name is Jo Beth Sidden. I breed and train bloodhounds to mantrail, drug search, discover arson, and find cadavers. Each living person has an individual scent that is like no others. Just like fingerprints, a person's individual scent is unique. It consists of dead skin we shed, body odor, fallen hair follicles, perspiration, and other bodily fluids that we excrete. This scent surrounds us like a fog, and sheds thousands of tiny invisible pieces with each step we take.

"Simply explained, the dog searches out the individual scent of the person he is seeking. This is called the bloodhound's testimony in a court of law. Now I hear a few titters, and I can understand why. Everyone is picturing a large bloodhound with his hand on the Bible, baying and pointing a paw at the guilty party. This isn't what happens. A bloodhound has a rigid test of ability, right to judge, and strict rules to follow before he can give testimony. He has to have been recognized as an expert, such as having several prior successes in court, being certified by the AKC, and successively trail from the point of the crime to the conclusion of the search.

"The only exception to this rule is the scent machine that gathers the air from the crime scene and stores it in a concentrated form on a sterile gauze pad; then the pad is frozen until a possible subject is found. If the chain of evidence is proven, the dog successfully picks the suspect out of an impartial lineup. Then and only then is his testimony accepted in a courtroom.

"I would now like to tell the defense that this dog is highly qualified, the evidence chain unbroken, and the bloodhound's testimony will be allowed into a trial." I looked into space between the lawyer and the reporter, pretending I didn't know which one was the lawyer. The young lawyer gave me a small nod, to say he would take my word until court time, and then beware, he'd challenge every minute detail. I nodded my acceptance to his implied challenge.

"Now, scent evidence is hard to prove from a scent pad when taken from a convenience store robbery that has maybe two hundred or more people passing in and out of the store each day. All those scents mingled together, no dog could pick out any one scent with any accuracy *unless* we know what the culprit touched while he was in the store, and the exact locations where he stood. If we have this information, we can contain the area, plug in the scent machine, and it draws the scent from certain areas that the suspect inhabited last.

"It's nice that we have a bank bag with the suspect's fingerprints and smell on the surface, as we do on the third robbery, but we only have scent from the first two robberies. I believe after this lineup, you'll understand why law enforcement calls scent from the crime scene the 'forgotten evidence.'

"Since this kind of lineup is new to this area, I want to prove wrong the people who will guess that I have trained a dog to do tricks. Or can give a certain hand signal to the dog that only he will see or understand. Or that I might tug his leash in a way to point out a suspect.

"I think we will let someone neutral handle the dog."

I looked at the reporter. "Do you know me, sir?"

"Me?" He asked with surprise. "I'm not going near that dog!" A lot of laughter followed.

I smiled. "The dog is very gentle. It is trained only to trail a person's scent. He's not a catch dog or an attack dog. He'd happily greet you and lick your face if you were breaking into my home, and expect to be petted."

More laughter and the bolder ones began calling out to the cub reporter, "Give it a try," "You can sue if he bites," and the one that convinced him, "I dare you!" He must have recognized a voice. He stared behind him and must have found the source of the taunt. He stood suddenly and boldly walked toward me.

"What do you want me to do?"

I gave him a warm smile and held out a pair of thin gloves for him. "Put these on, we don't want your scent on the pad.

"Sheriff, would you please ask the men to leave the jury box and line up about three feet apart in front of the judge's bench area?" I checked each door to see if they were closed. I was going to unhook Caesar's leash and let him roam at will. At least, I was going to have Hank release him. I was afraid to lean over; I might not be able to straighten up again.

The reporter said his name was Tim. I gave him instructions on how to present the pad and pet Caesar, and had him place pieces of deer jerky in his mouth. I gave Caesar the okay to eat them, and Tim had an instant friend. Caesar kept his eyes glued on Tim's hands.

I nudged Hank, and after he released Caesar I nodded at my chair and made a small circle with my finger. He turned the chair around and I eased down into it, facing the onlookers instead of the lineup.

"Give Caesar the command," I whispered. "Remember to sound excited, like it's a game you're playing." Tim played his role to perfection, even ad-libbing from time to time.

"Go get him, Caesar, get your man, get your man!"

He opened the plastic bag, and thrust the open bag under Caesar's nose. "Go get him, boy, go get that sucker! You can do it, get him boy! Sic him! Sic him!"

Caesar took off down the aisle, stopping to smell each person who was sitting in the seats. Men were scrambling to pull their arms out of his way and leaning over seats to move out of his reach, which only spurred Caesar on.

He cornered each one and got a good sniff of his pants and shoes before he moved on to the next selected scent carrier. He circled back up the aisle and started with Sheriff Beaman, who seem surprised to be a target. He gave Caesar a look that plainly showed he thought he should know the good guys from the bad guys. Even Hank got a nose to his gabardine uniform pants, as did Tim, the reporter who had put Caesar on the scent, and the lawyer. Caesar didn't take anyone for granted. The bailiff who had escorted the teenagers was leaning against the wall with his arms folded and looked amused when Caesar gave him the onceover with his nose.

The tension had been building. Every eye in the room had been on Caesar's merry romp through the unsuspected; now we were waiting for the finale. I knew that it was just coincidence that Caesar had saved the suspects for last. He couldn't have known; he was just eliminating everyone in the room and searching for a particular scent.

The black youths had slouched, laughed, jeered, and postured according to their temperaments throughout the procedure, but now they were subdued and apprehensive, and more than one set of eyes were showing fear. I had read an article once that discussed racial fears that were inherent and bred into their genes, but I couldn't go along with the theory.

I believe that all people, white or black, have a latent fear of large animals, such as bloodhounds; but only to the extent of their knowledge learned from birth. Remember Little Eva on the ice? Who wouldn't fear dogs when they knew they had been used to hunt down their ancestors? I challenge anyone who has ever glimpsed a group of crowd control canines being released on a rioting mob: Who hasn't had some sort of visceral reaction and thought, what if it were me?

Caesar scampered toward them, ears flapping, tail high, his toenails clicking and sliding on the varnished floor. The fairly straight line of black boys broke and pandemonium reigned. The sudden eruption caught everyone off guard. Grunts, yells, and sudden flight brought fallen bodies and confusion; but one scream of fear overrode all the other voices.

"Get him off me! Call him off, I did it! I did it!"

I had jumped up like all the rest. My desire to reach Caesar and get him leashed was paramount. No telling what a panicked deputy with a gun on his hip or someone rushing in on the chaotic scene might do. I had forgotten my injury and the back of my leg struck the chair when I pushed back on rising. My vision blurred with dark spots and unshed tears of pain. I was completely helpless and could only watch the action unfold.

Caesar had found his target. He was standing over a youth on the floor, licking his face and pausing to lift his head in a joyous bay, then return for another lick. He was overcome with his victory, and wanted his praise for a job well done.

"Get him, help, I did it, I did it!"

"I object, I object!" screamed the young lawyer, who was still prudently behind the table.

"This ain't a court of law, boy! What are you objecting to? Your client is guilty!" Sheriff Beaman pounded on the table in front of the lawyer, and roared.

"Quiet. Everybody be quiet!" No one was listening.

After an eternity I saw Hank pull Caesar back, clip on his leash, and start back toward me. Even with the confusion Hank remembered to bring Caesar back to my right side, so he wouldn't bump my left one. He was a cool dude.

The noise was abating and the sheriff yelled at the bailiff who was trying to round up the runaways.

"Arrest that man!"

I glanced at the kid with his body contorted in a fetal position, sobbing, and felt a twinge of sympathy, then pushed it away. The three people he had held at gunpoint to rob had also feared for their lives.

"Well, the scent machine worked, and should clear up three robberies."

"Yes, indeedy," Hank agreed.

It took us another hour until we were able to leave. Hank took my crutches at his car door and helped me into the back seat.

"Sure you won't sit up front with me?"

"Absolutely."

When he climbed in front, he twisted to face me.

"You handled yourself well with Jeff in there, Sidden, I'm proud of you!"

"It made me want to puke," I hissed in his ear. "You males have to be fed pap in every sentence, just to receive cooperation you would extend to any male without hesitation. We have to be the helpless second-class citizen and salve your damn superior-feeling ego just to do our jobs. Come the revolution, y'all will be our prime target!"

I sank back in pain and braced Caesar and myself for a fast getaway. I wasn't disappointed.

26

"Working on the Murder"

October 17, Tuesday, 8:00 A.M.

I leaned back in my desk chair and rubbed my eyes. I had read a sentence twice and it just wasn't registering. For the past hour I had been poring over the mountain of information that had been sent by fax from Chet in New York. I'd been too pooped to even glance at it last night. I had hobbled to the kitchen, drank two glasses of milk, brushed my teeth, and fallen into bed, all before nine.

The puppies were twelve days old. Wayne had proudly shown me their charts this morning when I had used my crutches at daybreak to visit them. He had left them in Judy's care last night and had his first solid uninterrupted sleep since the birthing.

All was well in the nursery. Not so on the home front. Hank had dropped me at the door last night without returning my civil good night. Jasmine was conspicuous in her absence. She was leaving me to fend for myself. I had met her briefly this morning in the grooming room while returning to the house. She discussed her proposed activities of the day, and when I agreed she had nodded and moved on quickly. Her schedule hadn't included fixing my lunch, or doing any fetching on my behalf. I released a martyred sigh. So be it. I hate apologizing when I know I'm in the wrong. I'd just wait until she cooled down before I had to grovel at her feet. I took care of myself before I met her and could continue to do so.

There were glowing words of praise in this morning's *Dunston County Daily News*. Our fast-acting sheriff and the intrepid dog handler were mentioned several times. I decided to call Susan. I needed to schmooze with someone.

"Browse and Bargain Books."

"Did you see the paper this morning and read about your fearless friend's exploits yesterday?"

"Who is this calling?"

"Jo Beth?" I feared the worst.

"No, no, you aren't my friend Jo Beth! My friend Jo Beth is in the hospital and might be released yesterday or today. She promised she'd call me the minute she headed home so I could run over and settle her in comfort. If you're that liar Jo Beth, whom I wasted a trip to the hospital on my lunch hour yesterday to visit, you can just hang up, because I'm not speaking to her!"

"Something happened," I lamely began . . .

I listened to the dial tone a while before I hung up. Then I listened to the silence of the morning. It was something that I had lived with from the time that I was ten until two and a half years ago, when Jasmine had started working here. A silence I hadn't missed or mourned. I hadn't realized until just this minute what a loner I was and always had been. I looked out my office window and knew with certainty that with three of my closest friends no longer interested in conversing with me, I had no one to converse with. I shrugged. I owned eight phones and had no one to call.

"It's just you and me now," I whispered aloud to my ego. I didn't expect or receive an answer and presently went back to work.

What I was going to attempt to do in this murder investigation sounded amateurish and impractical at first blush. Simply stated, I was going to take all the information the operatives had found about the ten people who stood to inherit a good chunk of money from Miz

Cancannon's estate and look for a motive large enough to commit murder over.

I wasn't going to depend on the old method of a detective going around looking up people, questioning them, and by brilliant deduction saying "Aha!" while pointing to the guilty party during the denouement in the library.

No, my idea sounded even sillier than that. I was going to put all my eggs in one basket and go with the premise that whoever murdered her was also the one who kidnapped Amelia, the cat. Think about it. The kidnapping was the catalyst that caused the murder. All ten were present on the island the night Miz Cancannon died. All had an equal opportunity to slip into her room and shoot her, and time to hide the weapon. Their alibis were the same. They were all asleep. If no one broke and they stuck to their tale, who could prove otherwise? Certainly not Sheriff Beaman, he was scratching his head in frustration. Certainly not me, with very little time to spare and a kennel to run.

I was truly going to attempt to be an armchair detective. To sit on my duff and focus on the twenty-four-hour window directly before and after Amelia was snatched. If the person who kidnapped Amelia and the killer were not one and the same, then my theory would go down in flames. I would like to be the hero who solved the murder, but even if I couldn't, I still wanted to have generated enough paperwork to prove that I had honestly worked diligently to reach that goal. I didn't want to fail and miss the chance of selecting one of my father's paintings to be my own.

When I had formulated this plan, I had envisioned Jasmine and I spending cool nights in front of the fireplace, tossing different versions of what we thought back and forth, and arguing the merits of each one. This no longer looked possible, so I would have to try it alone.

I stopped at noon and made a peanut butter and banana sandwich on white bread slathered with mayonnaise, one of my favorites. The only nice thing about Jasmine's abandonment being I could eat anything I damned well pleased, I decided to take advantage and pig out on what she declared was not good for me. After my sandwich was finished, I read until the phone rang at three.

"Hello."

"Is this Jo Beth Sidden?"

"Yes, it is." I didn't recognize the voice.

"I hope you remember me from high school. I'm Alice Mae Petrie now, but I used to be—"

"Alice Mae Carter! Of course I remember you! Lord, how are you? I haven't seen you in, ah . . . lo these many years!"

I had drawn a complete blank. How long had she been gone?

Alice Mae laughed. "I had to figure up when I moved back home last year. We moved the week after graduation, so we haven't seen each other for fourteen years, as of last June!"

"God," I groaned. "Where have the years gone? Are you still married, and who is Petrie?"

"Petrie is out of the picture; we were divorced about eighteen months ago. I've been living in Richmond, Virginia, for the last ten years."

"Any children?"

"Nope, how about you?"

"Me neither," I said. "I got rid of Bubba eight years ago."

"Mother told me about him. I was so sorry to hear he attacked you when he was released from prison. I meant to call or write, but I just never did. I'm sorry I didn't."

"Don't be. I was in the same boat. I would run into your mother from time to time and I'd always ask about you, but I should have asked for your address and written."

"I should have called you sooner. Are you in the middle of something, should I call back another time?"

"This is the perfect time. I have a banged-up leg and can't do anything but sit here and gossip."

"How bad is the leg, or do you want to discuss it?"

"I can talk freely, but you're gonna think I'm pulling yours when I tell you about mine. A gator swatted me with his tail."

She giggled. "Same ol' Jo Beth."

"Scout's honor, it's true. I train bloodhounds for search and rescue in the Okefenokee. I guided in a pilot who had lost his plane—"

Her squeal of laughter disconcerted me until I remembered she only knew Jo Beth, the jokester in high school, not the grown-up one who tramped through the swamp for a living.

"It's the truth," I said softly.

"You weren't kidding, were you? I'm sorry for laughing, but you used to always be pulling pranks on us."

"Give me a break, I grew up."

"Start again, and I promise I won't laugh."

"Anyway, this guy waded out in a shallow stream and a gator started toward us. I shot him but he flipped over at my feet and lashed out with his tail. This was last Tuesday and it's feeling a lot better. The swelling is disappearing and the bruises are fading."

"I had no idea that you led such an interesting life," Alice Mae exclaimed.

"Well, it isn't all shooting gators. The rest is cleaning pens and training dogs. Nothing exciting about that unless you slip up and step in dog doo-doo."

She giggled. "I've heard about your scent machine from Sheri Bennett. She had a dinner party last month and she kept the whole table entertained with your adventures. It seems almost impossible to believe that those bloodhounds of yours are so talented. Tim was really impressed."

And I wasn't invited, I brooded. It was my own fault. When you're asked and turn down several opportunities in a row, they stop calling. I would have to start making myself available more often if I wanted to attend any future dinner parties.

"Tim?" I inquired.

"He's part of the problem I wanted to talk to you about. I'm going about this the wrong way. Now it sounds like the only reason I called is that I have a problem I want you to help me with. I don't want you to think that."

"Why should I think that?" I'm glad she couldn't see the wry expression pulling at the corners of my mouth. "Friends are friends, if it's a week or fourteen years since we've seen each other. Tell me about your problem."

"Thanks, Jo Beth, I appreciate you listening to me. Let me tell you a story. I went through a nasty divorce. We'd been married almost nine years when I found out he had been cutting a swath through my married women friends on our party list. No singles or divorcées, he only wanted to bonk the married ones. He explained it to me after the divorce. They gossiped less and were cheap dates because they couldn't be seen together out in public. I was soured on men and didn't date for a year.

"Six months ago Mother got sick and wanted me to move back and live with her. She needed me, so I came home. She's better now and I'm living in a small studio apartment that her and Dad built years ago. It's attached to the back of the house and I have my own entrance. It's around back and can't be seen from the street. I've been enjoying the peace and quiet until a month ago.

"Wait, I'm getting ahead of myself. Right after Mom got better and I started going around with old friends, I started dating again. Not often, and not just with one guy. There is one at work, a friend of a friend, and now Tim."

"Send me your leftovers," I joked.

"I'm not serious about any of them and the most I've gone out with one of them is three times and I'm not sleeping with any of them!"

"Okay, take it easy, I was kidding," I cautioned.

"Sorry, but it's getting to me."

"What?" I said helpfully.

"Two months ago, I started looking over my shoulder when I'm out of the house and going to work, or let's just say when I'm going anywhere."

"Uh-oh."

"God, I'm glad you understand so quickly. Sheri said that Bubba had stalked you for years, and that if anyone could understand, you could. I really don't think she did."

"Have you ever seen anyone following you?"

"No one. I see nothing that looks suspicious. I feel like I'm becoming a basket case. I feel eyes on me, Jo Beth. Someone is out there, I know it!"

"I believe that you've seen something or heard something that registered in your subconscious, only you can't remember what it is. I have a simple way of explaining what's happening. Your cavewoman's senses have been activated. They're warning you that you are in danger from someone. It's sorta like when you have a spider on your shoulder and someone brushes it off. Hours later, you still can feel a spider crawling in the most unlikely places and try to keep brushing it away. Have you ever had that happen? The tiny sensors on the surface of your skin and hair follicles have been activated and minuscule particles like a snip of hair or even scaling skin can trigger that feeling again."

"The weirdest thing happened a month ago."

"Tell me."

"I came home and my front door was unlocked. I tried the key and couldn't turn it. I reached out and pushed and it swung open. Jo Beth, I can't positively swear I locked it, but it's a faithful habit with me. I always lock it!"

"Did you go inside without anyone with you?"

"Yes, I convinced myself that I had forgotten that morning to lock it."

"Bad move. Don't ever do it again. Did you find anything disturbed inside?"

"My imagination did. My toothbrush was in the wrong slot in the holder. I thought I could see an impression on the bedspread where a head had rested, but I had been running late that morning and more or less flipped the spread over the pillows, so I couldn't be sure. My mother is shaking her head right now, saying I'm talking nonsense."

No wonder she had told me she wasn't sleeping with any of the three hopefuls. A daughter is always chaste in a Southern religious mother's opinion, even after motherhood or divorce. If Alice Mae was having a male guest sleep over, she had to be discreet and slip him in after dark and out before daylight.

"You're calling from your mother's house?"

"My door to my cottage was standing ajar when I came home from work at two-thirty this afternoon."

"You haven't been inside?"

"I remembered Sheri's dinner conversation about you and decided to call."

"Stay inside with your mother. I'll be there in less than thirty minutes."

27

"The Forgotten Evidence"

October 17, Tuesday, 3:30 P.M.

I called Donnie Ray. He picked up the phone in Wayne's office.

"Are you and Wayne busy right now?"

"No, ma'am. Wayne just finished feeding the new puppies, and I fed the rest. The dogs' suppers are mixed. We're just waiting until time to feed them. I'm playing a computer game and Wayne is reading. Need anything?"

"I need you to bring my van around to the porch steps, and for you to load the scent machine in my car and follow me. When we get to our destination, I'll tell you what to do. Don't forget the gauze pad. Tell Wayne you'll be back in thirty minutes."

"Should you be driving?"

"I can drive and use my right leg. It's the left leg that's sore. No problem, okay?"

"Yes'em. Be right there."

Bobby Lee was delirious when I told him to fetch his leash and that he could go.

We waited in the drive until Donnie Ray drove out of the garage and pulled up beside us. He ran back to get my car while I loaded Bobby Lee and eased into the driver's seat using the crutches. I saw

Jasmine running down the apartment stairs, taking two or more steps at a time. I lowered both windows as she walked up to the van door.

"Do you need me to drive you?"

She spoke in a neutral tone of voice, but I sensed her disapproval.

"I'm fine," I said with a smile. "But thanks for asking."

She stood there expecting an explanation. She turned her head and watched Donnie Ray pull my car behind the van and wait with the motor running.

"Are you sure you don't need me?"

She now looked worried. A small frown appeared.

"Positive. See you later." I pulled off and left her standing there. As I slowed at the inside gate to pull onto the driveway, I glanced back and she was staring at me. I felt better. She was worried about me. I should have relieved her mind, or invited her to join me, but I still felt betrayed to a certain extent. I knew it was silly, but I was just perverse enough to leave her in the dark and let her stew.

It was less than two miles to Alice Mae's mother's home. I pulled up to the modest house on Sycamore Drive and tooted the horn. She ran out to greet me, and stopped short when she saw Bobby Lee with his head out the window.

"Meet Bobby Lee," I said as I moved him over to the empty space between the seat and connected him to his seat belt.

"Does he bite?"

"One caress and he's a friend for life. Hop in and ride around to your door with me." She slid into the seat and closed the door cautiously, keeping her eye on him. I put my hand on his left shoulder.

"Shake hands with your left paw, Bobby Lee."

He solemnly offered his left. She laughed. "He always puts out his left paw, right?"

I casually dropped my right hand on Bobby Lee's right shoulder.

"Use your right, sweetheart."

He obligingly stuck out his right. She gasped. "He really knows his left from his right!"

"Not really. He was born blind, and I trained him with hand signals on his shoulders. He has the ability to see now, but he still needs the hand signals."

"How did he gain his sight, with surgery?"

"Nope. Over a few weeks' period, he acted skittish and had me worried. The vet thinks it was a blood clot that eventually was absorbed into his system that had been blocking the optic nerve."

"It doesn't surprise me that you're working with dogs now. I remember the dog you had in the third grade that got run over. We all thought you were gonna die. I heard my mother tell a neighbor that you were gonna dry up and blow away, you had lost so much weight."

"It was a bad time for me; I had just lost my mother. All I ever wanted to do was raise bloodhounds. I just had to work for several years to be able to start."

"Are you having fun?"

"They are my reason for rising early every morning. They are eating me into bankruptcy, but I couldn't imagine life without them."

I pulled around the driveway and stopped at the door of the cottage.

"Who's in the car behind us?" Alice's voice was sharp.

"Donnie Ray, my videographer for the kennel. He's bringing the scent machine, and will set it up. I don't get around too well on these crutches."

We got out, and I hobbled to the door. Donnie Ray joined us, and I introduced Alice. Mrs. Carter had walked around the house, and appeared with a baseball bat.

"Just in case," she said defensively as she saw the three of us staring at her.

Alice was embarrassed. "Mother, for Pete's sake!"

"A practical woman is a prepared woman," I said, grinning at Mrs. Carter. "Do you know how to use it?"

"Alice's father liked to shag flies in the spring. I was the one who hit them to him. I can handle a bat."

"Good. I'm sure if there was an intruder, he's long gone, but we'll stay out here until Donnie Ray checks."

I put on a pair of thin gloves, opened the filter that Donnie Ray brought, and loaded it in the top of the scent machine.

"Set the machine on the floor by the bed. Plug it in, and take a quick glance under the bed, behind the shower curtain, and in the closet. I want you back out here in thirty seconds, don't dally."

I held the screen door and gave the front door a nudge. He slipped in, and I pulled it shut behind him.

"Want to contain the existing air inside," I explained. We stood waiting for him to return. He was back in forty seconds.

"What took you so long?"

"There were three closets," he replied, aiming his glance upward. He knew I was kidding.

"How long does it have to run?" Mrs. Carter inquired.

"I'll give it five minutes. That should be sufficient."

"I understand the concept, from Alice's explanation, but won't the air have other scents?"

"Well, the theory is that Alice's and yours have had time to settle in the several hours since you've been in there. The prevalent scent, of the intruder, if there has been an intruder, should be still floating around in the dust motes and tiny currents of air. That's why I had Donnie Ray in and out so quickly."

We all stood and listened to the small hum we could barely hear coming from the cottage. It sounded as if a vacuum was being used in a faraway bedroom.

When the five minutes had passed, I sent Donnie Ray back inside to retrieve it. On the small stoop, I removed the filter pad of gauze, still wearing my gloves, and double-bagged it into gallon Ziploc bags.

"Label it and stick it in the freezer. I'll be along shortly," I told Donnie Ray.

Alice and her mother insisted that I stay and visit for a while, but I begged off, pleading some heavy reading on a present case.

"Invite your three suspects and a few people over for drinks as soon as possible. Put me on the guest list. I don't want to drag this out; I'm worried about you being stalked. Get a new lock on your door tomorrow. See you soon."

Back home, I settled in the office, and decided that ten suspects to juggle was way too many. I would make a list of all of them, showing only their city of residence, occupation, and brief alibi for the time when Amelia was kidnapped. Maybe I could narrow the number of suspects while being sure their alibis were airtight. An hour later, with the list finished, I stood up to stretch, and admired how neat it looked. I typed it so I would be able to read it in the future.

SUSPECTS

1. Celia Cancannon, private secretary, on island, inside working.
2. Rand Finch, helicopter pilot, off island, picking up supplies.
3. Cathy Cancannon Kingsley, unemployed, Bethesda, MD, home alone.
4. Larry (Cathy's husband) Kingsley, unemployed, Bethesda, MD, fund-raising party, Washington, D.C.
5. Teri Cancannon Halbert, designer, Lathrap, CA, her office, then home alone.
6. Phillip (Teri's husband) Halbert, CPA, Lathrap, CA, works in his home office, then home alone.
7. Sabrina Cancannon Wilder, public radio, Atlanta, GA, on the air, then home.
8. Paul (Sabrina's husband) Wilder, real estate broker, Atlanta, GA, his office, then dinner out.
9. Cynthia Cancannon Ross, unemployed, Kalamazoo, MI, shopping, then home alone.
10. Steven (Cynthia's husband) Ross, lawyer, Kalamazoo, MI, office, dinner with client, then home alone.

I studied the list, then eyed the heavy stack of reports already accumulated, and decided to make them more manageable. I pulled out one of the many summaries and began clipping them, and pasting the articles on an individual page for each suspect.

I heard the first gate alarm and from my kitchen window watched Jasmine drive through the second gate and garage her car. I stood in the dark and watched her climb her stairs and enter her apartment without glancing once in my direction.

I resented the fact that she was ignoring me. She was making too much of our little spat. Common courtesy dictated that she should have stuck her nose in my door and asked how I felt, and if I needed anything. It was only 10:00 P.M. and my light was on in the office. She knew I would be checking to make sure it was her returning from her college class and not Bubba with his baseball bat. I hardened my heart. There would be no apology from me tomorrow, or in this millennium. I could out-stubborn her any day of the week.

I went back to my pile of papers, and finally finished cutting out and pasting all the alibis that had been verified on their individual sheets. It was after midnight. My eye settled on the top sheet, which was number ten on the list. It was Steven Ross, Cynthia's husband, from Kalamazoo, Michigan. His alibi had been checked several different ways. His client, who had been his dinner companion, had been questioned, and the waiter had picked out Ross's picture. The restaurant had looked up the dinner check that had been charged on Ross's credit card, which had a register printout time of 10:35 P.M.

He couldn't have traveled even by private jet to get to the island within the time frame.

I felt justified in using an orange-colored highlight pen and boldly crossing him off the list, thus eliminating my first suspect. *And then there were nine.*

28

"Nailing the Stalker"

October 21, Saturday, 3:00 P.M.

Wayne was weighing the masterpiece litter, and I was charting their gains with satisfaction. They were little wrinkled butterballs.

Wayne grinned at the last one as he placed him back in the puppy cart.

"They are doing great!" I signed. "I regret that we can't keep one, but we don't have the time to show it and give it the right ring training. All of these deserve to be champions. At least we'll be mentioned as the breeder, that should give the kennel some good publicity. I suspect we'll be getting a lot of phone calls seven or eight months down the road about these guys when they start in the ring."

Wayne nodded his agreement and began signing.

"Can I ask you a personal question without you getting angry at me?"

"Certainly." I bit back my reluctance. I might as well answer him and get it over with. The situation between Jasmine and myself still remained mired in an impasse. I couldn't very well tell Wayne it was none of his business. I suspected that he and Donnie Ray were on the receiving end of our short tempers and had gotten a lot of snappy retorts they didn't deserve. You could cut the tension with a knife.

Jasmine and I were trying to act cool, disinterested, and haughty to each other. All our nerves were wearing thin. Ours from the strained relationship, and theirs from being available and within firing range.

"When are you and Jasmine gonna make up?"

"She started it, not me."

"But you're the boss. It's up to you, not her, to smooth it over."

"Sounds like you're now choosing sides, and you think it's my fault. You can tell her, if you wish, that I will be glad to accept her apology and end this nonsense."

The speed of his signing accelerated.

"I wouldn't pass on that message on a bet. I'm too young to die. It's your place to apologize!"

"In a pig's eye."

"Donnie Ray and I are serving notice. Any time in the future when you and Jasmine meet in our presence, we are going to disappear, regardless of what we're doing. We don't want to be victims or witnesses. Okay?"

"Read and understood. Anything else you wish to add?"

He signed so rapidly, I couldn't assimilate his message. He threw up his hands and left. If I didn't know better I would swear he had been cursing, but Wayne never uses cuss words.

Back in the office I decided to call Patricia Ann Newton and thank her on the phone instead of writing a bread-and-butter note for the lovely dinner she prepared for me last evening. I'm sure Miss Manners wouldn't approve.

Yesterday I had visited the SPCA kennel at five. I ran into Patricia, who spends many hours there each week doing volunteer work. I had met her at the beginning of this year, while I was working to solve an old murder case, and we had become casual friends. She donated a lot of money to the kennel, and also gave freely to some of my special projects.

On the spur of the moment, she urged me to go home with her, promising to prepare dinner for us. I accepted the invitation with alacrity. I had dreaded the thought of sitting home alone, waiting to see if either Jasmine or Susan would come to our regular Friday girl's night. I suspected both of them would be no-shows. I had an excellent dinner, stimulating conversation, and was back home before ten. I read more reports and went to bed at midnight, without eliminating any of the remaining suspects.

Patricia answered her own phone, something she wouldn't have done back in January.

"This is Jo Beth, and I wanted to thank you again for the lovely dinner last night."

"I'm glad you enjoyed it. I was spellbound with some of the local stories you shared with me. I've fallen more deeply in love with this town of ours with each day that passes. I'll be a Southerner before you know it."

"You were born in the South, and don't you forget it. Spending thirty years in the Big Apple doesn't cancel your Southern heritage."

We chatted for a while before I ended the call.

At seven, I filled the bathtub with unscented bubble bath and relaxed in the soothing hot water. Bobby Lee would be working tonight, and I didn't want to distract his nose. I was invited for drinks at Alice Mae Petrie's house. My plan to identify her intruder/stalker was in progress. I had taken the precaution of eating a large salad loaded with olive oil, and two slices of wheat bread slathered with butter. The olive oil and butter were to coat my stomach, so the hard liquor wouldn't go to my head. I'm a beer drinker, but Alice Mae wouldn't be serving beer. There would probably be three choices of booze: vodka, bourbon, and gin. I didn't particularly care for any of them, but I could tolerate vodka. If a male guest was filling in for a bartender, the Standing Operating Procedure was to load every female glass to the brim with liquor and add only a token splash of mix. The men seemed to believe that it increased the male's chance of getting lucky. When it had happened to me in the past, I had always gotten sick quickly and thrown up on my male escort, which tends to cool down even the most ardent Casanova.

Alice Mae had called me Thursday and informed me she had invited twelve: her three suspected suitors, three more males, and four females. A total of twelve people in her small cottage would be a tight fit. It made me think of a packed tin of sardines. It should be an interesting evening.

When I arrived at a few minutes after eight, the room was somewhat as I had imagined. The couch and chairs were back against the wall, and Alice Mae had supplemented the seating with several of her mother's dinning room chairs. Everyone would be seated in an irregular circle with an opening at the front door for people to enter, and another opposite so we could trek to the kitchen for drinks.

She and I stood in the middle of the circle as she introduced me to the nine who were seated. Her three suspects were among them. She sent me to the kitchen for a drink. I knew the man who was mixing the drinks. He owned a service station facing the courthouse square downtown. We chatted as he worked at the dinette table. It was loaded with glasses, booze, and mixes. He added ice cubes scooped from an insulated cooler, filled the glass with vodka, and more or less waved the carafe of orange juice above it. Adding a swivel stick he presented it to me with a flourish. "Ta-da!"

I held the drink up to the light, and could only detect a faint tinge of yellow color. I looked at him.

"Orders from headquarters," he boomed across the table. He had been sampling his wares.

"Uh-huh," I said, and went back to the action.

I chose a seat next to a woman I hadn't seen in ages. She was a paralegal for the county defense league. She had spent a lot of time at the shelter for battered women as a volunteer. I worked a four-hour shift there once a month bringing in a bloodhound and sometimes a couple of puppies if any children were in residence. I hadn't seen her there in months. When I inquired if she was still working there, she shrugged her shoulders.

"I got married to Mr. Right. It was my second time around. In less than three months, I was a guest of the shelter for a week, and had filed for a divorce. My experience from working there helped. I knew just what to do when he beat the crap out of me for the fourth time in twelve weeks. I can't go back there as a volunteer until the divorce is final."

I murmured the appropriate words, patted her knee, and changed the subject. We played charades for a while, and when interest waned, conversation and something resembling musical chairs began. Men and women began to loosen up from the liquor and changed seats often. I was still nursing my first drink, but the others weren't so prudent. I slipped into the bedroom and called Donnie Ray.

After fifteen minutes, I wandered over to a window to make sure he had arrived, and flipped the porch light on and off. I gave Alice Mae a nod. She moved to the middle of the room.

"Listen to me, everyone, I have a surprise for you!"

She sounded nervous. The noise level dropped to zero. The three standing quickly took their seats.

"Jo Beth wants to tell you a story about her bloodhounds, and give you a demonstration of their abilities. Would you please remain seated, and give her your undivided attention. Jo Beth?"

I stood in front of the door.

"Before I begin the demonstration, I'm going to bring Bobby Lee, a very gifted bloodhound, inside so you can meet him. I don't think many of you have seen a bloodhound in person, so I will tell you first that bloodhounds aren't aggressive, and don't bite."

"Can I have that in writing?" called out one of the males who wasn't a suspect. He received a couple of snickers for his humor. I ignored him, trying to draw the eyes and attention of the others to me. I opened the door and took Bobby Lee's leash and the thawed scent pad from Donnie Ray, who had been standing with the screen door open. I quickly shut the door in his face, and ordered Bobby Lee to sit. I now had their attention.

"This bloodhound is trained for search and rescue. His ability to smell is many, many times greater than ours is. I'm going to tell you a story, and I want all of you to suspend any disbelief of his abilities so I can prove he can do things that seem impossible.

"Two months ago, Alice Mae began to have a feeling that she was being followed. She tried to ignore it, but it kept reappearing, and was stronger each time. She came home one evening and found her door unlocked. Had she forgotten to lock it, or had someone picked the lock, went inside, and wanted her to be aware of his uninvited visit? She wasn't sure until the second occurrence. That's when she called me."

The jokester began to hum a ghostly theme and received more laughs and a couple of hushes. A woman gave a large shudder and glared at the culprit.

"Don't interrupt again. I for one am very interested in what Jo Beth is telling us!"

I sneaked a glance at Alice Mae and I saw she was resigned to the fact that she might lose more than one friend tonight. She tightened her lips and nodded her approval for me to continue.

"I came over immediately after her call, and brought with me a fairly new invention called the scent machine. I'll explain briefly what it does. It captures the scent, or I should say the latest scent at a crime scene. In this instance, the person who entered Alice May's living quarters, who is unknown at this time, left his scent all over the house. The scent machine was placed near Alice Mae's bed, and I let it run for five minutes."

At the mention of her bed, I heard some suppressed snickers.

"Ah, but your thoughts are incorrect. This type of stalker, predator, or would-be rapist isn't lusting for sex. They want to prove they have power over women, to feel in control, and to dominate."

I didn't let my eyes roam around the room because I knew I might let my gaze linger on the three suspects to see how they were reacting to my statements.

"The machine draws the air from the room and forces it through a sterile gauze pad, like this one."

I held the pad in front of me so everyone could see.

"It can be frozen indefinitely, and thawed when you believe you have a suspect, and used to convict him, if he is identified by a bloodhound who has the right credentials."

"Let me get this straight, this sounds like the *Twilight Zone*. Are you telling us that you're gonna let that bloodhound there, what's his name, smell that gauze pad and he's then going to pick out a male in this room as the one who took an uninvited tour here, and has also been following her?"

The questioner was a stout dark-haired woman who owned the local car wash. I couldn't remember her name. I smiled and nodded.

"You are correct. Bobby Lee will point him out shortly."

"Man's best friend is going to fink on him? I think that's priceless!" Another woman heard from. This one had come with one of the three suspects. She had an infectious grin.

"That is correct."

I kneeled and held two pieces of deer jerky in my gloved hand. This was the signal to let Bobby Lee know it was time to put his nose to work. I opened the Ziploc freezer bag, removed the scent pad, and thrust it under his nose.

"Seek, Bobby Lee, seek!"

I slipped off his short lead and whispered the familiar command in his ear.

"Find your man, get your man, where's your man?"

He took one fast sniff, stared around the room as if he were searching for a perp hiding under a sofa, and padded softly across to the first person on his left in the ragged circle of possible suspects. It was a slight female who still looked like a teenager, when I knew she was at least thirty years old. She giggled when Bobby Lee's nose brushed against her slacks. He moved around the room, hesitating briefly to take a sniff.

In front of the seventh person, who was one of the three suspects,

203

Bobby Lee raised his head and begun his victorious bay while planting his enormous paws on Tom's shoulders.

Everyone was riveted by the loud bay, which stopped just short of rattling the rafters. I knew what to expect and was still startled by the suddenness of Bobby Lee's actions, so I could understand why the others were so shocked.

Tom came out of his trance and began to push Bobby Lee away from him, but being seated, he couldn't get purchase on the happy animal. I got over there quickly, slipped on Bobby Lee's short lead, and hauled him out of Tom's range.

As I worked to silence the mournful cry, I observed several faces turned toward Tom. It was the women. They were glaring at him, letting him know that they knew he was a pervert and a stalker. The men seemed doubtful and embarrassed. They wouldn't meet anyone's eyes. Any second now they would wake up and begin to rally around the male accused. I had to stop it before it got started.

"Tom, you have been positively identified in front of witnesses. You can be convicted of entering Alice Mae's residence and stalking her. I'm advising her to apply for a restraining order tomorrow. If you are seen within fifty yards of this residence, you will be arrested and tried under the new stalking act. I suggest you leave immediately."

Amid soft mutterings and glares, he rose and faced Alice Mae.

"I want you to tell me you don't really believe this garbage and that animal that slobbered all over me. What's gotten into you? Why didn't you ask me if I was coming over uninvited, and if I was following you, huh?"

His cheeks and ears had reddened with anger. She rose from her seat and glared at him.

"I believe the dog and will get a restraining order tomorrow, or Monday, if I have to wait until then. I want you out of my house, and don't you ever speak to me again!"

She was trembling but resolute. Tom stumbled past her without another word and left, slamming the door behind him.

I've been known to clear a room pretty fast working alone, but Bobby Lee and I working in tandem have to hold the record. Within ten minutes it was only Alice Mae, Bobby Lee, and me.

I helped her clean up the party debris and walked her around the house to spend the night with her mother. I told her I would go with her to secure a restraining order, and she said she would call me if she needed me.

I arrived home at a little after ten, and saw that Jasmine was home and had company. I counted the vehicles as Bobby Lee and I walked from the garage to the back porch. A pickup with a cab over camper, another pickup, a small motor home, and two cars. I smiled ruefully. She was having a party and I wasn't invited. Her college friends, no doubt. I wouldn't have fit in anyway. Six years is a large gap when you're still in school. Her friends and I would have little in common to talk about.

My leg was back to normal. I still had a slight limp when I was tired. It was from the deep bruising, so that meant no dancing. I wasn't missing much. I still resented not being asked. I wished she would be sensible; I was tired of this feud. I wanted her back as my friend. I sighed as I gathered my stacks of papers and headed for the bedroom. I would read another file tonight. Tomorrow I would bite the bullet, apologize to Jasmine, and get our relationship back on track.

This plan buoyed my spirits and I read for the next two hours. I decided I could eliminate Cynthia Cancannon Ross, Steven's wife, for mostly the same reasons that I had crossed him off my list of suspects. She also had a very good alibi for the twenty-four hours in question, and also didn't have time enough to travel so far. I crossed off number nine on my list and turned out my light. After consideration of all the facts, I was pleased to be able to shorten the list. *And then there were eight.*

29

"She's Gone, Gone, Gone"

October 22, Sunday, Noon

I put my feet on the desk and sat tilted backward at a precarious angle. I rubbed my eyes and looked out the office window at the gorgeous Indian summer day. It was warm with a fresh breeze, a perfect day for a picnic. Unfortunately, I didn't know a soul to call and invite to one. I was feeling impatient with Jasmine. Since I had decided to apologize to her, she hadn't even shown her face this morning. It must have been a late, late night last night. I just wanted to get the apology behind me and move on.

I walked out to the back porch and stared at her stairs, hoping my apparent interest would make her appear at the window. No such luck. I continued across the courtyard and found Wayne and Donnie Ray playing computer games in Wayne's office.

"Have either of you seen Jasmine this morning?"

They shook their heads negatively.

"Her car was gone when I went to pick up the papers. I noticed because her garage door was open, and she always keeps it closed." Wayne shrugged. "Maybe she went to church this morning."

"What time did you fetch the papers?"

"A little after six."

"Not hardly. Easter's the only day you go to church before day-break. She must have gone home with some of her party people."

"Party people?" Donnie Ray seemed surprised. "She had a party last night?"

"Yep, they must have come after you two left. I went to the bedroom to read in bed, and didn't hear them leave."

"We didn't see them. We came home at one, and all the lights were off." Wayne looked thoughtful. "Did anything else happen yesterday, another quarrel or something?"

"No, Wayne, our relationship was the same as Friday and all of last week. She'll be back this afternoon."

I sounded more confident than I felt. My stomach churned.

Back in the office I settled with my tall stack of papers, and read every scrap of information on the third name on my list, Cathy Cancannon Kingsley, Bethesda, Maryland, who had been home alone. Feeling hungry, I made two sandwiches out of the small beef pot roast that Rosie had brought over yesterday, and ate them while I read.

After four hours, I had read her entire file and matched the time during the crucial period to her phone calls. There was no way this woman was guilty. She didn't have time to plan and commit a murder. She volunteered for every club, charity, and function in Washington, D.C., plus Bethesda. Her phone bill listed twenty-nine calls she had made during the crucial period, and the detectives had interviewed each recipient. I felt nary a qualm about eliminating her name from the list. *And then there were seven.*

I tried to study Cathy's husband Larry Kingsley's file, but my eyes kept wandering to my watch, and my ears were cocked for the sound of Jasmine's return. I stepped over Bobby Lee's tail. He was stretched out full length and snoring softly. I wandered to the window and gazed with unseeing eyes in the direction of Jasmine's staircase.

I went back to my chair and tried to talk myself out of what I had decided to do as I pulled open the shallow middle drawer of my desk. I reached way in the back, searching for Jasmine's spare key to her apartment. She had left it with me when she moved in. My finger located the cold metal object and I drew it out slowly.

If she comes home and catches you, you'll be sorry! My mind warned. *Shut up!* I admonished. I detoured to the kitchen and took two Alka-Seltzers.

I marched up the stairs, held the screen door open, inserted the key, and hesitated. I took a deep breath and opened the door.

"Jasmine?" I called softly. I didn't expect an answer. I was several steps into the room when I paused. Jasmine didn't live here anymore. The furniture was still here because it belonged to me. She had picked out the style she liked. All the other things she had added in the past two years, a Tiffany-like table lamp, pictures, tossed pillows, and her glass figurines, were absent.

I started humming an aimless tune under my breath as I toured the other rooms. I couldn't remember the title or any of the lyrics. I hummed a few bars over and over as I noticed small details. She had changed the kitchen cabinet's shelf paper. The last one I had noticed had been blue. This new pattern was yellow and brightened the small, empty, clean, and sterile surroundings. I moved to the bathroom. The shower curtain of small lavender flowers was also new. I guess she didn't have time to wash the old one. The medicine cabinet was empty except for a small blue bowl of potpourri. The dried petals' attar of roses filled the compact room with its pleasant scent.

The tiny bedroom looked larger with only the white mattress covers and white mini-blinds. There was no color in the room. With the drapes, matching bedspread, and the pictures missing, it looked barren and deserted. I locked the door and left.

Downstairs, Wayne and Donnie Ray were feeding puppies when I walked into the grooming room. I couldn't look them in the eye and deliver my news. I picked up a squirmy bundle of wrinkles and spoke in his ear as I was looking at nothing on the far wall.

"Jasmine has moved out, bag and baggage. I'm sure she won't be back. Wayne, you'll have to adjust for her absence the best you can.

Give me her sweeps and her puppy feedings. Donnie Ray, you'll have to assume her training schedule for now."

I returned the puppy to the cart, turned on my heel, and got out of there. I couldn't bear to hear how they felt about me. I knew they would blame me for driving her away. I would have to face them, but I wanted it to happen later, not this minute. I had to call Hank. He would get her back for me.

I reached his answering machine at home, and left an urgent request for him to call me ASAP. I had a pan of store-bought biscuits in the oven, and was nuking the beef roast when he returned my call at six-thirty.

"I need a favor, Hank," I began.

"I didn't think you were calling to discuss world events," he retorted. "What now?"

"I need you to find Jasmine for me."

I heard a thud, and knew he had dropped his booted feet from his desktop to the floor.

"Jasmine is missing? Since when? What happened?"

"She had some people over Saturday evening. I guess they helped her pack. I went over about one this afternoon, and all her things are gone. You have to help me get her back. You can put out an all-points bulletin on her, can't you? Find her for me, and I will talk her into coming back."

"Let me see if I understand what you're saying," he said, in a more relaxed tone of voice. "She packed and left on her own, no one forced her, and it was her decision to leave?"

"Yes. How long do you think it will take to find her?"

"I ought to come over there and beat on your bottom! You put it like she had been abducted and scared the hell outta me!"

"You're wasting time, Hank. She's been gone——"

"Shut up and listen!" He sounded furious. "You ran her off with your highfalutin' ways and acting like you're always right, when you aren't, more than half the time. If she calls me, and I hope she will,

I'll tell her the same thing. I'm glad she's had enough of you, and I wish her every success. She's smart, and too good for you. Now you'll know what it feels like to be dumped and deserted."

I held the receiver tightly and let him have his say. I didn't try to stop him or object to any of his remarks.

"Are you finished?" My voice was polite.

"I'm surprised that you let me finish. Why didn't you hang up, like you usually do, when you don't want to hear what I'm saying?"

"I didn't hang up because everything you said is true. I should have apologized to her when the incident first happened, but I didn't, so I have to live with the aftermath. I also want to apologize to you, Hank. I've treated you real shabby."

"Ah, Jo Beth, you're making me feel sorry for you when I should be mad. Don't be trying to sweet-talk me."

"I'm not doing that, Hank. Honest. I know I have been hanging on the fence too long, trying to keep you in reserve and not being able to make up my mind. This isn't right. I hope we can be good friends, Hank, for the rest of our lives, and not just because you're the sheriff, and can do favors for me—"

"Hold it right there!" He suddenly sounded hoarse. "Don't say the words that I think you're gonna say. String me along, lie to me, or just let it alone for a while, but please . . . don't end it."

"Don't make it any harder than it is, Hank. I want you for a friend. I'm not the one for you. Find a nice woman and have lots of babies. I wish you a happy life."

"This rollercoaster romance, on and off and on again, hasn't been a picnic. I want you to search your heart and be very sure, Jo Beth. Last call for love, fidelity, and adoration for all the rest of my allotted days."

"I'm sure, Hank."

"I'm shaking like a leaf," he admitted, half in sorrow and half in jest. "You're my friend for life. So long, kid."

"Good-bye, Hank." He wasn't the only one shaking. My hand was far from steady as I replaced the phone.

30

"Keep on Keeping on"

October 23, Monday, 8:30 A.M.

I felt more organized this morning than I really was. I was Ms. Efficiency personified. The computer entry tray was bare. Wayne and I had met at seven, and my schedule for the week was listed in my daily planner. I had toured the kennel and had a nice chat with Harvey, my vet. We agreed that the dogs were healthy and the masterpiece litter were gaining nicely and looking like champions already. We were kidding each other. It would be months before their stance, bone structure, and even their amount of wrinkles could be judged and evaluated. We were literally whistling in the dark, hoping that by saying they were perfect often enough, it would become gospel.

I decided to beard the lion in its den. I dialed Susan's number.

"Am I still on your list of people that you don't talk to, or am I forgiven?" I asked contritely when she answered.

"At this stage of my life, I can't be too choosy with my short list of friends, so you're back in my good graces. How've you been?"

"Do you know of anyone who needs to rent a small apartment?"

"I can always count on you to keep me supplied with news. You know how I hate facing Monday mornings without plenty of weekend gossip. Whose apartment is involved, who left, and why?"

"Mine, Jasmine, and because I never apologized to her."

"Oh God," she moaned softly. "You really tore it this time!"

"Yes, indeedy," I agreed.

"Is she really and truly gone, as in 'Gone, gone, gone'? or did she leave something essential that she has to come back for, thus giving you a chance to talk her into coming back?"

Susan had just put a name on the tune I had been incessantly humming since I had viewed Jasmine's empty apartment. Knowing the title might help me erase it from my mind.

"She didn't leave even a dust bunny, and she is 'Gone, gone, gone,' for good, and she won't be back."

"Stop sounding so casual about it all," Susan said. "I know you're hurting. I don't feel so hot, either. She was my friend too, you know. We'll get her back. Have you called Hank? Has he talked to her? Do you think he knows where she is?"

"Crying now wouldn't do much good, so I'm trying to keep a stiff upper lip. Hank won't lift a finger. He says he hasn't heard from her, and I believe him. And as long as we're on the subject of Hank, I should tell you that I kissed him off for good yesterday over the telephone. Tacky, but effective. Now he's just a friend."

"Jesus." She was silent for several seconds. "I still had hopes you two would get back together. You're sure?"

"Absolutely."

"That sounds final. You and I will find Jasmine. Do you know any of her instructors or classmates?"

"Not a one."

"Well, I do. I have a friend that has or had her in one of his classes. I do a lot of ordering of special books for him, and he doesn't always buy them. He owes me. I'll call him. Maybe she hasn't dropped her classes, and she's still in town."

"Thanks, Susan."

"She's my friend too. Remember?"

"I meant thanks for being my friend and for forgiving me again and again when I screw up."

"You are my forever friend," she said staunchly before hanging up. "And don't you ever forget it!"

What can I say? Some days I feel blessed. This was one of them.

I called Chet and told him to send info.

The fax machine rang soon after, and I jerked with surprise. I rolled my chair over close enough to read who was sending a message and settled back when I saw it was Chet from the detective agency in Washington, D.C.

I picked up the first completed sheet, and read that it was page one of thirty-three. I lost interest. He hadn't discovered anything new. If he had, it would have been one page for maximum effect. He was only giving me another summary of facts already reported, while trying to look productive and worthy of their hefty fee. I'd read it later.

At a little after four I was back home from two industrial building drug searches that we visited two and three times a month. Nothing unusual had been found. A few home-rolled marijuana cigarettes were tossed in the wide aisles, which the users called "no-man's land." A tin of Copenhagen snuff revealed several rocks of crack. When I showed the manager what Tolstoy had found discarded in the aisles, he was ecstatic.

"Now we can arrest someone. I'm was getting tired of you finding drugs and not being able to prosecute. Good work!"

"We still are unable to prosecute," I said evenly.

I sure wish these guys would listen more closely when I present the facts about what constitutes evidence. I knew he was going to be unhappy with what I had to tell him and also knew he would want to blame me.

"The snuff tin was on the floor in open sight. Tolstoy didn't find it in anyone's possession."

"Yea, but there will be fingerprints on the can. That proves who is guilty!"

"I'm afraid not," I said with a sigh.

"Why not?" He now sounded belligerent.

"In the first place, the District Attorney won't present it to a grand jury. And even if he did and got an indictment, he wouldn't get a conviction because of reasonable doubt. I can hear his lawyer now. 'Sure my client dips snuff, and his fingerprints will be on every can he finishes and discards in the trash. Anyone can pick up an empty can from a public trash receptacle, or from any of the large drums that are available in his place of employment.' That's reasonable doubt."

"That's bull," he said angrily. "What is America coming to? Why am I paying you each month if you can't convict them?"

It had taken an additional fifteen minutes to soothe his ruffled feathers and pump some hope into him for possible future arrests. Our visits were a deterrent, and they tried to second-guess when we would search. They could get sloppy and be caught. They could also stick their hand inside the machinery where it didn't belong while under the influence of drugs and get pulled in and pulverized. A machine operator who used drugs was dangerous to himself and all those around him.

My answering machine held three messages. Alice Mae Petrie informed me that the judge had signed the restraining order that her lawyer had prepared. She thanked me again for solving her problem.

I hoped for her sake that I had. From personal experience I didn't hold much trust in restraining orders, but hers had to be in place if Tom continued to stalk her. I mentally wished her well. Maybe the scent machine evidence would never be needed. It could have frightened him enough that he wouldn't be stupid and continue to harass her.

Thinking of the devil brought Tom near. The next call was from him. He tried to sound indignant and righteous. He warned me that he had consulted an attorney, and if he heard of any rumor I started about him, he would take action against me. I knew he was lying. The first thing any attorney would advise would be that he was not to contact me either by phone or mail. Why hire a lawyer if you're not going to follow his advice? His posturing didn't worry me.

The third call was a big surprise. It was my handsome helicopter pilot, Randall Finch. He said he wanted to talk, and would try again later in the day.

I couldn't call him back. I could only wait for him to call me. My thoughts were scattered. I really had no firm opinion. Part of me wanted him to be calling because he was interested in me, and another part was having serious thoughts about the fact that I was investigating him and all the Cancannons.

I had been ignoring all clippings about Celia Cancannon and Rand. I had met them and wanted to wait and see if I uncovered a possible motive or murderer before I considered them. I knew that both of them were available during the time that Amelia had been snatched. They were my prime suspects, but I wanted the easier alibis checked out and verified before I started concentrating on them.

I stacked the hefty thirty-three-page fax in front of me, and began attaching each page to the correct suspect's dossier. I didn't read any of them while sorting; I'd tackle them after supper.

I nuked a Lean Cuisine of stuffed bell peppers with tomato sauce and tossed a small salad. I was gonna try to eat healthy while waiting for Jasmine's return. I had to get her back, so I was thinking positive. When, not if, she returned, she'd be angry if I had pigged out on junk food and gained weight during her absence.

A few pages into the report, I was reading an agent's surveillance log on Sabrina Cancannon Wilder's husband, Paul Wilder. He was a real estate broker, and had been dining with a woman. Living in Atlanta, he had been close enough that he could have possibly made it to the island, kidnapped Amelia, and returned in the allotted time frame. His alibi didn't cover all of the period in question, and I thought he was one of the more viable suspects.

The agent had written, "As per your instructions, in the past three days in tailing the subject, I have been overt in letting the subject see me. I have been obvious to the point of seeming foolish and inept. It took him until tonight to realize my continued presence in his life meant he was being followed. He placed his dinner companion (identified in the previous report) in a cab, then walked over to confront me, where I was twelve feet away and watching his every move.

"Subject: 'Why are you following me?'"

"I answered him as you had advised, by telling him the truth.

"Agent: 'My agency has been employed to do a complete study on you because you are a prime suspect in the murder of your wife's aunt. Her estate attorney is footing the bill. We will continue to monitor your every move until the killer is caught.'

"You wanted a detailed description of his appearance and demeanor when I delivered the news. I won't attempt to describe the look on his face, I'll just tell you what he did. He literally jumped for joy, and was so elated he slapped me on my back and pumped my hand in a frenzied handshake. It seems that when he finally tumbled to the fact that he was being followed, he thought it was because he had been engaged in working dinners with the wife of an infamous person who is rumored to be connected. (Identity in previous report.) My personal opinion is that this man is not responsible in any way for the disappearance of the cat or the murder."

I had to laugh. I, too, believed the guy to be innocent after reading about his reaction to the tail. A man guilty of catnapping and murder for profit would not have shown such obvious relief. He would have been afraid that the man following him was lying, and that the investigation had turned up something that he had overlooked or forgotten.

Smiling, I drew my highlighting pen through his name. *And then there were six.*

I glanced at my watch and was surprised to see that it was almost eight. I was on my way to the kitchen for a Coke when the phone rang. I made myself finish my errand before I hurried back to answer. It wouldn't pay to seem too eager. I picked up the receiver after the fourth ring, and just before my voice mail would activate.

"Hello."

"I'm sitting here in Waycross afraid to call you, and afraid not to. Are you still speaking to me?"

I gripped the phone tighter when I recognized Jasmine's voice. I had to swallow before I could speak.

"Oh, Jasmine, I'm so glad you called. I'm going crazy here without you. Come back. Please come back. I'm so sorry I made you leave by being so stupid!"

I was pushing the words out as fast as I could, and it seemed they were taking forever.

"Are you sure?" Her voice seemed muffled.

"Get back here, please. Please come home."

"I'm in Waycross, and I can't drive too fast, I have lots of junk piled on top of the car. It will take me a couple of hours or more—"

"Don't waste any more time, get in the car and drive. Don't go too fast, but don't stop for anything. I'll be here waiting. Okay?"

After I hung up, I put my head in my arms on the desk and bawled like a baby.

31

"All My Chickens Have Come Home to Roost"

October 23, Monday, 8:30 P.M.

After my therapeutic tears, I sat in awe and contemplated Jasmine's call. I realized that I was very lucky that she had had second thoughts. If she had gone further away, unpacked, started looking for employment . . . I knew that each day that passed she would have been emotionally stronger and it would have been more difficult to get in touch.

When the phone rang, my heart leaped into my throat. She had changed her mind! It rang three times before I could find the courage to answer it.

"Please don't say you've changed your mind," I began.

"Hello? Jo Beth? I can barely hear you. What did you say?"

I sagged with relief. Although he sounded like he was speaking through a tin can, I recognized the voice. It was Rand. I had forgotten all about him promising to call back.

"Where are you?" I asked. There was a great deal of static on the line, like a radio station fading in and out.

"In a phone booth in downtown Balsa City with a frayed cord and with what I pray is peanut butter smeared all over the glass enclosure.

I borrowed a car from a friend. I'm driving to your house, should be there in ten minutes."

"Not tonight, Rand. I'm expecting company. Let's make it another night." The noise on the line was getting worse.

"Great. See you in ten minutes!"

"No, Rand, you misunderstood!" I stopped speaking because I was talking into a dead phone. I jiggled the hook, but it didn't change anything. We were disconnected.

Well, let him come. I could visit for a few minutes, and then run him out. It would take Jasmine over two hours to make the trip. It was sixty miles of only two lanes. I knew she would be driving slower because she had a load on top of the vehicle, and if she got behind a slowpoke who was doing thirty-five, it would be difficult to pass. The road had a steady stream of traffic even on a Monday night, up until the wee hours.

I went to the bedroom to change. I decided to wear something more feminine than jeans and a T-shirt. It was all that he had seen me wear. I had the shirt off and my jeans were around my knees when I head the first gate alarm. That had been quick, much sooner than ten minutes. I quickly refastened my jeans and grabbed a heavy new rust-colored T-shirt that I had never worn. I was brushing my frizzy hair when the second alarm sounded. I walked to the back porch with Rudy and Bobby Lee right behind me. When Rand came into view, I received a jolt. The pickup he was driving was decorated with all the symbols of a good ol' redneck from South Georgia. The body of the truck was raised a good five inches, a coon tail was tied to the radio antenna, and there were glittering mud flaps and the obligatory window-tinted Confederate flag on the back window.

I suppressed a smirk as he approached us.

"You borrowed that from a *friend?*"

"Yep, not all Southerners are as touchy as you are. I have a couple of Southern friends."

"Surprise, surprise," I murmured. "Let me introduce you to my roommates. The small one is Rudy, and the big one is Bobby Lee. Shake hands, guys."

I was shocked speechless when Rudy casually raised a paw to Rand, who had squatted before him. He acted as if he had been shaking hands daily since he was a kitten. I could only stare as Rand reached out and rubbed his knuckles under Rudy's chin.

"It's rare to see a such a well-trained cat," Rand commented.

"If you only knew," I said with awe.

I was still having trouble believing what I had seen, that Rudy had actually shaken hands with a stranger. I dropped my hand to Bobby Lee's shoulder, and he stuck out a paw.

Rand rubbed Bobby Lee's ears and leaned closer, and said something that I couldn't hear. Rising, he gave me a warm smile.

"What did you tell him?"

"That he was a lucky dog."

"Uh-huh." Staring into his eyes, I felt uncomfortable. "Where are my manners? Come on in."

I held the screen door until he was inside, then the animals and I followed him in. He stood and surveyed the room slowly, turning so he could see it all. I sat in an armchair and, when I caught his eye, nodded to indicate that he sit opposite me. He remained standing.

"Have long have you lived here?"

"Almost seven years."

"Do the two young men I saw on my earlier visit live here with you?"

"They live in an upstairs apartment to the left of the kennels."

"Are they currently upstairs?"

"I suppose so, I haven't heard them leave." My ears began to tingle. The questions were innocent enough, but I was beginning to feel as if I was being interrogated, not just having a casual conversation.

"Who lives next door?" He nodded his head in the direction of Jasmine's apartment.

My ear tingle was augmented with a flush starting at my neckline and slowly rising to cover my face and creep into my hair. What was with this guy?

"No one." I didn't expand my answer to cover Jasmine's expected arrival. I wanted to know where he was going with this.

"I thought you had a female associate who lived here, at least that was what I was told."

The ear tingle increased, although the blush had faded. His question had been quick and sharp. I shifted in the chair, and crossed my leg.

"I did until Saturday night," I said smoothly. "That's when she moved out. Are we playing twenty questions?"

"Sorry," he said, giving me a boyish grin and sliding into the chair in front of me. He didn't sit back relaxed, but perched on the edge of the seat with his hands clasped between his knees

"I did sound odd, didn't I? I wanted to make sure that you would be free to go out tonight for a little while. I have something I want to show you. It will only take a few minutes."

"I'm sorry, Rand, I tried to tell you over the phone when you called, but you didn't hear me because of a lousy connection. I can't go anywhere tonight. I have someone coming over later."

Rand tipped his head and regarded me somberly.

"When's he due?"

"Within the hour."

Don't ask me why I lied. I was relying on my ear tingle. It has fooled me a few times, but generally its presence signals that something isn't quite right. Mostly I feel it when the motor doesn't run smooth in the van, and I anticipate major surgery will be required on its innards. It also appeared last month when the refrigerator added a strange *ping* whenever the fan motor came on. I joke about intuition, but I pay attention every time I experience it.

I stood quickly and stepped out of his reach, and forced a laugh.

"Sorry, I have to use the restroom, be right back."

I took off down the hall, with Bobby Lee right behind me.

"You silly boy," I said cheerfully to Bobby Lee, "I don't need you along!"

I was talking to cover my steps. I rattled the doorknob once, pulled it closed, then released the knob and left the door standing open. Moving quickly, I tiptoed silently into my bedroom, and eased open the nightstand drawer. I grabbed the .32, opened the cylinder, and fed six rounds in the chamber one by one, trying not to let them clink together as I handled them.

I stuffed the small gun in the back of my jeans and rested it against my lower spine. God knows the jeans were tight enough that it wouldn't slip. I pulled the heavy shirt over the slight bulge to hide it.

I walked gingerly back to the bathroom, flushed, and rattled the knob again. We went back into the office a lot slower than when we left it.

"Where were we?" I inquired good-naturedly as I returned to my seat.

Rand was sitting in the same chair, but he had slid back in its depths and crossed his legs. He didn't look threatening at all. I began to feel silly. Maybe my sneaky trip to arm myself hadn't been necessary. I relaxed in the chair, very aware of the cold steel on my skin and the pressure on my backside.

"I was telling you that I have something I want you to see. I want you to come with me. Ten minutes there, five minutes to see it, and ten minutes back. Will you come?"

I checked his voice and his lazy smile. I knew right then that I wouldn't get in a car with this man if he was the last man on earth and owned the only car that functioned.

I returned his smile. "Sorry, not tonight."

He shrugged. "How's the investigation going? Imagine our surprise when Master John Jason Jackson told us that you would be handling a private investigation into Alyce's murder, independent from the official one."

"We?" I raised one brow.

"There I go grouping myself with the Cancannons, and everybody knows I'm not part of the clan. I am, however, one of the people named in the will, and it was that *we* I meant."

"You're also one of the prime suspects in her murder."

"Prime? Why do you say prime? I'm no more of a suspect that any of the other nine. What gave you that idea?"

He had managed to sound indignant. I laughed at his expression. This is one of the reasons I wanted to be a problem-solver. These conversations charged with innuendoes are right up my alley.

"Come on, you were on the scene and don't have an airtight alibi."

"Don't you think I'm smart enough if I knew I would need an alibi, meaning if I snatched the cat and killed Alyce, that I would have a good one in place? The fact that I don't have a perfect one should point to my innocence, not guilt."

"Uh-huh. What about Celia's alibi? Are you saying her lack of an alibi means she's innocent also?"

"Celia doesn't mean squat to me. She's not my problem. Neither are the others."

"Really? That's strange. It's obvious that she adores you. You're gonna abandon her?"

"Abandon her, what do you mean by that? She's nothing to me. How many times do I have to tell you?"

His voice had risen with each sentence uttered. He squirmed in his seat and seemed agitated. I decided I had pushed him as far as I cared to tonight.

"Relax. I'm just trying to fit everyone's relationships that are germane into the proper prospective. Sorry if I upset you." I made a show of staring at my watch and producing a frown. "I wish we could continue this conversation, but I'm running late. My company will be here soon."

I rose briskly to make my point. I wanted him out of here. My ears were not only tingling; they felt like they were on fire. The flush had returned to my face. My eyes were lowered, and I was straightening the waistband of my new T-shirt. I saw him beginning to rise from his seat, and I turned to escort him to the door when he struck.

Before I knew what was happening, he caught me during my turn and wrapped his left arm around my neck, and with my right arm behind me, he was forcing it upward to a painful height. I rose on my toes, trying to ease the pain. I was attempting to arch my back to keep his body away from mine. I didn't want him to feel the hard object lodged near my spine. He snickered.

"Ready for a little ride?"

32

"Riding the Terror Train"

October 23, Monday, 10:00 P.M.

I was completely powerless, and it's hard to think while someone's trying to separate your right arm from your shoulder. I decided to act like a helpless female, which was exactly what I was.

"Please . . . Stop . . . You're hurting me! Please . . ."

While I was giving an Oscar performance, he was forcing me into the kitchen. It was essential for him to keep me on my feet so I could help him navigate, so the pressure on my arm eased somewhat.

"You got any duct tape?"

He was breathing heavily through his mouth. He had expended a lot of effort moving a reluctant one hundred-thirty-pounder, which should have given me an edge, but unfortunately my own breath was more labored than his. I felt like I had gone a round with Ali.

After two upward yanks on my arm, I told him where the duct tape was kept. He forced me to my knees, put a knee in my chest, and stretched me out flat. I knew my spine was splintered by the gun that was between the floor and me. Hope died as he brought my arms forward and began taping them in front. I had already mentally practiced flexing my wrists bound behind me, so I wouldn't drop the gun when I fished it out and shot him dead. Scratch that plan.

He pulled me up and wrestled me back into the office, prudently keeping me more or less by his side. Our thoughts were on the same subject. I longed to get a strong kick in his nether region and he was determined to deter me. He pushed me into a chair and stood close, his legs hugging mine.

"You try to scream for your boys, and I'll gag you with my socks."

"I promise I won't scream."

I meant it; it would be wasted energy. Wayne was deaf, and Donnie Ray's radio earplugs appeared surgically implanted during his waking hours. There was no one to hear.

He paced restlessly around the room, keeping me within view at all times. Time was passing and I knew that Jasmine would walk right into this nightmare if he kept delaying whatever he was gonna do. I had to do something.

"Why are you doing this?"

"All I wanted to do was take you for a little ride, introduce you to my new buddy, but no. You wouldn't go willingly. All this hassle is your fault!"

"Well, now that you've explained, I think I'd like to go. I like surprises."

"Now you decide to go," he jeered. "Why didn't you do that a while ago? Then I wouldn't have missed the first meet. You women are all alike!"

I was filing away his skimpy clues and trying to decide how to get him moving.

"I gather that you arranged a later date to meet this buddy? Tell you what. Why don't we drive around while we're waiting for the time to pass? Let's go."

I stood. He was behind me, and I couldn't see his face to gauge his reaction to my suggestion. I was pulled backward and shoved back into the seat.

"Sit and shut up!"

"Listen," I said, trying to judge his reaction to my inability to keep quiet. "Why do this the hard way? If you move me one foot from this chair while I'm bound and without my permission, it's kidnapping. You're an intelligent man, and know I'm telling the truth. Why risk something going wrong and serving a long prison sentence? You can avoid this by simply cutting this tape off and escorting me to your car. Surely you can see I'm sincere.

"You haven't threatened me with a weapon or told me that I was going to be hurt in any way. Let's just get out of here, and on our way to meet your friend. I'll hush now and let you think it over. What have you got to lose?"

I tried to read his expression as he listened, and I thought I saw apprehension and fear flit across his face. He opened his mouth and laughed. Guess not.

He spoke slowly and seemed to be enjoying himself. Some men get off on having a woman beg for favors when she is in a precarious position. I couldn't tell if he was one of them.

"Jo Beth, you are something else. All you have said is true. I would be wise to listen, if I was only taking you to meet my friend, having a few drinks, and bringing you back before midnight, but it's a little more intense than that. Let this be a lesson to you, that you really shouldn't stick your nose where it doesn't belong. What do you think your big dog will do if I drag you out of here?"

"What he's doing right now, sleeping. I could be kicking and screaming and calling out to him, and he wouldn't do a blasted thing!"

I tried to sound disgusted that Bobby Lee wouldn't be any help. I must have convinced him. He gave me a confident smile.

"You don't have a clue what's in store for you, do you?"

"Why don't you enlighten me, so we'll both know?"

I said it quietly and without rancor. My chest felt tight, and I didn't want to explore his clues. They were too scary.

"My new friend is your old friend. Technically speaking, he was at one time. Sure you don't want three guesses?"

I couldn't speak. My chest turned to ice and I struggled to breathe in a lung full of air.

"If you mean my ex-husband, Bubba Sidden, you will be guilty of conspiracy to murder one. You'll get the chair!"

My words were whispered, but I was proud I managed to tell him the crime he would be committing, and the punishment. At least I let him know *I knew his fate,* if he were caught. I felt numb. The icy feeling was spreading into my limbs and up into my head. I rested my head on the chair back and closed my eyes. I wanted to sleep.

"Don't be so melodramatic!" he said, seemingly enjoying himself. "I can understand that you don't look forward to a beating. It'll be a few broken bones, which is only assault, and I won't be the one wielding the bat. You are as healthy as a horse, for God's sake. It won't kill you!"

I roused from my stupor when his words penetrated my brain. Might as well give it a go.

"You idiot," I said, temporarily silenced by a wide yawn. I didn't open my eyes. "You call up . . . You call up the editor of the *Dunston County Daily Times.* Tell him that someone told you that Bubba would kill Jo Beth, if he can get his hands on her. Say you're a friend of his, and don't believe it. Fred will set you straight and won't ask any questions. What have you got to lose but the rest of your life?"

"You're lying," he yelled.

"Like hell I am," I said without emphasis.

I raised my head and watched him as he thought it over. I saw resolve and the tiny negative motion of his head and knew I had failed.

"I'm going to the kitchen, and watching you every second. You move out of that chair, you will be sorry!"

"I'm too scared to run," I whimpered.

I counted several seconds, then leaned my head around the chair back to see what he was doing. He was coming toward me with a pair of scissors in his hand. I screwed up my face and started whining.

"Don't hurt me . . . Please . . . I was just looking . . . Please!"

"Shut up," he said with contempt. "I liked you better when you acted like a bitch! Dreading that beating, I guess. I'm going to cut the

228

tape off your hands. You try anything, anything at all, I'll stab you with these, okay?"

"Please, please don't . . ."

I lowered my lids so he couldn't read the expression on my face as he pulled and whacked at the tape. I was elated. I didn't know his reasoning, but I was hoping he no longer considered me a flight risk. I would be easier to move without the secured wrists, and he could deny any wrongdoing up to minute he handed me over to Bubba. He might have been listening to what I said. I didn't care what made him change his mind, all I cared about was that I had a chance to get free.

He ripped the cut tape from my wrists, taking all the hairs that were caught underneath, and several small hunks of hide and flesh. I'm allergic to the glue in duct tape, and most other types of stickums. I flinched and gave little jumps and grimaced, but I didn't feel a thing. I was so pumped with adrenaline, I could have floated on air out the door and into the borrowed truck.

He had me drawn close to his side with a strong grip on my arm. I leaned my weight against him, and pretended weakness. He had to assist me into the truck because of the extra five inches from the ground. I sat there and didn't attempt to close the door. He was halfway around the truck when he saw I hadn't closed it. He came back and slammed it harder than necessary, mumbling something under his breath.

I had been clenching and unclenching my fingers from the second he cut the tape. They were fine and would react as fast as they always did. I saw myself reaching for the hidden gun, and shooting Rand as he climbed into the truck. I had plenty of time and knew I was capable of pulling the trigger to save my life. I sat there calmly and didn't move a muscle. I didn't like the thoughts that were running through my mind.

I could end all the uncertainty tonight. It was within my power to shoot Bubba and Rand, and not be censured. There was the tape with Rand's fingerprints and my bloody wrists. A pair of my scissors was in his pocket. I banished the thoughts, but they came back quickly, settling in and assuring me that I could do this, that I had the right to do this. I shook them off.

As Rand climbed into the truck, the front gate alarm sounded. It startled Rand.

"What was that?" He must have been playing his radio with the windows rolled up in the truck when he arrived; it had rung then too.

"The front gate," I whined. "If it's my boyfriend coming in the drive, let me get rid of him. I don't want him hurt. If it's my maid, let me leave her orders, or she will alert the others, and he still might get hurt. Please? I'll take the beating."

"I'll stab either one of them if you get cute!"

"Oh, I won't, I won't."

"Start up and meet whoever it is in the drive. The light is dimmer there."

I was surprised that he was following my orders. Either I had totally convinced him that I was jelly, or he was unsure of his own reaction.

When I saw that it was Jasmine coming up the drive, I put my hand tentatively over his on the wheel.

"Dim your lights, and slow to a crawl. Stop the truck where the windows are together. It won't take more than two or three sentences."

"Don't make me use the scissors!" He dimmed his lights and rolled down his window.

"Oh, I won't," I whispered.

Rand and Jasmine stopped when their windows were even with each other. I leaned forward so she could see me in the dim light.

"Jasmine, it's Miz Sidden. You're late again! I've got a good mind to tell Hank! If my boyfriend comes, tell him I don't know when I'll be back!"

I could see Jasmine's eyes widen as I began talking. I held my breath.

"Yes'em, I's sorry I's late. I's tell 'em."

Her voice had been shrill and she had sounded scared. Absolutely perfect. I let out the breath I had been holding and started listening to the voices, as Rand drove the terror train toward Bubba.

"You know he's gonna keep going 'til he succeeds in killing you," my mind asserted.

"Don't do it, my dear, it would be very difficult to live with, in fact, I don't believe you could. You'll be confessing before New Year's!" My heart was practicing her usual bleeding-heart routine.

My gut rumbled. *"I need some fizzy stuff. You two have got me upset with your bickering!"*

"Shut up, you guys! Leave me alone!"

The voices ended. They could tell I meant business. They knew what I was planning. I was being delivered to the slaughter, willingly. I could have stopped the trip half a dozen times in the last fifteen minutes. I was gonna take this get-out-of-jail-free card and blow the sucker away.

33

"Who's Doing What to Whom?"

October 23, Monday, Midnight

Rand drove with confidence. He didn't hesitate on turns and seemed to be heading in a southeasterly direction. If he knew where he was going, he was using the back streets well to get there. He was staying off all the main roads. I didn't know that he knew Balsa City at street level. He must have been here several times to drive so effortlessly in the maze of small suburban streets lined with rows of houses that were mostly dark at this hour.

Bypassing the main part of town, he worked his way over near Johnson's Landing, pulled off in a small lot with a turnaround, shut off the engine, and killed the lights.

I removed my arm from the door panel, slid my hand behind my back, and closed my fingers around the gun. I didn't want to be surprised by any sudden move, from him or an unexpected visitor sneaking up to the window. I sat and listened to the occasional *ping* of the hot engine cooling, cicadas in the brush, and a lonesome grunt of a bullfrog in a drainage ditch a foot from the right wheels.

Neither of us spoke. I don't know why he was keeping quiet, but I didn't want my voice to cover the small rustlings that would signal a clandestine approach. After several minutes Rand turned on the cab light, checked his watch, cranked up, and pulled back on the road. Killing time, or checking to see if someone was following? Whatever, he seemed content to drive slower. He turned onto a paved area in front of the old Bleeker warehouses that had been abandoned years ago.

Turning left, he drove into a small alley between the two rusted tin structures and pulled up to a double door that was closed. He gave a single tap on the horn button.

Adrenaline surged through my veins and my knees felt weak. The door started slowly sliding open with assorted creaks and groans. There were absolutely no traffic sounds, although I knew we were only two blocks from Highway 301. Rand pulled slowly into the inky blackness and I shut my eyes, hoping to build up some night vision. When the truck stopped moving I opened them to see a single shaded bulb suspended from a high rafter shedding a dim light on the gray concrete floor. The darkness outside of the dim cone of light felt cold and empty.

My bare arms were covered with chill bumps. Rand opened his door and alighted, and walked forward. I eased open my door after a careful 360-degree scan, and dropped lightly to the floor. I placed both hands under my T-shirt in the back and ran them just inside my jeans. I thought both arms would look more natural than just one.

"Yo, Rand!" rang out from the darkness. It seemed to quiver and bounce in the cavernous space. I spread my legs slightly, so I could swivel easier, and tried to remember which direction the now-echoing voice had came from. I took a quick peek at Rand, but he hadn't changed position. His head hadn't turned and he continued to face the space in front of the truck, so I did likewise.

"Brought me the bitch and almost on schedule!" This blast came from behind the truck. I turned without haste to see a parody of my first love step into the light. This travesty was a disgusting sight of bulging ropy muscles that looked grotesque on his six-foot frame, beer-keg thighs straining against their denim restraints, with an impossibly tiny waist between the two abnormalities. His hair was a prison bleach job, yellowish-orange shocks of dried-out corn shucks falling to his shoulders. Both arms were twisted snakes of sinew and muscle. His right hand held a bat.

I shuddered with distaste. The unformed boyish face I had married fourteen years ago had gained creases and rough-looking pitted skin adorned with crudely carved tattoos. Twin daggers, one on each cheek. Could he possibly think he was handsome?

He could. "See what you been missing?"

My mind searched for an explanation of his weird looks and could only guess that maybe he had tried the forbidden fruit and was now wired for both AC and DC. It was the only answer I could think of at the moment.

He swaggered toward Rand, putting the width and bulk of the truck between us. I was glad to get them closer together; it had been a strain trying to keep an eye on both of them while they were twenty feet apart.

Bubba spoke under his breath to Rand. I couldn't make out Bubba's mumble, and only caught the last of Rand's answer. ". . . leaving now."

"Not yet!" Bubba spoke sharply. "You haven't been paid yet."

He moved his bat under his left arm and reached back for his wallet. Neither one of them were looking at me. It was as if they had forgotten me. I could have faded back into the darkness, or made a break for the door. I didn't do either. I stood rooted in place, a yard from the truck door, and watched them both across the hood of the truck.

Bubba slid a sheath of money out, and Rand looked uncomfortable. I couldn't make out the denomination of the bills. I wondered what my capture and delivery was worth to Bubba. Five hundred? A thousand? Rand was protesting.

"No need, no need." He raised both hands in front of him as he swiveled his head. ". . . wanted . . . way . . . also."

I wished they would quit mumbling. Did he possibly mean he

wanted me out of the way also? From what I saw, I would guess yes. So . . . that meant that I was investigating him and his past couldn't stand to be scrutinized, or was it possible he was the one who had snatched Amelia and murdered Alyce? I couldn't think about Rand now, he was the lesser of two evils. I had to concentrate on Bubba.

"Listen, I was for this one hundred percent!" My head spoke nervously. *"Now I'm not so sure. What if they both want you dead? Are you capable of killing both of them?"*

"It won't come to that! You're the one that gave me the idea in the first place. Are you chickening out?"

"Not exactly. I just didn't count on Rand interfering and being present when you shoot Bubba. You are *still planning on shooting him? Huh?"*

"He won't. Trust me. Rand will take off at the first opportunity."

"But what if he doesn't?"

"Hush! I can't think when you're nagging at me!"

"You are taking the money," Bubba said, with cold resolve steeling his voice. "You brought her here, and you'll be paid! That way you will keep your mouth shut because you'll be just as guilty as I am when I kill the bitch!"

He punctuated his speech by rubbing his left hand back and forth on the smooth surface of the bat. His action was slow and deliberate and quite mesmerizing. I followed the movement of his hand and wondered woodenly if death was waiting in the wings to take just me, just him, or both of us.

Bubba's face lit up with a grin displayed from ear to ear. He took a step closer to Rand, who hastily stepped backward to compensate for Bubba's advance. He looked terrified.

"Maybe I should do both of you, make it a doubleheader. That way I won't have to worry about you squealing."

I shook my head to clear it, taking a deep breath.

"Hey, you bastard! What's this talk about killing! Haven't you learned anything from all those years in prison?"

As usual, I didn't know when to keep quiet. They both stared at me.

Baiting Bubba was akin to grabbing a wild bull by the horns, but I was tired of standing on the sidelines sweating the outcome of tonight. I was psyched and ready.

"Just hold on there, tootsie!" Bubba yelled, his mouth releasing the rictus of his deadly grin. "Don't be so impatient. I'll get to you in a minute!"

Bubba's head jerked back to stare at the spot that Rand had been occupying before he decided to run like a stripped ape. We both listened to his fading footfalls, Bubba cursing with frustration, while I smiled at my small victory. I had gotten Rand out of the picture without bloodshed. Neither one of us wanted a witness at this last confrontation, I was sure.

"See what you did?" Bubba screamed. "Now I'll have to go looking for him. You've messed up my life for the last time, bitch!"

"Freeze!" shouted a familiar voice.

I couldn't believe this was happening. I turned my head quickly and saw Jasmine step into the cone of light, bracing her gun with both hands, correctly positioned, and aiming it steadily at my ex-husband.

Oh shit! I just had time to remember that her revolver hadn't been left in her empty apartment. She had kept it for her journey, I suppose. I wanted to yawn from the tension of the moment, but just then time turned into slow motion. I began my mad dash to get around the truck to get in front of Jasmine. I didn't want her killing him, it would be the worst thing that could happen to her now, and I didn't want him attacking her. My bullets had to enter him from the *front* to successfully claim I shot him in fear of my life.

God, why couldn't I run? My knees were pumping and I could feel my harsh breath leaving my lips, but it was like I floated around the back of the truck.

Jasmine was still pointing the gun at Bubba when I came up behind her. Too slow, too slow. Bubba was in full stride and bringing the bat around in a roundhouse swing, less than six feet away.

"Nooo!" I shouted. I had time to hear it echo in the dark open empty spaces and up to the faraway high-pitched roof. Moving dreamily, I brushed effortlessly against Jasmine and sent her falling softly to the right like a downy feather. Off balance, I took my time raising the gun with my right hand. I knew at this moment that the rest of my life would be changed forever.

I wished that Tom Selph, dead these past nine months, could have seen my aim. He had taught me how to shoot at the county firing range. We had never been buddies. Hank had insisted that Tom was the best shot on the force and made Tom spend his time and effort so I would be prepared with the knowledge I needed.

"Hold it steady, and squeeze, until the chamber is empty," he had drummed into my head when I had pulled up the muzzle with each shot.

"*Thanks, Tom,*" I breathed silently. "*You would have been proud of your student. I placed all six in the chest at point-blank range.*"

It was done. I had deliberately murdered my ex-husband, Buford Sidden Jr., and the only emotion that I felt was enormous relief that it was over.

34

"The Investigation Is Ongoing"

October 24, Tuesday, 1:00 A.M.

The bullets didn't stop Bubba's forward motion. He hung there above us for an incredibly long time, it seemed, before he toppled toward us like a fallen oak. He landed on top of us, as if he wanted to smash us flat for our part in ending his life. I didn't hear him fall, just felt his warm blood all over me as the air was knocked out of my lungs.

I couldn't hear anything except the ringing in my ears from the close blasts of the .32, and now I couldn't breathe. I worked to draw in precious air to keep from blacking out. The first inhalation made my chest burn, and I heaved in more to clear the black dots from my vision.

Jasmine hadn't moved beneath me. I scrambled around like a crazy person, trying to push the heavy body off me, and drag her away from the pool of blood. His heart would have stopped pumping when I hit it bang-on, but it must have been the final bullet. It seemed as if we were drenched with gore.

I fumbled for Jasmine's pulse and felt her move her hand to push mine away. She sat up and looked at me. I must have been a sight. I could feel the wetness covering my face.

"Are you hurt?" My hearing had returned with a vengeance. Her voice was too loud for normal conversation, but we weren't exactly in a normal situation. At least we were still breathing.

"The blood is all his."

I saw her glance wildly around until her eyes found his body.

"He's dead." My voice was matter-of-fact.

"Did I shoot him?" she asked, in the same tone.

Her question surprised me. It seemed to have taken an eternity to kill him. I had had time to memorize every move and have it indelibly engraved in my memory.

"Of course not!" I answered quickly. "Whatever gave you that idea?"

"It happened so fast." She tried to smile. "Can you fill me in?"

Fast? How could two memories be so different? Maybe it was for the best. I wanted us to be able to tell the same story to whoever got here first, and if her memory was cloudy, *maybe I could make her believe my sanitized version.* It was worth a try.

"Rand kidnapped me, brought me here so Bubba could beat me. He became scared when he found out Bubba was going to kill me, and ran away. Bubba had the bat raised to beat my brains to a pulp, and I had to kill him to save my life. Do you remember it now?"

"Sorta . . . Didn't I yell freeze or something?"

I forced a laugh. "Boy, you're really out of it. What makes you think you yelled freeze?"

I had dropped my gun, and it was beside the body. Jasmine's was under my left hip, the one away from her, and I was going to keep it out of this murder scene, if I could possibly manage it.

"I thought I brought my gun inside," she said with a frown.

"Listen, let's get this over with as quickly as possible. Someone may have heard the shots and reported them. I want you to go call Hank, and don't settle for anyone else. Wait till you are speaking to Hank before you tell what happened. Okay?"

"Yes, all right." She acted as if she needed to have some reason to move. She stood awkwardly, and held out a hand to help me up.

"Nope." I gave her a grin. "I'm not gonna attempt to stand until I think I can without falling back down. I'll be fine. Go make the call."

"You're sure?"

"Positive. Scat!"

The minute she left I picked up her gun and scuffed my shoe soles every step to keep from leaving clear prints because they were bloody. I walked around the truck and opened the passenger side, pulled the wide seat back, and searched for something to wipe the gun clean. I found a pile of oily rags, and used two of them. I placed her gun beside my backbone, and holding onto the oily waste, I began cleaning my face and hands as I strolled out to where she was in the van, attempting to reach Hank.

I opened the door of the van and saw Jasmine's purse on the passenger seat. I slid in, picking up her purse and resting it in my lap.

"Got any tissues in here?" I said, as I causally opened it and moved around its contents.

"I think so—Hank? Oh, I'm so glad I found you. Please come quickly, there's been an accident." She turned in the seat away from me, so she didn't have to look in my eyes when she told Hank that I had shot Bubba.

I quickly placed the gun in her purse and pulled out several tissues.

"I'm afraid so." Her voice was low.

Hank had asked if Bubba was dead.

She turned back to me with a startled expression.

"Do you know where we are? I can't direct him here."

"In the alley between Bleeker's old warehouses," I said.

Jasmine replaced the mike with a trembling hand. I slid between the seats and squatted in front of the storage locker, searching for baby wipes. I crammed the oily rags into the locker and returned to the passenger seat and offered the box to her.

We began cleaning our hands and face, and dabbing on our soiled, spotted clothing.

"How did you manage to switch from your car to the van and still tail us?" I asked as we worked on the stains.

"I was terrified that I took too long, and wouldn't know which way he turned on the highway. I hit the left side of the gate when I turned onto the lane. I felt the bump, but kept on going. I couldn't see his truck when I got there. I guessed and turned right. I must have been doing ninety when I spotted his taillights when he turned onto Oak Street. I almost lost control when I made the turn because I hadn't slowed enough."

"You did great," I said when she paused.

"Yeah, just great," she said wryly. "I lost him after about five turns. I was like a lost dog in the meat house, running from one intersection to another trying to find out where y'all had gone. It was pure luck when I finally spotted him pulling out of a small road later. His lights shone my way for a second as he made his turn. I was one street over. Tell me, he actually was the helicopter pilot? Was he really delivering you to Bubba? They didn't know each other, did they?"

"It was Rand. He must have looked up Bubba when he found out I was investigating Mrs. Alyce Cancannon's murder. He didn't want me nosing into his past, I guess. He is a suspect because he inherits the same amount as the nieces. He could be the murderer, for all I know. I'd been saving him and Celia Cancannon for last. Maybe I should have started with him."

"Did he hurt you?"

"Just my dignity. He bound my hands with duct tape. I promised him that I wouldn't run away and he eventually freed them, before he took me to Bubba. Then he feared for his own worthless hide and ran away and left me there. I'm looking forward to future conversations with the jerk. He almost got me killed."

"Why did you agree to go with him?" Jasmine asked, trying to get oriented.

"Wayne and Donnie Ray were upstairs. I didn't want them involved." I didn't mention that she was also on the way home, and could wander in unsuspecting.

"I would have seen Rand's truck outside your door," she said softly. "I wouldn't have blundered in, I would have gone upstairs and called you. You could have warned me over the phone, just as you did when we met on the driveway. That way, you wouldn't have had to confront Bubba."

"I couldn't take the chance," I lied.

Jasmine studied my face and I had to lower my eyes. I covered it by rubbing at a stain on my pants. It's difficult to lie to Jasmine. She seems to have X-ray vision into my soul.

After a short silence, she spoke.

"Tell me what to say."

"You came home just as we were leaving. You didn't know Rand, and knew I was expecting you, and wouldn't have left except for a dire emergency. You quickly exchanged your car for the van and followed us. When you reached the warehouse, you went inside, just in time to hear Bubba threatening me. You started forward, spotted Bubba advancing toward me, you rushed to help me, and I shot Bubba. It's simple."

"But not the entire story, is it?"

I pulled the truck door closed, the dome light went out, and her face was in shadow. I hoped mine was also.

"It's close enough. We have to tell the same story," I stressed.

She pulled her purse toward her, and took out the gun.

"You put it back when you got the Kleenex. I will tell your version, but I want to know why."

"Why do you think I put it in your purse?"

"Because I had it under the seat, and if I hadn't taken it inside and yelled freeze, and prepared to fire before you knocked me aside, it would still be under the seat."

I sighed. "Will you tell it my way, and stay out of it? I'm expecting Hank to come roaring up any minute with a whole pile of people in tow. I have to know what you're going to say. I can't be caught in a lie at this stage."

"I'll tell it like you say. I now understand why you want me out of it, so they can't question me about my past and embarrass me on the stand. Don't you realize they will do exactly that, if I'm on the stand telling your version?"

"Of course I do, I just don't want two women pointing a weapon at Bubba. Even if the ballistics report proves I'm the only one—"

A faint squeal of tires sounded down the block, then we could hear Hank's engine before we could see his car. He wasn't using the siren, or the flashers.

He skidded to a stop and quickly started toward the van. Jasmine jumped out of the van and ran toward him. He hugged her while patting her on her back and never once took his eyes off mine while he stared over her shoulder.

It was the first time I had thought of myself, and now I realized I was in for a rough night. You just didn't empty a gun into a person and go home and get a good night's sleep with everyone's blessings ringing in your ears. Self-defense was bad enough, but if they discovered I had plotted and planned in advance to murder him in cold blood, I might have a lifetime of rough nights.

With his arm around Jasmine, Hank walked to the truck window.

"Are you all right?"

"Sure," I replied, and promptly burst into tears.

35

"Picking up the Pieces"

October 30, Monday, 7:00 A.M.

In the week since the shooting, I had tried to get back to a normal routine, but it was foolish of me to think that I could. I was sitting on my back porch with my third cup of coffee. The birds were flitting through the dying garden, and the last blooms of the early roses. Their chirping must be the same but it now sounded foreign, as if I had been in a time warp and returned incorrectly to a different planet.

I had seen more of my lawyer, Wade Bennett, this week than I had the entire time I had known him. He made daily visits to question, probe, and furnish uplifting comments. I knew he would do his very best for me, but after a week I was very sick of any mention of Bubba, the shooting, and the depositions that he was planning. I just wanted to go away and hide, but since that was out of the question, I just sat a lot and stared at the kennel across the courtyard.

Hank had walked us through the whole nightmare last Monday night, or early Tuesday morning, several times. I understood he was drilling us to make sure our stories matched and Jasmine and I could repeat our statements in our sleep. I was so tired of the repetitions that both Hank and his second-in-command, Lieutenant P. C. Sirmons, finally relented. Jasmine and I were being led to the van when Charlene Stevens drove up in a bright red Corvette.

I was so startled I stumbled into Hank and gave him a glowering stare.

Hardly moving his lips, he said under his breath, "Don't say a word. I'll handle this."

Charlene had a wide smile as she strode toward us. Her nickname is the Barracuda, used only behind her back by all who have to deal with her. You would have to see her teeth to understand. Nice, large, even white teeth, the better-to-eat-you-with kind. She hated me with a purple passion. She had been seeing Hank occasionally when he and I began our brief affair. She hadn't appreciated being dumped, and apparently I was still on her list.

"What are you doing here?" Hank asked her in a reasonable tone of voice.

"Why, Hank, you know I catch the first three nights of the week. Why didn't *you call me*?"

"This isn't a crime, Charlene. It's self-defense. No charges, so your services are not required."

"Don't you think that the district attorney's office should make that decision? You know that we are to be called for all homicides, even justified?"

"You thanked me when I didn't get you out of bed for the Henderson shooting last week."

"Well, that didn't involve your girlfriend, did it?"

She hadn't even glanced at me during their discussion. I was beneath consideration.

"I'll just listen while you reconstruct the crime *again* for me."

Charlotte's eyes gleamed as she spoke. She was a true blond, short hair, slim as a pond weed, and two inches taller than I was. As a rising assistant DA working under district attorney Bobby Don Robbins, she was climbing the political ladder on Bobby Don's back. He had been trying to protect his flank since Charlene had won her first case. He knew she was after his job.

We trudged back in and started telling the story again. When I mentioned that Randall Finch had brought me here, Charlene held up her hand for silence.

"Is this Randall Finch in custody?"

"Not yet," Hank replied.

"Put out an APB on him at once," she said, directing her command to P. C.

"It's been on the air and wire since we first arrived," P. C. reported.

She waved for Hank to continue. We finally finished, using the same words we had used in the first walk-through. Jasmine and I were finally told to go home, but I knew that Charlene wouldn't let it go. I proved to be correct.

Wade gave me daily reports on her actions. On Tuesday, Rand turned himself in, lawyer in tow. Charlene had obtained a deposition. Wade was still trying to find Rand to obtain one for our side. We both suspected Charlene had advised him to vanish for a few days.

On Wednesday, Charlene had jumped over several cases waiting in the wings, and presented Bubba's shooting to the grand jury. They dutifully returned the indictment that she requested, second-degree murder.

Hank was shocked and Wade was incensed. They both came to deliver this news. My guess was they didn't relish telling me one on one. Hank had gone over Charlene's head and appealed to Bobby Don.

"I should have known better, he's got his nose up Sidden Senior's ass. He's afraid of the next election!"

Wade was pacing the floor and questioning Charlene's lineage.

"That's not helping, Wade," I said quietly. "What happens next?"

Hank answered for him.

"Wade has assured me that you will turn yourself in on Friday at noon."

"Why the wait?" I asked, directing my gaze at Wade.

"I've already requested a bond hearing. It won't be heard until the Friday afternoon session. I don't want you to have to sit in jail for two days."

"Amen to that," I replied dully.

Thursday morning early, Hank called.

"Charlene is on the warpath, she wants you incarcerated immediately. Get out of the compound until Friday noon. I'm on the way to serve the warrant, and Charlene insists on accompanying me. I can only stall for thirty minutes."

I hit the panic button, and Wayne, Donnie Ray, and Jasmine came running. Donnie gassed up his truck while Wayne packed food and camping equipment and Jasmine filled an overnight bag. I made two phone calls, and was halfway to the Fargo landing before Hank and Charlene turned into Bloodhound Lane.

Entering Stephen Foster State Park, I turned off the tourist entrance and followed the small blacktop road that wound through planted pines, old growth, and thick brambles to the game warden's residence, James Phelps. He was waiting on his screened porch and came down the steps to greet me.

"The only time I see you is when you want a favor," he said gruffly.

I ignored his tone, threw my arms around him, and gave him a grateful hug. James is fifty-two now, has quite a bit of gray in his dark hair, and has added at least ten pounds since I had last seen him. Patrolling his area of the Okefenokee Swamp kept him looking capable and hardy.

He had helped me several years ago to keep Leroy Moore, my very best male friend and his cousin, out of a jam. I still owed him a big one.

He eyed my wraparound sunshades and the colorful bandanna covering my hair.

"I read about the indictment in yesterday's *Dunston County Daily News*. This is a bad move, Jo Beth. You aren't planning on taking up permanent residence on Billy's Island, are you?"

I stepped back and flung out both arms to indicate the beauty around me.

"Don't I wish! Just overnight, James. My lawyer wanted to set up a bail hearing, and I didn't fancy spending the night in the slammer. It's much nicer out here. I turn myself in at noon tomorrow."

"Who's this?" James squatted and began rubbing Bobby Lee's ears.

"The best dog I have. Meet Bobby Lee."

"Your guide came up to the porch about fifteen minutes ago," he said, straightening. "Said his boat was tied up at my dock. Sure you can trust him? He looks like a poacher to me."

I held back a smile.

"Which one came, the big one or the little one?"

"He was small, wouldn't weigh a hundred and forty dripping wet—wait a minute here—he's one of the Conner brothers? No wonder he looks like a poacher, both of them are!"

"His name is Ray. His brother Sam weighs two-fifty-plus. Calm down. They are *rumored* to be poachers. They've never been arrested. Where's your sense of fair play?"

"That little twerp is not spending the night in my territory! I mean it, Jo Beth!"

"He isn't planning to spend the night," I soothed. "He's just taking me to the island, and will fetch me in the morning and bring me back here in time for me to get the courthouse by noon. Stop your fretting."

James helped me carry my gear down to his small dock and stood glaring at Ray until we rounded a small promontory and were out of sight. As we unloaded, Ray finally asked.

"You told him my name?"

"Without knowing how popular you are. He's heard *rumors*."

We grinned at each other, and he left.

After I had set up camp, Bobby Lee and I explored the island for hours. I tried to imagine how it must have looked a hundred years ago. At that time, there were over twenty families living on this eight-mile island of marshes, bogs, and some fairly high ground. They farmed, hunted, fished, and lived completely off the land. They had chickens, cows, pigs, and goats, and grew their own food and silage for their livestock. Nothing was wasted. Chicken feathers made mattresses and pillows, tanned cowhides were the seats and backs for chairs. Wild honey for their table, berries for their pies and wine, corn for their moonshine, and a great bounty of venison, turkey, coon, wild hogs, bear, and possum.

In exploring, Bobby Lee and I spotted a few relics of the past, a tumbled chimney with bricks that fell apart in my hand, fragments of fence wire, and one broken dish, half submerged in dirt and water.

I had buried two ears of partially shucked corn and two Idaho bakers before I had built the fire on top of them. When we returned there were only hot coals left from the dead wood. I raked the coals back with a metal spoon and set the veggies aside to cool. I opened my short iron stand, and placed a cast-iron skillet directly above the coals. When the seasoned pan was hot, I added two large hamburger patties, which had thawed during the mild afternoon. As the meat cooked, I fed Bobby Lee a half-portion of dog food.

He raised his head often to stare at the sizzling meat and to breathe in the tantalizing smells, making sure to cast his eyes my way.

"Never fear, dear heart, half is yours as always."

I broke up his hamburger to cool faster, and shucked both ears of corn, dividing them between us on the paper plates. I buttered my corn and added sour cream and chives to the potato.

Before I started eating, I put on a small pot of water for instant coffee. No food had ever tasted so good. Bobby Lee polished off his share, and lay contentedly across from me noisily sucking all the juice from the corncob. I removed it from his jaws before he decided to chew it up.

Bobby Lee sometimes acts as if he has psychic abilities. He moved to my side and laid his large head on my leg. He seemed to sense my distress. I had been looking longingly at my two true loves—my mysterious, beautiful swamp and him.

I explained to him why I was so sad. There was a good possibility I would have to leave him forever, and the swamp for a great chunk of the rest of my life. The penalty for murder in the second degree is fifteen years to life.

In the morning, after cooking bacon, eggs, and fried bread, I broke camp. Ray picked us up and deposited us on James's dock. I borrowed Ray's shower and dressed in a navy suit and heels. At noon I met Wade in front of the Sheriff's Department.

He delivered me to Hank, who guided me through the fingerprinting and having my picture taken with a sign around my neck with large black numbers. I had to fight the impulse to stick out my tongue for my mug shot. Frivolity is frowned upon here. They were making this county safe from a dangerous person who had the audacity to kill a founding father's son. I sometimes wonder about my stupidity. I should have secretly stalked the sucker and planted him in an unmarked grave. But being a borderline law-abiding citizen, I had still believed that the system would protect a woman being terrorized and promised an agonizing premature death. That was then. Now I know better.

I was numb as I awaited the judge's entrance at the hearing, with Hank sitting on my left and Wade on my right. Sinclair Adams, my CPA, was seated directly behind me. He had patted my shoulder and gave me a smile. I saw he had his ever-present briefcase beside him. I wondered idly how much this fiasco would cost me. He had cashed in my tiny pile of assets, most of them prematurely, and arranged a second mortgage on my homestead just to scrape up bail money. My defense of a murder charge would not come cheap. I moved my anticipated retirement date at age fifty-five to seventy.

When a robed Constance Dalby entered the courtroom and sat on the bench, I lowered my head and spoke softly to Wade through gritted teeth.

"Christ, Wade, you requested her, didn't you? You have just caused me to be assured of no bail."

"Trust your lawyer, Sidden."

"But you don't—"

I shut up. I couldn't tell him that I'd been blackmailing his favorite judge for several years now. He'd demand to know why. This I could never tell him. It would get his wife and me a long jail term for tax evasion. It seemed that all my chickens were coming home to roost.

Judge Dalby conferred with the clerk and we were called forward. Charlene, the barracuda, was already seated at the prosecutor's table.

"This is a bail hearing for the defendant, Jo Beth Sidden. Counselor?"

"Your Honor, Ms. Sidden is a respected member of this community. She has lived her entire life here, and owns a thriving business. She works with local law enforcement finding lawbreakers with her bloodhounds, and rescuing her fellow citizens in distress. She is no flight risk. We ask that she be released on her own recognizance without bail until her trial."

"Ms. Stevens?" Judge Dalby sounded bored.

"We request that bail be denied. This was a cold-blooded murder, Your Honor. The victim was armed only with a baseball bat, and the defendant shot him six times in the chest. Her life was never in danger. Her response was excessive and uncalled for. The victim would never have hurt her, while she was holding a gun. She saw her chance to rid herself of an annoyance and deliberately murdered him. The defendant has no family ties here, and so little equity in her business, she is definitely a flight risk. If convicted, she faces at least fifteen years in prison. I ask for no bail."

Wade quickly responded, "Your Honor, I would like to remind the district attorney that bail is not punitive, nor an instrument for revenge. It is to assure the court of the defendant's appearance in court. If you decide on asking for bail, we plead for a reasonable amount. The defendant works for a living and has limited resources."

"Bail is set in the amount of fifty thousand dollars. Cash only. Pay the clerk or be remanded to jail."

Judge Dalby rapped the gavel once, stood, and departed.

I sat limp with relief. Sinclair had exactly fifty thousand in the briefcase that he sat on the clerk's desk and began to empty. I could sleep in my own bed tonight. If worse came to worst and I was convicted, I now had a few months before the trial to train Bobby Lee that Jasmine's apartment was his new home. These two facts were worth every penny of the bail.

I thanked Wade and Hank and walked over and waited for Sinclair to finish so I could thank him. I noticed that there were several packets of bank-banded money left in the open briefcase while he waited for the clerk to write out the receipt. He joined me at the dividing rail.

"Let's pull a shepherd, and get the flock out of here," he whispered while guiding me to the door.

"You had more money than fifty thousand. Where did the rest come from?"

"It's for something else," he replied lamely.

"Sinclair, you still haven't learned how to lie convincingly. Give!"

"Hank was afraid that she might say one hundred thousand. He, Wade and Sheri, and Sylvia and I floated a loan. Please don't tell them you know, they'd be embarrassed."

"I won't. Thanks."

Wade was wrong when he told the judge I had limited resources. I have faithful friends and that means I have it all.

36

"Problem-Solving Time"

February 28, Wednesday, 9:00 A.M.

During the four months preceding the trial I tried to put my house in order.

I worked diligently, knowing I was racing the calendar on several projects. The most important one was retraining Bobby Lee. Then I wanted to solve the murder of Alyce Cancannon. I also desired to have another go at trying to find Captain Evan Danglish and the USAF's downed plane.

I started with Bobby Lee. Jasmine spent her days with him attached to her belt. He went willingly, not knowing that it was possibly a permanent arrangement. I had Wayne put two screen door hooks and eyes at the bottom of the pet door in my office. Rudy spent two uncomfortable nights on the back porch before he folded and accepted Jasmine's hospitality. He might have missed me a little, but he loved his comfort more. He didn't come to the pet door and scratch to be let in. He had his bed, his food dish filled on time, and his ears scratched nightly. He possibly missed the occasional treat I fed him that Jasmine wouldn't provide because he was obese. Cats are very sensitive. He caught on quick that I was avoiding him, so he avoided me. He complained vocally to Jasmine about the loss of his treats, but artfully stayed out of my way. I was surprised that I ached so much from missing him.

Bobby Lee's love was unconditional and he had a tough heart. It took months to break it. Every morning when Jasmine let him out for his morning run, he hastened to my door and scratched and whined miserably when he couldn't get it open. I started avoiding him; I couldn't bear his bewildered and questioning glances. He seemed to be asking, What have I done?

We all lost weight; Rudy from eating correctly, Jasmine and I from lack of sleep worrying about Bobby Lee's condition. He seldom ate and his coat looked dull and lifeless. He lost ten pounds quickly. Harvey, my vet, patted my back and held me when I consulted with him on Bobby Lee's condition. He told me that I was doing the right thing. I asked him when the pain of betrayal would end, but he had no answer.

In the third month, Bobby Lee began to change. He ate more, and he stopped shedding so much of his hair. Gone was the vibrant dog that so enjoyed life he danced with butterflies. He had a different demeanor. He seemed ashamed. He carried his tail limp, not curled dramatically over his back. He knew that he had failed to please. He was now resigned to his banishment.

Jasmine praised him extravagantly with every simple exercise that he completed. He was pathetically grateful and quivered with gratitude for her kind words. She slipped him a lot of treats when Rudy wasn't watching.

I didn't rebound as well as he. I kept moving and working feverishly to finish my goals. I dropped twenty pounds. For the first time in my life I was fashionably thin, and I couldn't care less. Rosie, Wayne's mother, nipped and tucked and took up seams in all my clothes. Susan tried to entice me with shopping sprees. She insisted I looked like a displaced refugee. I finally convinced her I didn't have time and that I might be wearing prison garb in the near future.

I tackled the stacks of reports on my six remaining suspects. After several days of reading and comparing the first reports and the most recent ones, I realized I was just making busywork for myself. The reports didn't vary over an hour's difference from the first to the last. Their distant locations and corroborated affidavits of sightings completely eliminated four of the six.

With a marker I boldly slashed through four names: Cathy's husband, Larry Kingsley; Teri Cancannon Halbert; Teri's husband, Phillip Halbert; and Sabrina Cancannon Wilder.

And then there were two.

Celia Cancannon, private secretary, and Rand Finch, helicopter pilot and *bastard extraordinaire.* Oh God, I wanted Rand to be the murderer so bad, I could taste it! I examined my conscience to see if I had let this fact sway my decision. No. I had picked these two way back while I still thought of him as a nice guy and Celia as a victim. Proximity to the crime and opportunity were obvious from the beginning. When obvious is all you have left, it must be so, but I couldn't prove it.

Something flickered across my mind like a falling star in a black sky and was gone just as quickly. I sat with my eyes closed and tried to make it reappear. Nothing came to mind. Damn! I sat down determined to read every line word by word. There had to be something.

The next morning when Jasmine came for coffee, she commented on my condition.

"You look terrible!"

"I read and studied these lousy reports until four this morning. My throat is sore, my head hurts, and my eyes feel like they've been scrubbed with sandpaper. What's your schedule like for today?"

"You're in luck, I don't have a thing planned until my eight P.M. class. Want me to read something?"

I gave her the two files.

"Something's not right. I'm missing something I've either heard or read. I can't put my finger on it and it's driving me nuts!"

"As if you didn't have enough on your plate right now." She shook her head in sadness. "I realize you have been under a terrible strain for these past several months and I'm worried about your health. You haven't gained any of your weight back that you lost worrying about Bobby Lee. The body and mind can only take so much stress, Jo Beth. You should try running a few minutes each morning. It just might relieve some of the stress you're under."

I faked some chuckles.

"If I started to run south I wouldn't stop until I hit Key West. I don't know what would halt my northern run, the North Pole?"

"Don't even kid about running. Surely you aren't thinking along those lines . . . are you?"

"I could get fifteen years, or more, and have to serve at least eighty-five percent of it. I'd be forty-six or older when released. I don't know what I'm thinking about, except it would be too late for babies, and I can't seem to generate any enthusiasm for romance near fifty."

"Stop it," Jasmine ordered. "You are not going to be convicted because you're innocent! Quit talking like this. Hank and Wade will not let you be sent to prison."

"Sure. Will you read the files for me?"

"I'll take them upstairs now and study them. Will you be all right?"

"Right as rain," I told her, and tried to look that way. "Where's Bobby Lee?"

"He's on the porch."

"You could have brought him in, he's over me now. He's transferred his affection to you."

"He . . . he didn't want to come in."

"Good." I held back the tears and smiled at her. I watched from the window and didn't weep until they were safely upstairs.

Jasmine came down at six with the files stuffed under her arm and carrying a crock pot with two pot holders wrapped around the handles to protect her hands. She kicked the screen door, and I ran to hold the door open for her.

"Irish stew, Southern style."

"Yummy," I said, not really caring, just thanking her for her effort. "Did you spot anything?"

"Let me plug this in." She disappeared into the kitchen. I waited three minutes and moved to the kitchen table. Jasmine was washing salad greens at the sink.

"Don't keep me in suspense. Did you see anything I missed?"

"I'm afraid not. There doesn't seem to be anything to find." Her back was to me.

I slumped in the chair and closed my eyes.

I heard her pull out a chair and sit across from me. I raised my head in time to see her pull the files in front of her. She tapped Celia's.

"This niece, the secretary, never really had a life of her own. For years, she only took one day a month off. The agents reported the mileage was almost the same for every trip in the rental cars she hired, a total of two hundred miles, but they couldn't find out where she went. She stopped these excursions over seventeen years ago."

"She must have lived vicariously through her Aunt Alyce's travels, who was always going someplace different and exciting. Why didn't Aunt Alyce ever take her secretary-niece with her?"

"Rand was always into something in his youth, chasing some job or dream, but he too stayed near the island after he landed the job of ferrying all the family around by helicopter. It must have been a requirement to always be available, but Rand should have gotten tired of the short hops back and forth to the mainland long ago. I think—"

I slapped the table.

"That's it, that's it!" My heart was pounding and this was the most animated and alive I had felt since the bond hearing. "Where's the phone, what time is it?"

I ran to my office, grabbed the cellular and my address book, and hurried back and dropped them on the table.

I looked up the number, and held up a hand while I was dialing the number with the other. "Just a second, and I'll tell you."

I listened to the recorded message and waited impatiently for the beep.

"This is Jo Beth Sidden. If anyone is there, please pick up the phone, now! This is an emergency!"

I listened for ten long seconds and disconnected.

"Clock-watchers!" I muttered as I flipped my address book to the A's. I dialed Chester Adams's home phone number. He was my contact at the detective agency in Washington. I hadn't called him or vice versa in over two months. After I got *his* answering machine, I left him a nasty message.

"This is Jo Beth Sidden. I hope to Christ that you have this phone connected to your beeper, or I'll boil you in oil! I need you. Get back to me ASAP!"

I gave Jasmine a genuine smile of pleasure, the first in ages.

"I have this theory . . ."

37

"A Good Day with an Ugly Ending"

March 1, Friday, Noon

It was a cool, bleak day when Captain Evan Danglish, USAF, and I penetrated the depths of the Okefenokee for the fourth time. The search for his crash site had proved just as elusive as I had anticipated.

The huge dead cypress still loomed over our heads as a friendly beacon and landmark, but the plane could have disappeared in the water and muck anywhere from one hundred feet away to a formidable one-thousand-foot distance in any direction.

Not counting the first disastrous probe that Mr. Gator had ended, this was our third trip here. I had promised Evan I would give him a week. Since we returned home each night, it only gave us about five hours to actually search. I chose to go out five hundred feet in one direction, move over approximately one hundred feet, and return to the tree. It was a pitiful amount of ground to cover compared to the projected area where the plane could be resting.

I had called a halt shortly before noon to check Marjorie's paws. We were traveling through and around large clusters of blackthorn vines. She stood patiently waiting while I inspected each pad and felt between her claws. She's my favorite drug sniffer. If she can find drugs sealed in steel drums, I figured that the pungent order of jet fuel and greasy metal would be a snap, even if it were several feet below the surface.

I was off-balance, leaning over a hind leg, when Marjorie suddenly jerked loose from my grasp and strained forward at the limit of her short lead.

"It better not be a possum!" I admonished as I took a couple of quick steps to keep from falling. Marjorie has broken training before, going off on an exciting scent and acting victorious when she treed a coon.

I let her pull me forward, and I could hear Evan crashing and lumbering through the underbrush behind me. Marjorie headed toward a large shallow-looking slough. She would have entered the water without slowing down if I hadn't been pulling her back and yelling the command to stay.

She raised her head and gave a full-throated celebrative bay. My heart pounded against my ribs, and I raised my free arm to the heavens with a clinched fist and yelled, "Yes, yes, yes!"

Evan was staring with open-mouthed astonishment and looking as if he thought we had both lost our minds. At that moment I completely forgot killing Bubba, the trial I had to face, and what the consequences could mean. I was alive and doing what I did best. Marjorie had found the plane, God was in His heaven, and all was right in the world!

Evan couldn't make himself hope. He couldn't see the plane, couldn't smell it or touch it, so therefore he didn't believe it was under the shallow water and mud.

"Evan, never doubt a miracle. It happened today, right here in front of your eyes. If the crash wasn't pilot error, your flying future is assured. With your luck, you will have a lustrous career, a wife and children who adore you, and a long and happy life!"

His thanks didn't sound completely sincere until the plane was raised from the swamp. The FAA eventually completed its investigation, citing mechanical failure and absolving him of any blame.

Hank called me late in the evening, a few minutes after I retired. "Were you asleep?"

"Yes, Hank, you woke me up." Stretching straight beneath the quilt, I fought the urge to yawn. "What's up?"

"I didn't want you reading about it while you were alone. I'm sorry, Jo Beth. It's bad news. I knew she was your friend and that you had tried to help her."

I sat up straight clutching the phone. I was fully awake in a heartbeat.

"Who?" I choked the word out dreading to hear her name.

"Alice Mae Petrie."

"Oh God, the bastard attacked her? Tom raped her, didn't he? Is she in the hospital? I'll have to call her mother, is she at the hospital now?"

"She's dead, Jo Beth."

"Dead?" I echoed.

"When she didn't come home from work, her mother called me. I drove her route home, and found her car abandoned and immediately put out an APB on Tom, since she had a current restraining order on him. Two deputies worked the area where her car was left and found three eyewitnesses to her abduction. They thought it was a lover's quarrel, unfortunately, an all too common reaction when people see a man dragging a protesting woman away. We had him in custody by seven P.M. It took only thirty minutes before he confessed and told us where he had hidden her body.

"She didn't suffer long, Jo Beth. He strangled her within fifteen minutes of picking her up. She wasn't molested. He said if she wouldn't have him, she didn't deserve to live. He's flaky, but I bet my badge he's sane and will be tried."

"Another woman lost because he has to rape or kill her before the law can act." I was bitter but calm.

"I know how you feel, kiddo, just don't let this get you down any more than you already are. Promise?"

"Sure, Hank, you're right. I need all my strength to face a murder

261

trial because I protected my life and refused to be a victim!"

"If it makes you feel any better, go ahead and scream and rant and rave at me, but you know I couldn't do anything to him without provocation."

"I know, Hank. I'm just remembering that small, slim girl who played with me on the monkey bars during recess in the first grade. I know it wasn't your fault, but who do you blame?"

"Congress? Fate? Weak and ineffective laws? Beats me, kid."

"Thanks for calling, Hank."

It was close to dawn before I could sleep.

38

"Testing the Theory"

March 2, Saturday, 11:00 A.M.

The rented helicopter's pilot and I were flying over the Okefenokee Swamp on the way to the island to visit Rand and Celia. It had seemed to take forever, but in reality it took only forty-eight hours to get the answers I needed from Chester Adams. I have to admit that I was sure it would take longer, because the files I wanted were thirty-five years old.

Chester had a formidable machine of agents, which easily uncovered the proof that I needed when told where to look. He apologized for missing the information the first time around. I forgave him and wished him well. I told him to send in the final bill, I had found the murderer. He was dying to know how I had arrived at the solution, but he had too much class to ask.

The pilot set the plane down in the clearing in front of the Cancannon mansion, and the rotors went silent.

"What's that awful smell in here?" I complained. "My eyes are stinging!" He had introduced himself when he lifted me off my grass and took me aloft, but I had forgotten his name.

"Insecticide residue, probably," he remarked cheerfully. "I spray crops most days in the spring."

"I'll probably come down with respiratory problems," I grumbled.

"If you've never smoked, there's no danger."

"That's reassuring!"

"Spraying crops beats hauling pot."

"I want you to sit here for one hour," I explained. "If I'm not back by then, contact Sheriff Jeff Beaman of Camden County and tell him I need rescuing."

"Y'all be back."

"What makes you so sure?" I snapped.

"You sound like you have it together. If you're smart enough to know you might need rescuing, you're smart enough to go in with more than just a crop sprayer waiting outside without a working radio."

I glanced around the tiny cockpit in dismay and gave him a dirty look.

"Y'all be back," he repeated, nodding his head.

I stalked angrily across the grass, and hoped that both Rand and Celia were here. I wanted to confront them together.

I stood patiently and waited for someone to answer my summons. Rand opened the door.

"Ah, if it isn't Miz Jo Beth!" he sneered. "I'm shocked that a murderer is standing at my door!"

"Takes one to know one," I answered calmly.

"I have no idea what you're talking about. If you've come to beg me to change my story about the fatal night, forget it. I'm going to enjoy sending you to prison for a very long time."

"I've read your deposition, Rand. The lie that I shot Bubba in cold blood without provocation doesn't bother me. By the time I'm tried, you might be in jail yourself. I want to talk to both you and Celia right now."

"I'm not going to let you bother her."

"Then I'll talk to Sheriff Beaman, it's all the same to me."

Frowning while he studied my expression, he finally swung the door wide.

"Come in then, by all means! I for one would like to know what you *think you know.*"

I walked around him and straight into Celia's office. She looked up from her desk and her eyes widened in shock. She directed her gaze behind me.

"Rand?"

"Right here, Celia. Don't worry, I'll protect you. She insisted on speaking with you."

"What do you want?"

I sat without an invitation in an armchair with the desk between us. Rand took a seat in its mate.

"As you know, I've been hired by the estate to investigate your aunt's murder. I would like to ask you a few questions."

She looked at Rand. He gave her a brief nod.

"All right." She didn't look nervous.

Nothing like getting right to the point. "When you finished your sophomore year in high school you were sixteen. You and your Aunt Alyce went to Florence, Italy, during your summer vacation. Why didn't you return in the fall and resume your studies here?"

She answered immediately.

"I had a severe bout of flu. It sapped my strength so much that Aunt Alyce thought it best for me to remain in Florence and convalesce under the clinic's care since they had taken such good care of me. I had a private tutor, as I was unable to attend regular classes."

"That's what your aunt wrote to your school, and you both told the same story to your cousins, but it wasn't true. But let's continue. When you returned, from nineteen sixty-one until nineteen seventy-nine, a total of eighteen years, you rented a car once a month and traveled approximately two hundred miles. Would you care to tell me who you were visiting?"

"A . . . an old friend." She suddenly had moisture on her carefully made-up brow.

"Another lie, but we'll continue. After eighteen years you stopped visiting and never rented another car. Did your 'friend' move or die?"

"She moved." Her answer was so low I could barely hear her. Her head was drooping.

"Another lie." I slid forward in my seat so I could catch her if she fainted; she really looked ill.

"That's enough!" Rand yelled. "Get out of here, you are upsetting her! Just get to hell out of here!"

"Why can't I tell her?" Celia whispered. "I'm not ashamed of—"

"Shut up!" he yelled. "Don't say another word!"

"You leave her alone," I told him. "I will not let you speak to your mother in that tone of voice in my presence!"

It worked. Celia slid from her chair in a dead faint. Rand stood frozen and his face lost all color. I got a glimpse of what he would look like when he was a very old man. He turned and walked out the door. I straightened Celia's body and hollered for the maid. Between the two of us, we got her on a couch. She moaned once before she opened her eyes and saw me kneeling beside her.

"Where's Rand?" she whispered.

"He left you laying on the floor," I said. "Give it up, Celia. Don't cover for him any longer. He killed Alyce."

"His father was so beautiful. I loved him and Florence and the whole world when I found out I was going to have a child. Aunt Alyce paid him money to go away. I refused to have an abortion. I wish you could have seen Rand when he was a baby, he was the most beautiful baby in the world."

She looked feverish. I wiped her brow with a damp washcloth the maid had fetched.

"You didn't know that he was going to kill her, did you?"

"He was tired of waiting for the money. Aunt Alyce had promised me that she would leave him money in her will if I never told anyone. He said she could live for another twenty years."

And then there was one.

"You're planning on taking the blame if he's arrested, aren't you?"

"He's my son." She closed her eyes.

I guess that said it all. I left. I never would have gone and gotten conformation of my guesses if I had known that the love between a

266

woman and her illegitimate child would make her sacrifice the rest of her life for him, not even for *all four* of my father's paintings. Chester Adams was smart enough that he would figure it out shortly. If I didn't tell the sheriff, he would. I called John Jason Jackson and told him the whole story. I also told him there wasn't any evidence that would convict either of them.

Two days, later on March fourth, the first day of my trial, Celia Cancannon turned herself in to Sheriff Beaman and confessed to killing Alyce Cancannon because she wanted her money and didn't want to wait twenty years. Rand was not by her side. He was waiting with the other witnesses at my trial to testify against me.

And then there were none.

39

"The Verdict"

March 8, Friday, 10:45 A.M.

Jasmine and I had been sitting on my back porch dressed in our court finery since eight-thirty this morning. It was a few minutes before eleven. Today was March eighth. My trial had lasted four days, Monday through most of Thursday.

The judge had charged the jury and sent them to deliberate my fate at three yesterday afternoon. Hank, Wade, Jasmine, and I had waited in the courtroom until eight. The judge sent the jury home and Jasmine and I came back to find that Rosie had left a full meal warming on the stove. Surprisingly, I was hungry. I ate well, but Jasmine picked at her food.

"The condemned-man syndrome," I said with a shrug, to explain my appetite.

"Don't say that!" Jasmine snapped. Her nerves were as strung out as mine were. "Wade said that it was a good sign they were taking so long. The longer they are out, the better it is for you. Don't you remember?"

I had agreed with her last night and again this morning on three separate occasions when she voiced the very same sentiment using the exact same words. It was too cold on the porch to be sitting out here; I had tried to get her to go in several times. She went in and brought out two quilts and we were cocooned within their folds. My feet were like ice, but I didn't mention the fact. Jasmine would have run for a hot water bottle.

I stared into the bleak, cool sunshine and remembered the trial. There had been a short burglary trial that was heard before mine. My case started about eleven. Wade and Charlene had agreed on two jurors before the dinner break, and it took the rest of the afternoon to choose the rest.

I had been shocked when Hank came over that evening and gave us the news about Celia confessing to her aunt's murder. I brought Hank up to date on my last visit to Little Cat Island.

"You idiot," he stated without heat. "You shouldn't have confronted him alone, and on his territory, to boot."

"The only thing I accomplished was to show Celia that she had to protect her son," I said wearily. "If she had kept quiet, they both would be home free but without their inheritance. The estate would never have been settled without the murder being solved. Litigation could have stalled the division of assets for years. I know the bastard convinced her that he would never get the money with the murder investigation still open, so she happily threw away her life so he could collect. Case closed."

Tuesday was opening statements. Charlene's hatred of me fueled her voice and made her sound assured as she outlined the case against me.

"Ladies and gentlemen of the jury, I will prove to you beyond a reasonable doubt that the defendant deliberately murdered Buford Sidden Junior, her ex-husband, with malice aforethought on the night of October twenty-third of last year. The coroner will testify that Mr. Sidden was shot in the chest and torso area a total of six times with the defendant's gun. Not once, not twice, but a total of *six bullets was fired at point-blank range.*

"In the confrontation that resulted in Mr. Sidden's death, he was not armed with a gun. Mr. Sidden didn't own a gun. All his friends knew he kept a favorite baseball bat in his truck. He had been a hero, winning several crucial baseball games during his senior year in high school. The bat was a memento of happier times, not a weapon, as the defense will claim. Don't also be fooled by the defense's claim that the defendant killed him in self-defense. Mr. Sidden was not a foolish man. Only a foolish man would charge a vindictive, embittered ex-wife who was pointing a loaded weapon at him, especially an ex-wife who had *previously killed an unarmed man with the same gun!*

"A grieving father asks for justice for the deliberate murder of his only son. I ask you in the name of the State of Georgia to listen to the evidence presented and return the rightful verdict of guilty as charged. Thank you."

As Charlene returned to her seat in the silent courtroom, I whispered into Wade's ear.

"She's convinced me. I'm ready to be fitted with prison twill."

"Now it's my turn." He patted my arm, rose, and went to stand before the jury.

"Good morning, ladies and gentlemen. My name is Wade Bennett. I'm a local attorney, and was hired by Jo Beth Sidden, the defendant, to clear her name of this ridiculous charge of second-degree murder. We should not be in this courtroom today. Jo Beth Sidden was defending her life when she shot her enraged husband, and I will prove it to you beyond any reasonable doubt. It was justifiable homicide.

"Before I start giving you the unassailable facts of what occurred on the night of the shooting last October, it is my unpleasant duty to clear up a gross misrepresentation of facts that the prosecutor told you about a prior shooting involving my client and her work weapon.

"Jo Beth Sidden raises and trains bloodhounds for search and rescue and trailing escaped felons. She is currently under contract for furnishing bloodhounds and a trainer to track all prison escapees in Dunston, Herdon, and Shelton counties.

"Almost three years ago, three vicious felons escaped from Monroe Correctional Institute in Shelton County. Jo Beth Sidden and her mantrailing bloodhounds were called in. They tracked the felons to an isolated farmhouse, where they discovered the bodies of John and Ellen Stevenson, an elderly couple, repeatedly stabbed to death in their bedroom. They were killed for their truck, which was not there, but at a son's home to have the oil changed. A thirty-thirty rifle, a twelve-gauge, and a twenty-gauge shotgun were missing. The search team comprised of Jo Beth Sidden, one bloodhound, and three Shelton County deputies continued to track the felons into heavy brush in the Okefenokee Swamp.

"During the confrontation when the felons were found, a talented bloodhound's throat was cut. From less than six feet away, Jo Beth Sidden stood, walked around the brush, and fired six times, hitting the felon three times, as he was reaching for a shotgun lying beside him. Jo Beth Sidden was given a commendation for bravery for saving three law enforcement men's lives and her own.

"This was the unarmed man that the assistant district attorney referred to in her opening statement. She owes the court an apology for misleading you so badly.

"On the night in question, Jo Beth Sidden was taken from her home and driven to a deserted warehouse, where her ex-husband from whom she had been divorced for eleven years was waiting for her with a baseball bat. This bat was not a memento of happier times, as the prosecution claims, but a *deadly weapon!* I will show you in testimony from an expert that it was drilled and the hole filled with lead shot!"

He had been eloquent and I again felt hope.

Jasmine and I didn't talk much as we waited. We had said it all the past few nights as we lingered over each word spoken during the trial, the jurors' expressions, Wade's passionate defense, and Charlene's determination to bury me.

We were waiting for *the* phone call. It came at eleven.

Wade sounded a little breathless.

"The judge is bringing in the jury in fifteen minutes."

"We're on our way."

Jasmine and I entered a packed courtroom. Every day there had been more spectators than the day before. As I walked down the center aisle beside Jasmine, I felt that all eyes were focused on me.

271

It made me wonder if all these people really cared about my fate, or whether they didn't have anything else to do on a nippy March morning. I casually glanced back at the gathering as we waited for the judge. The room was awash with whispered conversations. I saw the usual hangers-on, the bored retirees, and many more. I spotted several lawyers. Wade was earning a deserved reputation for winning. He was good. I didn't know if his peers had come to cheer or jeer.

I saw four off-duty deputies. I knew they were off-duty because Hank was seated one row behind me. I spotted Susan, Rosie, her fire chief, and a few of my friends. I also spotted Rand sitting on a back bench. He gave me a grin and held a thumb upside down, in case I didn't catch on to why he was still here. Bubba's father, Buford Sidden Sr., was sitting behind Charlene's chair in the first row. He had been there every day in the same seat, trying to bore holes into my back with his beady eyes.

Judge Dalby entered the courtroom from her chambers and the crowd went silent. No one wanted to get thrown out before the verdict was read.

We all sat expectantly as the jury filed in and took their seats. None of them looked my way.

"Has the jury reached a verdict?" Judge Dalby's voice sounded neutral. Maybe she liked me, even if I had been blackmailing her into doing me favors. Maybe not.

A downtown druggist, where I didn't trade, handed a folded paper to the bailiff, who carried it to the judge, waited until she had read it, and carried it back to the foreman, or madam foreperson, or whoever.

"Will the defendant please rise?"

Wade put his hand under my elbow, and I managed to stand erect without disgracing myself.

"Will you please read the verdict?"

The fat lady druggist had a nice baritone voice.

"On the charge of murder in the second degree, we find the defendant guilty."

Epilogue

I was sitting at my kitchen table attempting to eat a banana and peanut butter sandwich. It was noon and I hadn't eaten since last night. When I prepared it, it had looked appetizing, and the first bite was delicious. Then Wade had called and informed me that he and Hank were coming out with news. The second bite was difficult to swallow, and I threw the remainder in the kitchen trash and sat there sipping iced tea.

I was still free on bond, pending the appeal of my conviction. Wade had explained the procedure.

"Judge Dalby knew you were innocent, but the only way she could help was to make sure there were sufficient grounds for appeal. She let not one, but three beauties slip by her. I could drive a semi through these openings! She was a fine trial attorney, and is an excellent judge. The errors in the trial were deliberate. She risked getting her name bandied about doing it. You owe her."

"Give her this message from me the next time you see her, and quote it exactly as I state it.

"'I know our paths will never cross again, so I want to take this last opportunity to thank you.' Can you remember it?"

"Of course." He sat for a few seconds staring at his desk before raising his eyes to mine. A small frown appeared on his brow.

"Is there something you're not sharing with me?"

"Not a thing," I lied, and spent several minutes making him believe it. I had informed Constance that I would never bug her again or threaten to reveal her indiscretion. She was free of my blackmailing her for favors, forever.

I gazed out the window and remembered Rand as he had looked that first day when he flew me to the island. He had been carefree, good-looking, sexy, and seemed worthy of future consideration. It's sobering to realize with hindsight how easily one could be deceived by appearances.

As much as I loathed Rand for hanging a murder charge around my neck, and conning his mother into confessing to a murder she didn't commit, I regretted the fact that his life had ended. He was buried last week on Little Cat Island, and the sheriff had allowed Celia to attend the funeral.

Two fishermen just offshore in a skiff had seen his helicopter drop out of the sky belching smoke, and barely make land before crashing and burning. A quarter-acre of wild brush was turned into a smoldering circle of soot and ashes before the two could approach the small pile of burnt metal. He was an evil man and deserved punishment for his actions, but fate had produced an ending too horrific to contemplate. The FAA was investigating. Hank had seen photos of the crash site, and told me that I shouldn't view them. I took his word.

I heard car doors slam and rose to go greet my support team that was trying to get my life back on track. I hadn't wasted any time in removing my two gate alarms after I had eliminated the reason I needed them. The speaker at the front gate had been sent back for a refund and I had Wayne and Donnie Ray take both gates off their hinges and store them in the barn. It still felt strange that people could now drive into the courtyard unaccompanied by loud noises.

They greeted me politely, and followed me back into the kitchen with unreadable expressions. I served coffee with a dry mouth and an accelerated pulse. I sat and folded my arms on the table.

"I'm ready. Tell me."

"We came bearing gifts!" Hank was grinning from ear to ear. I switched my gaze to Wade.

"Judge Dalby is writing a decision on your trial to set aside the jury's guilty verdict, based on new evidence. It will take a few weeks, but it's all over but the shouting."

"You won't be retried, Jo Beth," Hank butted in. "In fact, I had to listen to the pompous district attorney, our own Bobby Don Robbins, explaining that he knew you should have never been tried in the first place, and how happy he was that justice prevailed."

"I will want all the details later, but right now, this minute, are you both one hundred percent sure that I will remain free, not have to serve time, and won't be tried again? Please think before you answer, my sanity depends on honest appraisals."

"You are free of all charges, you have my word," Wade declared.

Hank pumped his arm and raised it dramatically. "Ditto, Jo Beth, it's over. The nightmare is over!"

I pushed back my chair and fled to the bedroom. It is easier to get a heart and pulse racing than it is to calm them down and feel normal. I cried for two reasons. Relief that I had gotten away with removing Bubba from my life, and regret for being pushed into taking his life to protect mine.

I knew I wouldn't be riding off in the sunset feeling cleansed and rid of all guilt. I would be paying for my action for the rest of my life. The nightmare came each night. I was on my back and a bloody Bubba was towering over me, falling in slow motion to smother me with his blood. I would wake and be unable to sleep again. I'd read, catch up on my paperwork, or simply sit and wait for the dawn.

When I returned to the kitchen Hank and Wade were on their second cup of coffee and Jasmine had joined them.

"Tell us about the new evidence."

Hank began. "When Celia confessed, it seems that Rand went to a lawyer and had him draw up a will. He anticipated getting his share of the estate. Now, I don't believe that he had a conscience. My guess is that he wanted to brag about his ability in manipulating Celia and sandbagging you, and the only way to do that was to leave a signed confession to be opened after his death.

"He wasn't thinking of dying so soon, he thought that it would happen years and years from now, and possibly he saw it as a future payback for his illegitimate birth. I'll even give the sucker a little credit. He might have realized that he might die in an accident or illness while his mother was still languishing in jail. Whatever his reason for leaving a detailed statement in his handwriting exonerating Celia, he had to include you, Jo Beth, detailing where and when he lied on the stand about the night he witnessed the shooting. Upon his death the lawyer opened this document, and notified Judge Dalby. She notified the district attorney, Wade, and me. It is enough, Wade tells me, for her to reverse the jury's decision and render a verdict of acquittal."

"Could the appeals court or any higher court find that she erred, and possibly reverse it, again?" Jasmine was exploring all possibilities of what could go wrong. We both are prone to looking a gift horse in the mouth, not only to discover his age but also to check for a tattoo to make sure that he wasn't stolen. We both turned to Wade.

"Absolutely not. In fact, she should have done so the minute I asked for a directed verdict of acquittal, immediately after the state presented its case. I still don't understand her reasoning for letting the trial go forward. Maybe she thought when the circumstances were placed into evidence that Jo Beth's peers would fully exonerate her. She had to realize that she shouldn't have been tried for murder two, it was clearly justifiable homicide."

And just maybe, I reasoned, she wanted to extract a pound of flesh and make me suffer for the humiliation that her pride had suffered when I asked and she had to grant me favors. We are now even, Constance. We should both go forth and sin no more.

The questions asked and answered then turned into laughter and suggestions of different ways to celebrate.

I stood. "Sorry, guys, I'm going to be really busy the next few days, maybe we can celebrate next week."

"Doing what?" Hank asked.

"Winning back Bobby Lee and proving to him that he's the love of my life, and bringing him home forever." And that is when I ran for the door.

"Bobby Lee!" I yelled, "Come here, you big lug! It's time to come home!"

Two months later, on a warm May day, I was sitting in John Jason Jackson's office waiting impatiently for him to finish his long-winded speech about the trials and tribulations of closing the probate file for Alyce Cancannon's estate.

Finally, with a flourish, he had presented me with the promised check. I barely glanced at the figure; just enough to make sure that it had enough zeros as I tucked it into my purse.

When he realized I wasn't going to thank him, he sighed and waved a hand toward the right side of the room.

"If the check didn't excite you, I'm sure the four canvases your father painted will. I guess you didn't notice them when you arrived. They are displayed on the south wall. I can't wait to see the expression on your face when you pick the one that you'll take home with you."

I had spotted the pictures in my peripheral vision when I had entered his office, but hadn't taken my eyes from his face to study them.

"I noticed," I said softly. "I would rather be alone when I examine them."

He opened his mouth to say something but had second thoughts. His ears were turning pink. He pushed back his chair and departed in haste, closing the door with more force than was necessary.

I stood and walked slowly to the wall and took my time on the first three. They were beautiful. Three different views of Cumberland's coastline, gentle surf rolling in on the beach, sea oats waving in a soft breeze, and pine and oak trees looking majestic in the background.

When I moved to the fourth, I gasped with pleasure. Suddenly I was eight years old again, standing under a hot summer sun, sandy and perspiring, watching my father while he painted this picture.

The small stone cairn that I had leaned on was in the foreground. The view was of surf at low tide. A black-as-midnight, strong-limbed stallion ran in the shallow water leading his twelve mares. They were a herd of the famous wild horses of Cumberland Island. I could hear their hooves slapping the water's edge and see the droplets sprayed into the air reflecting the sunlight. They were carelessly tossed jewels, a possible tribute from a benign deity.

Muscles rippled under warm hides and haunches bunched and relaxed in unison as they ran free and unfettered by man-made restraints.

I felt dizzy and placed a hand on the wall to brace myself. I shook my head to clear my vision and drew in tiny breaths so I wouldn't hyperventilate. The painting was a glorious remembrance of a magical day I had spent with my father.

With great joy and a cheerful heart I went to tell Jackson my decision. The painting would protect me on the black nights when Bubba came to call, bearing his twin gifts of blood and guilt. I realized I was tentatively beginning to feel contentment.